The Seven Days of Man

The Seven Days of Man

Abdel-Hakim Kassem

With a Foreword by Ahmed Abdel-Mu'ti Higazi

Translated by Joseph Norment Bell

hydra books

Hydra Books
Northwestern University Press
Evanston, Illinois 60208-4210

First published 1969 in Arabic as *Ayyam al-insan al-sab'a.* Translation

Printed in the United States of America

Library of Congress Cataloging-in-Publication Data

Qāsim, 'Abd al-Hakīm.
[Ayyām al-insān al-sab' ah. English.]
The seven days of man / Abdel-Hakim Kassem ; with a foreword by Ahmed Abdel-Mu 'ti Higazi ; translated by Joseph Norment Bell.
p. cm.
ISBN 0-8101-1415-1 (alk. paper)
1. Villages—Egypt—Fiction. I. Bell, Joseph Norment.
II. Title.
PJ7858.A76A913 1996
892'.736—dc20 96-3731
CIP

The paper used in this publication meets the minimum requirements of the American National Standard for Information Sciences—Permanence of Paper for Printed Library Materials, ANSI Z39.48-1984.

The dream of my life
All my hope
My ships with their longing sails
Yearn for distant ports

Contents

Foreword by Ahmed Abdel Mu'ti Higazi ix

Translator's Preface xviii

1. The Evening Gathering 1

2. The Baking 40

3. The Journey 72

4. The Lodgings 102

5. The Big Night 136

6. The Farewell 161

7. The Path 184

Foreword

I do not believe that the Egyptian village has been dealt with in any book in our recent literature that can rival Abdel-Hakim Kassem's *Seven Days of Man.* I read this unique work once again after its author had left us at the height of his maturity and fertility, leaving behind him an empty place in the circles of contemporary literary art and a silence interrupted only by our expressions of grief at our great loss.

Kassem combined qualities not found together in any novelist who wrote about the Egyptian village before him—the experiences and the memory of a peasant, the sensibility and the language of a poet, and the poet's concern for essentials rather than for the superficial. His was a broad experience laden with the fruits of firsthand knowledge and detailed retrospection. The image of the village, the faces of its people, the characteristic traits, the distinctive expressions, the penchants and the habits of each one of them. What goes on around them and the homes they live in—their wives or their husbands, their children, their animals, and their belongings. The fields surrounding the village, the palm trees and the willows, the water wheels and the lanes, the feasts and the festivals, the love and affection that bind its people together, the strife and enmity that at times divide them. The house and the animal pen, the mosque and the graveyard, the slaughtering of animals and the baking of bread. The bond between husband and wife, the relations between fellow wives, the flowering of full-fleshed adolescence. Day in the village and evening in the village, the guest house and the coffeehouse, weddings and funerals, degrading poverty and indomitable spirit. How the sun rises, how the shadows retreat, the burning of the noonday heat, and the fall of evening. Cries and whispers, sounds and echoes, the harshness and the tenderness of the men, the misery of the women and their occasional little joys. The fatigue of the day, the ecstasy of the *zikr*,[1] and the dreams of the journey to the feast of Saint Ahmed Bedawi in Tanta. The old world passing away, and the new world coming into being.

Kassem is loyal to his experience and to his perceptions in the minutest detail. The village in his perspective is the capital of the universe. Everything he sees is measured by its standards, and everything he writes springs from its life.

But how does he write? With a language drawn from the Koran, from Arabic poetry, from popular epic, and from devotional literature like *Dalâ'il al-khayrât* (The tokens of his blessings) and hagiographic works like *Manâqib al-sâlihîn* (The deeds of the righteous). A language that is neither remote from its object nor artificial,[2] that insists on the image or the thought, encompassing it on all sides and calling it by its real names. It observes every glance, records every feature, traces every shadow. Yet it is a caring and affectionate language that embraces its subject warmly, and follows its steps and its extensions into the soul. In Kassem's language poetry is blended with prose in such a way that the novel takes on the character of authentic folk literature.

One is struck by this feeling not only when reading Kassem's works about life in the village, such as the present novel or works such as *al-Mahdî* (The Mahdi), *Taraf min khabar al-âkhira* (A little information on the next world), *al-Ukht li-ab* (The half-sister), and *Sutûr min daftar al-ahwâl* (Lines from the daily record). One senses it also when reading his short story *al-Sawt* (The voice), in which he wrote about his experiences in Germany, or his short story *Ruju' al-shaykh* (The return of old man),[3] which he wrote about his visit to Fez and which he dedicated to the writers of Morocco. Could it be anyone but an

Egyptian peasant who describes Berlin with these words?

> The rows of lights on either side of the street perceive the sound of my footsteps on the snowy sidewalk with disbelief. One after the other they stare at me amazed with their wide yellow eyes. As I quicken my pace, my steps sink into the crispness of this eternal silence, with its secrets of pale shadows and yellow light.
>
> The day in this land is short, and the ailing sun shines weakly on the snow-covered earth. The night hides under the cover of its wings three-fourths of the cycle of the day. And I turn in unison with this cold, wet cycle with a constricted heart, knowing that I will go on walking until the Day of Judgment. It saddens me that my steps will leave no trace on the layers of snow covering the earth.

What language will he use, then, when he is writing in the bright sun of Egypt rather than the ailing light of Berlin, when his feeling is one of belonging and involvement rather than of loss and alienation?

The road to the Egyptian village will from now on pass through the works of Abdel-Hakim Kassem, just as the road to Cairo passes through the works of Naguib Mahfouz. Whoever wishes to understand the Egyptian village, to come into contact with its eternal spirit and to uncover its most carefully preserved secrets, must read Abdel-Hakim Kassem, and the road to Abdel-Hakim Kassem begins with his first novel, *The Seven Days of Man.*

It is a human Book of Genesis that corresponds to the divine book, a history of the village microcosm that reflects the story of the universe. In seven days the creation was completed: a day for the day and the night, a day for the heavens and the seas, a day for the earth and the trees, a day for the sun and the moon, a day for the animals and the birds, and a day for man. Then God "seated himself upon the throne."[4] In like manner the life of the village begins and ends in seven days: the day of the evening gathering, the day of the baking, the day of the journey, the day of service in the lodgings, the Big Night, the day of the farewell, and the day of the Path.

The Egyptian village is not just an earthly phenomenon. It towers like a palm with its roots in the earth and its fronds in the sky. Throughout the day the village toils, in order to water in the evening a heart thirsting for the light of God and his saints. Though engrossed in the everyday tasks of tilling the soil, bearing children, cooking, and baking, it does not forget its divine origin. On the eve of every Monday and Friday devotional meetings are held in the village, and its weary spirit, freed of material fetters, flutters up through the festive pennants like a white dove and loses itself in the heavens.

What writer could grasp this moment and thus put his hand on the soul of Egypt? Who could discover in the tilled brown soil the throbbing golden vein that runs from the beginning of history to its end, the tiny specks of earth in which sparkle the purest of hearts and in which can be heard the echoes of their prayers?

> But men are merely guardians of what they have. . . . "Pitchers of light are pouring down from heaven over your house, Ali Khalil." . . . "Sunset is a jewel. Seize it." . . . Sometimes the men's hearts were stubborn, like ill-tempered donkeys. . . .

This is how the heavenly world reveals itself to people of the village. Everything they do is holy, whether in the evening gathering when they meet for devotions, or during the day when they bake. The baking day is a terrestrial day that follows the heavenly day of the evening devotions, a festival of the flesh after the feast of the spirit. And it is the day of the women after the day of the men.

On the day of the baking we see only women—busy housewives absorbed in their chores, and laughing girls with ripening bodies who pant breathlessly as they work, their loose shifts revealing swelling breasts and little brown nipples. They almost die of laughter in the fever of kneading the dough.

But the day of the baking is only a prelude to the day of the journey to Tanta to attend the moulid of Sayyid Bedawi, and the day of the journey, in turn, is a fulfillment of the dreams of the evening gathering and a prelude to the day of service in the lodgings and the Big Night. The evening gathering is an expression of longing to meet the beloved, and the journey is the act of setting out for the long-awaited meeting. It is a corporeal journey, but one without the burdens that weigh the body down and delay the moment of encounter. It is a liberation from the preoccupations of house and village, work and custom, a release into blissful horizons where the soul takes flight, or rather where the body itself, as if transformed into a bird, soars up on the wings of the letters "BE," the divine command of creation.

The journey is a ritual ablution—freshly washed galabiyas, walking canes hung over forearms, and faces beaming with joy. It is anticipation and the elated apprehension of unforeseeable events to come. The journey is also an intrusion into the city through which the villagers recover their self-respect when they meet in the mosque of Ahmed Bedawi to perform their thundering ritual dance, imposing themselves and their presence on the city dwellers.

When the band of travelers arrives in Tanta, the day of service in the lodgings begins. Pilgrims to the tomb of Sayyid Bedawi are his servants, and the servants of his followers and his loved ones. They offer them food in the form of the bread and the moulid cookies they have brought with them. It is common for the people from a given village to rent a single house or apartment in which to stay during the moulid. These lodgings are their home in the city as they carry out the rites of the pilgrimage and perform their devotions and ritual dances. And from here they share their provisions with the needy.

The day of service in the lodgings is the day we discover the city, with its geometrical promenades, its pruned trees, its houses and its tall buildings. Under the street down which we walk there was in former times a canal, but it was filled in long ago, and over its course now stand these long rows of trees and these tall buildings. In the past Tanta still preserved something of its rural features, the most important of them being that buried canal that now has become a street, that old canal that visitors from the countryside still recall in a mournful song.

A satanic machine has replaced the water and the trees. The city has become something remote for the peasants, something that looks down on them. To welcome them in the square before the railway station it has stationed its terrifying instruments, squads of uniformed policemen on horseback and on foot, angry-faced marionettes wielding long sticks of bamboo in their hands.

In the city, despite its beauty and its cleanliness, everything is hostile and contaminated. The asphalt streets are crowded with carriages and noisy automobiles spewing smoke and steam from front and rear. On either side of the street stand tall buildings with plaques advertising the offices of doctors or lawyers. Then appear grocers' shops, cigarette stalls, shops offering chickpeas and sweets, and the workshops of automobile mechanics. As we reach the center of the city, the streets grow narrow and become crowded with townsfolk and wary visitors from the countryside. The peasants keep a tight grip on their bamboo sticks, which provide them with a sense of security. As they move through the streets in wide-eyed amazement, the town boys assail them, mocking their speech, tugging at their clothes, and snatching away their skullcaps.

The city is the malevolent antithesis of the good-natured and kindhearted village. Its inhabitants are unbelievers. It is an unclean and contaminated world. But in it stands the great mosque of Ahmed Bedawi with his mausoleum, the object of the peasants' longing, the reason why, in anticipation of the Big Night, they delight in visiting this hellish town.

The Big Night is the bridal crown that will sparkle on brows that have dripped with sweat from the ritual dance throughout the year. It is the culmination of the wedding feast and the gift of the saint to his followers who have longed to be with him, a blazing torch spreading light from the mosque of Ahmed Bedawi through the streets and the alleys and the squares.

Everywhere the city is filled with temporary pavilions, tents, and makeshift lodgings, tables spread for hungry dervishes, little groups sitting drinking coffee, and rows of devotees dancing the *zikr*.

The years pass, and the evening devotions are held twice every week. Each year the moulid of Ahmed Bedawi returns, and the women come together and devote a day to baking the provisions for the trip. Each year there is a new journey to Tanta, and the Big Night is repeated. But the author lingers only over some of these years. After the last Big Night that his characters attend, he takes us to the day of farewell.

The day of farewell is the prelude to death. Time has taken its toll on everyone and everything. The villagers have once again answered the call of the saint, but they have come broken in body and spirit. Their leader and spiritual father is frail and sickly. So are his men. One of them has nearly lost his sight, another has lost his wife, and all have lost their original enthusiasm. They are overcome by sorrow and lassitude. Everything is pale. Even the women of the city have lost their allure. The old houses have been torn down, the familiar narrow streets have been widened, and ugly new buildings have been built along them. Now one path must come to an end and a new path must begin, and the change of course marks the last day in the life of the traditional village.

The Seven Days of Man reflects a keen perception of the passage of time. The author of the novel appeared on the Egyptian literary scene in the middle of the sixties, when the world of the village was dying and a new world was being born in the Egyptian countryside. In the book it is the novelist himself who is the veiled hero. He stands in the shadows and observes the life of the village and chronicles its days, taking as his guide his father, the hero who stands in the light, who leads the brethren in the Path on their persistent journey until they come to the seventh day, which is the end of his story and the beginning of the story of his son. The son has left the village to complete his education at the university, but he comes home again to assume responsibility for the family when his father falls victim to a chronic illness.

Two paths leading in opposite directions. A man seeking a city in heaven, whose life ends with the end of the novel, and another from his loins seeking a city on earth, for whom the end of novel is the beginning. A clash between the two men is inevitable.

The boy grows up and rebels against the life of the village, while his father grows old and frail, exhausts his wealth, and is at length stricken with partial paralysis. In the clash between the two men, the lines of their destinies cross and are deflected in new directions. And in this change, Kassem's masterpiece reveals to us ourselves, our history, and the state of our land.

A desperate struggle between that which is being born and that which is dying. But it is a reclusive struggle that goes on for the most part in secret, and only a little in the open, just as happens in nature itself. Only a little violence, but a great deal of love. Yet time does its work. The sun shines on the home and on the grave, on youth and on old age, on those who laugh and on those who weep.

The author penetrates the lives of all his characters and reveals them to us, showing us their joys and their sorrows, and their hopes and their disappointments. We can hardly hold back our tears, for Kassem records in this novel the story of seven days we had forgotten.

Ahmed Abdel-Mu'ti Higazi

NOTES

This foreword is a translation, with minor changes, of the article "Ayyâm al-insân al-sab'a," published in *Al-Ahram,* December 26, 1990, shortly after the death of Abdel-Hakim Kassem. Notes are by the translator.

1. Sufi litany based on the repetition of the name of God, ritual dance.

2. The Arabic here is reminiscent of Koran 56:33.

3. Play on the title of *The Return of the Old Man to His Youth,* a sexual manual by al-Tîfâshî (d. 1253), which was translated into English by "an English Bohemian" under the title *The Old Man Young Again* (Paris, 1898).

4. Cf. Koran 7:54, 10:3, and other similar passages.

Translator's Preface

Abdel-Hakim Kassem was born on December 25, 1934, in the Nile Delta village of El-Bandara near Tanta. He attended secondary school in Tanta, commuting for most of the period but moving to the city in his last year. He continued his education at the Faculty of Law of the University of Alexandria, but after nearly three years of study, interrupted by a period of employment with the postal service, he was arrested on suspicion of leftist activity and sentenced to five years' internment in a concentration camp. In the spring of 1964, having served most of his sentence, he was released together with other political prisoners.

After spending about a year in his village, he went to Cairo, where he worked for some time in a bookshop in Zamalek owned by the widow of the leftist leader Shuhdi Atiyeh. Subsequently he resumed his studies at the University of Alexandria. After graduating, he began working in the State Organization for Insurance and Pensions. *The Seven Days of Man,* which was his first novel, appeared during this period.

In 1970 he married Zeinab Sallam, with whom he had two children. In January 1974 he was invited for some weeks to the Evangelical Academy in Berlin. Kassem was fond of Germany, and later in the same year, after having been accepted for advanced study by universities in both Britain and Germany, he chose to return to Berlin to the Free University, where he began work on a doctorate on Egyptian literature in the period of

Abdel Nasser. He soon became convinced, however, that concentration on academic goals would impair his creativity. It was in Berlin, at the cost of his doctorate, that he wrote most of the works he produced after *The Seven Days of Man.*

In 1985 Kassem returned with his family to Cairo, where he worked until his death in the General Egyptian Book Organization. For some months he was an associate editor of the literary and cultural periodical *Majallat al-Qâhira* (Cairo revue). In 1987 he began writing a weekly column in the fundamentalist newspaper *al-Sha'b.* In April of the same year, while running for a seat in the National Assembly for the leftist *Tajammu'* party, he suffered a severe stroke, which left him partially paralyzed for the rest of his life. His illness did not interrupt his activity for long, however. With the assistance of his wife Zeinab, to whom he dictated his works after his paralysis, he was soon able to resume writing. To this collaboration we owe his last two works, *Dîwân al-mulhaqât* (Collected epilogues) and the posthumously published *al-Dîwân al-akhîr* (The last diwan). Kassem died on November 13, 1990. He is survived by his widow and his two children.

The Seven Days of Man has been acknowledged in Egypt and among Western scholars of Arabic not only for its literary merit but also for its unique value as a social document. As translator, I felt it my duty to provide an English version that, while scrupulously accurate in its rendering of the many details relating to everyday life in rural Egypt, would still convey the feeling and the beauty of the original. To achieve both aims was not always an easy task. I must leave it to the reader to decide whether, or to what extent, I have been successful. The transliteration of Arabic words and names is deliberately inconsistent, being based on typical spellings used by Egyptians themselves and, particularly in the case of names, all I could muster of a sense for people's roles and personalities. Thus, to cite the most obvious example, the name of the Prophet is written "Muhammad," but "Mohammed" Kamel, whose first name in Arabic is precisely the same as that of the Prophet, has his name spelled more or less the way he himself would have written it if he had had the chance.

The foreword by Ahmed Abdel-Mu'ti Higazi and the biographical information on Kassem in this preface have been added in the present edition. Numerous changes and improvements have also been made in the text.

Many friends and colleagues have helped me along the way, and to all I wish to express my gratitude. Kassem's widow, Zeinab Sallam, his brother, Major-General Abdel-Moneim Kassem, Saeed El-Kafrawi, and Sonallah Ibrahim provided information for this preface. An English translation of the first chapter by Ben Bennani and a German translation of the fifth by Nagi Naguib were available to me. (A Dutch translation by Richard van Leeuwen and Johan de Bakker with an essay at the end by Hilary Kilpatrick appeared in 1984 [Antwerp: Standaard Uitgeverij] before my original manuscript was published. The translators kindly acknowledged my contribution to their work. I do not read Dutch and have unfortunately been able to use their translation to control my own only in a few places.) Abul Yazid El-Agami went over with me many problems in the first draft. Father G.-C. Anawati, Diana deTreville, John Hunwick, Séan O'Fahey, Frederick de Jong, Richard Pierce, and Hassan Mahmoud Abdel-Latif el-Shafei shared with me their knowledge of local customs and institutions and often helped me in choosing the right English words to render concepts and expressions particular to the rural Egyptian context. The people of El-Bandara kindly went out of their way to show me, one by one, virtually all the unfamiliar objects described or mentioned in the novel and explained to me a number of obscure points. Natasha Lewer read the text of this edition with great care and suggested a number of stylistic improvements. Most especially, however, I am indebted to the author, who not only went over the entire draft of the translation, providing help that no one else could have given, but who also graciously took time to show me Tanta and the village as the characters of the novel had seen them.

Much of the translation was completed while I was in Cairo on a grant from the American Research Center in Egypt, and the greater part of the remainder of my work was carried out with the generous support of the University of Bergen.

This translation is dedicated to Walter Herman Bell, Leonard Haines Bell, Earl Henry Carter, Robert Bagley Crallé, Jr., Frederick Holliday Jones, and John Andrew Lloyd, a generation of Virginians who, like the father of Abdel-Aziz in Kassem's novel, and indeed like Abdel-Aziz himself, have now left us.

1

The Evening Gathering

Abdel-Aziz had always loved the evening prayer. It came at the time when the day was growing faint, the sun was setting, and the lights were soft, perhaps even a little sad. His father, Hagg Karim, would say in his solemn, resonant voice:

"Sunset is a jewel. Seize it."

You had to pray right away, or the thin, delicate trace of light would vanish from the horizon and darkness would fall.

His father finished the prayer and went over to take his place on the bench on the guesthouse porch. His forehead was still dusty from his prostrations and his lips were still praising God. He was a good, lovable man with a special dignity about him, his father, Hagg Karim. No one ever sat in his place on that bench, even when he was away. If anyone were to do such a thing, he would surely sit there tense and nervous, leaning forward and cupping his hands on his knees, his legs dangling over the edge. It was Hagg Karim's guesthouse. He had inherited it from his father. It stood at the head of a lane where everyone belonged either to his family or his clan. He was their leader, and they were his proud, loving, and obedient followers.

Abdel-Aziz rolled up the reed prayer mat and stood it in a corner. Then he snuggled up to his father like a small kitten. His thin body was filled with excitement and anticipation for the delights of the evening.

How miserable the day was, when the sun blazed at its hottest and its harsh, unrelenting rays reached every corner, when the men labored long hours in the fields and the women hurried silently out to them with jugs of water and bundles of bread. The day was no time for pleasant words and storytelling. These were things for the evening.

Hagg Karim was good-humored in the evening. But during the day he was fearsome. He gripped the lead rope of his two animals with a rough fist and lashed their backs with his whip. The blade of his plow split the belly of the earth as the two beasts pulled and twisted beneath the yoke, dripping white foam from their mouths onto the cracked surface of the land. Around him all the men and children were single-minded and sullen, wholly taken up with what they were doing.

By day houses were sad places, flooded with light and dust. The lanes were silent, and Abdel-Aziz's heart was heavy. But now the houses seemed transparent as they glowed warmly in the subdued splendor of the twilight.

Abdel-Aziz snuggled up to his father and listened to his words of praise. They were obscure words whose mystery the boy could not grasp, but they unlocked in his imagination awesome images of men not like other men. Perhaps they were thin and frail and wore the most tattered garments, but they stood at the four corners of the earth, and when they chose to journey they covered huge distances with each step. They stretched out their hands and healed the sick. They filled udders with milk and granaries with grain. They lived among the people, and you could not tell them from the others. But when they died their light would break forth, and domed tombs would be built for them in the cities. The streets would be filled with people, like armies of ants, carrying their provisions to the feasts of the saints.

The boy snuggled up to his father and listened to that deep voice that seemed to be coming from his heart. He trembled with anticipation.

When his father had finished his recitations, he gathered his rosary in his hand and put it away in his pocket. Then he slapped the sole of his foot and with a long sigh invoked the name of Saint Ahmed Bedawi—the "Sultan." Hagg Karim's face was dark and fleshy, but well-proportioned. The boy could see his brown eyes take flight like two birds and lose themselves in the pink border of the evening twilight. This was the moment when he knew his father would tell him to fetch the lamp, and tonight everything happened as usual.

He brought back the big lamp, full of kerosene, its glass chimney polished and sparkling. His father lit it with a match, and Abdel-Aziz took it to the large reception room in the guesthouse. Climbing up on a chair, he placed it in the great lantern that hung from the ceiling and closed the door of the lantern over it. The dull yellow light spread across the walls, awakening the panels and floral designs painted on them and splashing them here and there with shining droplets of light. On the tiled floor was formed a big circular shadow that moved back and forth with the swinging of the lantern.

When the circle of shadow had come to rest beneath the lantern, and the rectangle of light that shone out through the door to the street, cutting the porch into two dark halves, had ceased to move, the people began to stir. They were coming back from the mosque after the night prayer, looking like feeble, broken ghosts, the remnants of their last recitations still on their lips. As they passed the porch of the guesthouse they mumbled faint greetings and then moved on to be swallowed up by the darkness of the lane. In their sad and dismal houses there awaited them darkened rooms and sleep until dawn. But ahead of the companions of Hagg Karim lay the delights of the evening gathering.

"Peace be upon you."

"And upon you be peace and the mercy of God."

A little storm of love and lighthearted laughter, and then the man climbed the few steps to the porch, greeted Hagg Karim, and sat down beside him on the bench. He caressed Abdel-Aziz's slender neck, and the boy felt the coolness of his hand, still moist from his ablutions.

Despite the darkness, Abdel-Aziz caught the glint of longing in his father's eyes as he spoke.

"God willing, may you pray in the holy sanctuary at Mecca, Sheikh Ahmed."

Ahmed Bedawi answered with pious humility:

"And you with us, God willing, Hagg Karim."

Every few moments another man would turn aside from the road that led by the guesthouse and climb the steps to join the gathering. He would greet the others and then take a seat and exchange a few pleasant words and good wishes. They kept coming until the whole group of friends had gathered.

Every evening this group of friends came together. They worked all day long on the land until their hands cracked. They yelled and screamed at their children and their wives and they beat their animals. They would become blind with rage. But in the evening they put on freshly laundered galabiyas and performed the night prayer together in the main mosque, saying amen from their hearts as they prayed behind the imam. Then they came to the guesthouse.

Now they were kind and wise. They looked at the toil and pains of the day with composure, and smiled. They regretted the storms of anger at their wives, their children, and their animals. But it was the hardship of life and the harshness of the day. It was that great and unfathomable secret hidden in the fertile earth on which they moved about in perplexity, worry, and anger during the heat of the day.

This was why God had created the evening and hidden the sun in the folds of the unknown for an appointed time. For if the world were an unending day and life were ceaseless toil, men would turn into devils who would not know God. There had to be the calm of the evening, when they could marvel at the wonders of the parting day, smile at its harshness, and question one another persistently about the secrets of growth and withering.

Hagg Karim was the lord of farmers. The land was his obedient wife, and he was its harsh master.

"If the blade of your plow is not right in the heart of the earth, there is no hope from the start."

They smiled with surprise to hear him make so much of plowing, but they agreed.

There had to be this calm every evening, when they could open their hearts to each other and talk. The conversation started, and stories began to unfold. In every breast there was a heart, and every heart had its own special concern. Life was a journey about which each of the men had something to tell, the things he had seen or heard, the hardships and the joys he had encountered. And so in the evening each of them came to the meeting of the brothers.

Each one of these faces, in all its minute details, was stamped on Abdel-Aziz's imagination. It could not be confused with any of the others. Each had its own character which he knew well and which he loved.

Ahmed Bedawi was the first to arrive for that evening's session. He was a young man of intelligence, the one who read books to the brothers. He had a round, childish face, with pink cheeks and narrow eyes, and he was always smiling.

Ali Khalil, the cautious and meticulous owner of the grocery shop, was the last to arrive, because he was slow and thorough in his prayers. He had a fat paunch, but his shoulders were narrow, his arms thin, and his face gaunt and pale. He seldom spoke, and he never laughed. He would only smile quietly, and a trace of blood would tinge the pallor of his cheeks.

Mohammed Kamel was tall and dark with broad shoulders. It was he who led the chants and the *zikr* at night. His head was graying, but he was still without children.

Iraqi the Deaf-Mute could neither hear nor speak. His only link with life was in his two sharp, flashing eyes, with which he recognized words as they were being formed on people's lips. He would answer with splintered sounds that provoked laughter more often than they conveyed meaning.

Mohammed the Dandy had a delicate frame and smooth white hands. Elegant and always smelling of cologne, he was the local ladies' man, and husband to the thieving Rawayih.

Then there was Omar Farhoud the camel-driver. Throughout

the day he would stay by his huge camel. He kept its halter wound around his arm, and he was constantly giving it something to eat. During the *zikr* his reason would abandon him, and white foam would run from his mouth. The men had to hold on to him until he calmed down. At the time of the moulid he would load the chests of provisions on his camel and take them to the city.

Selim Sherkasi was a carpenter, the remnant of a family whose minds had been destroyed by a strange form of madness. He would sit quietly without uttering a word. His only comment on what was said would be his obvious anger or a smile of approval.

There were many of them, but each one was a world of his own, a beloved world that Abdel-Aziz waited for every evening. He had an unquenchable thirst for the conversation of these men. Something bound them together in a strong and deep affection, and the day's cares, when they were thrown before the group in the evening, would always lead the brothers along a single path, toward former times and foggy images of the good old days, the days that had been full of blessings, to images of those men who spoke the wisest words, ate the coarsest food, and possessed divine power to heal the sick and fill udders with milk and granaries with grain. They would be led toward distant regions. There were their friends and the stories of rare meetings overflowing with love. There were the strange places and imposing shrines that one should journey to visit, the tombs of saints and righteous men in the big cities. In these moments there would emerge behind the limited world of everyday life another world, a marvelous and boundless world, one that awakened men's longings and filled their hearts with fervor.

Every evening was a new journey to another strange world, and the hero of the evening's journey would always be his incomparable father, Hagg Karim. He had traveled much and heard much. When he began to speak his gaze seemed to float in the pale yellow light. The designs painted on the wall looked on with eyes that sparkled. He heaved a deep sigh and slapped the sole of his left foot, which he had pulled up on his right thigh as he sat cross-legged in his place on the bench.

"By God, men! By the one who willed his death . . . "

Heads were bowed and hearts captivated as Hagg Karim told them about one of his friends or one of his sheikhs, or about a government official to whom he had spoken the bare truth without fearing a thing. When his story came to an end they sucked their lips in amazement and murmured inaudible words. Hagg Mohammed, Hagg Karim's father, had owned extensive lands, many animals, and even some riding horses. Then had come the crash and he had faithfully supported the brothers with all that he had. In the prime of his youth Hagg Karim used to ride around on a mare like a prince. But men are merely guardians of what they have; they own nothing. And the aim of this life is the afterlife, a misty, magical, pure world that kindles longing in men's breasts. Hagg Karim lit his lamp every night for the brothers, and he illumined their gatherings with his enchanting words. How happy were those men who opened their hearts to affection and sincerity. The few acres Hagg Karim still had were many, by the grace of God.

Ahmed Bedawi was speaking of his two small sons. Had they lived they would have been Abdel-Aziz's age now. On that day there had been no smile on Ahmed Bedawi's face. It was drenched with tears. His small frame lacked its usual sturdiness. He was weak and broken. Friends supported him on either side.

When Abdel-Aziz recalled those days, he would be overcome with sorrow and would not speak. The days of the cholera epidemic had been days of terror and dread. His young uncle had come to Hagg Karim.

"Death is crossing on the roofs from house to house, Hagg Karim. We must take our children and our things and leave."

Paralyzed by fear, Hagg Karim's brothers and children had looked on at him. He never took off his great cashmere galabiya or his turban. He went from one house to the other, wiping away vomit and excrement with his hands and bearing the victims on his shoulders to the vans. People shied and kept away from him, fearing the contagion. And the vans carried off those who had been stricken, blowing their sirens as they left the village with people who would never return, dead with no graves, bodies that would be thrown into ditches and covered with lime.

The morning of the Great Feast was a sorrowful one. The sun shone golden, and the lanes were freshly swept and sprinkled with water. But the village was wrapped in fear and silence. Ahmed Bedawi came leading his two little sons by the hand—four small white feet in new red slippers. That evening they died.

Ahmed Bedawi spoke of his two sons. Mohammed Kamel spoke of his wife Saddiqa, who was tall and dark like him, with big, wide eyes. Saddiqa went about in constant despair and oppressed with guilt. No sheikh or holy man ever came to the guesthouse without Mohammed Kamel taking the problem to him and without the man prescribing for him some prayer to say when he went in to his wife. Mohammed Kamel would say in a meek, broken voice that he never once neglected the prayer, when, in the evening, he went into the darkness of the room to Saddiqa. Abdel-Aziz looked at his brown face, his two withered cheeks. The man lowered his head. Perhaps. . . . Everything in its appointed time.

Each heart had its own special sorrow. But at times men's hearts were flooded with feelings of tenderness and affection. In such moments Ahmed Bedawi would speak of the girl he had loved. The sycamore fig trees beside the long canal had known of their love for each other. But her father had decided to marry her off to someone from a distant village. Ahmed Bedawi had been overwhelmed with grief, but she had told him to marry Fatma and to do his best for her. He loved his fair-skinned wife with the dark blue shawl. He loved her. She had a good heart and was obedient. But he remembered the girlfriend of his youth with fondness.

Sometimes the men's hearts were stubborn, like ill-tempered donkeys, and refused to be led along the path of decency and edification. Sometimes they yearned for idle words and scandalous talk. Then the rudder would turn toward the Dandy. His lips would part in a smile that revealed teeth ruined by tobacco and tea. Perhaps the problem in his eyes, too, had been caused by smoke rising from the water pipe. The whole gathering burst into laughter at the end of a story about his thieving wife Rawayih and his mistress El-Gazyeh. There was nothing illicit in his sharing the bed of El-Gazyeh, he said, since she had given herself to him as his possession. Ali Khalil grew pale at the Dandy's blasphemies. But no one could deny that El-Gazyeh had presented the Dandy with a treasure-trove of white flesh and kohl-blackened eyes fully equal to the treasures that Rawayih had given him, which included anything that could be stolen or carried off. El-Gazyeh would follow him around during the moulids. Once in a dark, narrow hallway Hagg Karim had caught them. He yelled at the Dandy, who jumped up off her in fright. Hagg Karim looked at him as he hastily arranged his turban. He was unable to restrain his anger.

"Leaving the others and playing around, son of a dog!"

The Dandy straightened his galabiya.

"I'll be right back, sir."

Within moments he was serving people food and coffee and seeing to the mantle lanterns that needed adjusting.

While the Dandy was talking, Hagg Karim kept his eyes lowered modestly and held back his laughter. But the suppressed laughter shook him visibly, and little Abdel-Aziz leaped up from his place with glee.

The Dandy owned no land other than a few square yards along the edge of the road. But he dressed like a pasha, in a clean white galabiya, and he protected his head with an expensive umbrella. Every afternoon he would go to inspect his "land," and the whole village would laugh. He was no farmer. He was only a servant who lit the mantle lanterns at funerals and weddings. His wife stole everything for him. Every day he ate meat and chicken and duck, all of it stolen. He put on the best cologne and the finest clothes and paid no attention to what the others thought.

Abdel-Aziz's heart would fill with laughter as he thought of the Dandy standing in the midst of a funeral reception, delicate and slender, wearing a striped satin caftan and holding a coffeepot in his hand. Only he did not call it a coffeepot, he called it a "weapon." He would lift the "weapon" up in the air with one hand and hold out a cup with the other. Down would come the stream of coffee, all that way, without ever missing the cup. Proud and arrogant, he would extend his hand to each person there, one after the other, offering him coffee. Whenever someone declined with a shake of his head, he would move on with an elegant sweep of his hand and pass the cup to the next person, never spilling a drop. That was how he was at the biggest funeral receptions, strutting around like a rooster, and glowering at the mantle lanterns as though he were a police sergeant making his rounds to check on the night watchmen.

Abdel-Aziz loved the Dandy and his jokes. He loved the way he made fun of Sherkasi and Farhoud. People said a lot of things about him. His wife was a thief, and he ate stolen food and wore stolen clothes. Abdel-Aziz could feel his heart pound when Ali Khalil came to see Hagg Karim. Ali Khalil was a man of few words. People could see distress in his face before he said a thing. He would bow his head, and his shoulders would seem narrower than ever. There would be a moment of silence, and all eyes would turn toward him. The eyes of Hagg Karim looked at him with compassion.

"Hagg Karim, the Dandy's whole life is sinful."

"But he dirties his hands with kerosene and lights the lamps at our weddings and funerals."

"His life is sinful."

"God has allowed him in his kingdom and in the Path. I can't throw him out."

But Ali Khalil insisted.

"His life is one sin after another."

The man's face grew pale with dread. It was a pallor that Abdel-Aziz knew, one that came over Ali Khalil's face when he sat listening to the preacher, that hulking giant who stood in the midst of the assembled peasants and shouted at the top of his voice terrifying things about the fire of hell, liars, thieves, and fornicators. The pallor of Ali Khalil's face as he spoke frightened Abdel-Aziz. He had never liked that preacher at all. He liked his donkey much better, a small white she-ass. Abdel-Aziz had thought she was little more than a baby, but he had learned that she was quite old. Nevertheless, he still hated to see the huge body of the preacher weighing her down, practically snapping her spine. When his father gave the word, Abdel-Aziz would lead her gently to the animal enclosure, where she would stand breathing heavily next to their big black donkey, which was also a female. Abdel-Aziz imagined the two donkeys becoming engrossed in friendly conversation as soon as he had left.

Hagg Karim went on speaking to Ali Khalil until he calmed his fears for the Dandy and brought back a feeble trace of good spirits to his face. Abdel-Aziz was pleased at his father's defense of the Dandy, that small, white-skinned man who was no bigger than a child, just like the preacher's donkey. His heart was full of compassion for these two, the skinny donkey and the sinful Dandy.

At times the merriment of the group would sweep away every remnant of decorum, and Iraqi the Deaf-Mute would stand in the middle of the gathering with his beard and his turban and his rosary made of big wooden beads—and talk.

How did Iraqi talk? He had a language of his own, splintered words whose meanings he completed by monkey-like gestures with his hands and body, contortions of his face, shrieks and whispers, and standing up and sitting down.

In earlier days Iraqi the Deaf-Mute had been as solitary as a wolf. He would crouch all day long in the sycamore fig tree at the head of his field, speaking to no one, looking about him with confusion in his eyes, glowering and alone. He had no link with the world other than his aged mother with her wrinkled black face. Then he fell ill, and from that time he would sit squatting on top of the mud heating oven that occupied half the dark room at the rear of their compound. Neither the amulets of the charm-writers nor the prescriptions of those who knew traditional medicine could cure him.

Then one day there came to the village a sheikh celebrated for his power to drive out the spirits that inhabit men's bodies. The old woman took him to her son, and the sheikh stayed on for months. He said that an obscure spell had been cast on Iraqi, a spell written on flakes of bran, and that the bran on which it had been written had been scattered to the four corners of the earth. There was no way to break the spell except by gathering the baneful bran and burning it. But that was an arduous task that only the sheikh's helpers, the good spirits who served him, could accomplish. Every morning he would bring a little bran, saying that it had been gathered from Iraq or from the Hejaz. The days passed and he would sit cross-legged on top of the heating oven, refusing to eat anything but pastry and honey for breakfast and meat and cooked dishes for lunch. From time to time he would burn incense and write out charms, at no little cost. When Hagg Karim heard of the matter, he grabbed his cloak and his cane and headed straight for the house of Iraqi the Deaf-Mute, taking two of the brothers with him. He dumped the sheikh's incense out and smashed his burner. Then he beat him and drove him out of the village. Iraqi looked on in astonishment, and then he laughed. Hagg Karim took him to the guesthouse and, in time, into the Path.

That night Iraqi had sat on the reed mat with the reciters, not knowing what was going on around him. He closed his eyes and began to move his head right and left, imitating the dervishes, but without any rhythm. All the while he kept muttering strange sounds. Abdel-Aziz had laughed his heart out at him. But Iraqi had become something different now, something that spoke. His words were splintered, but they conveyed some meaning, and he had a job in the nursery run by the Horticulture Service. He had bought a bicycle and was passionately in love with it. He decorated it with ribbons and red and green strips of paper. Whenever anything went wrong with it, he would grow sad and come to Hagg Karim.

"My bicycle's sick, Papa."

He called Hagg Karim his father. He would sit in front of him and laugh, carried away with delight. He was passionately attached to the brothers and to the Path. He had even let his beard grow and had bought himself a red turban and a red cloth belt with a shoulder harness that came down across his chest from right to left and bore the embroidered words "There is no god but God. Muhammad is the prophet of God." He was enraptured by candles, banners, and flags, and bought as many of them as he could afford. Early on the morning of the feast he would decorate the mosque, and in the dim half-light of the dawn you could see the mosque flooded with the glow of candles and virtually covered with standards and little triangles of colored cloth. Iraqi's delight bordered on madness. He would fly about the courtyard of the mosque, exchanging kisses with everyone and crying out for help from the Sultan.

Iraqi stood in the middle of the gathering, telling the story of his day at work in his own particular way, imitating everyone who worked with him. The brothers had a good laugh at the inspector, and at everyone else, pleasant or unpleasant, whom Iraqi had happened to run into.

This was the way it was from one evening to the next. At the end of the evening the lamp would be put out and they would return to their houses. But tonight was not like other nights. It was Thursday night, and Thursday night and Sunday night were blessed nights in the week. On these two nights would be held the sacred observance, with readings from *The Tokens of His Blessings* and *The Mantle of the Prophet* by El-Busiri.

When all the brothers had come together, they left the porch and went into the big hall with its great lantern and its two huge benches facing each other against opposite walls. Hagg Karim sat in his usual place and smiled to one of the brothers.

"Spread out the mats, my son."

"Yes, sir, Hagg Karim."

The shiny mats were spread out on the tiled floor. These mats had a white, waxlike sheen, broken by diamonds and squares of red and green. They were fine mats, woven by that godly man Sayyid from Mahallet Minouf. His eyes were so weak he could scarcely see and his voice so feeble his whispers could hardly be heard. But his hands had a roughness and an uncommon hardness, like the hooves of animals, the result perhaps of pressing sedge against twine as he wove his mats.

If he was especially pleased with a mat he had made, a prayer mat or a bench cover, he would roll it up and carry it on his hip, after the manner of the men of his craft, all the way from his village to Hagg Karim's house. The distance was great, and he passed many people on his way through the villages and the fields. He kept himself occupied on his journey with recitations and formulas of praise, and he greeted all those whom he met, even the children playing in the dust. When he arrived, he would lay down his burden and sit silently, looking very small. He reminded Abdel-Aziz of a pigeon. Not a sound could be heard from him except his sipping his coffee from the big painted china cup. When he got up to leave, Hagg Karim would object.

"You have hardly arrived, Sheikh Sayyid."

"It's the will of our Lord."

"Have a bite to eat, at least."

"It's not my lot."

Abdel-Aziz would be sad because this gentle guest would not share his father's meal. When he shook hands in farewell, the boy would ask himself if the will of God did not lie hidden in that strong, strange hand.

The mats woven by Sayyid, the godly man from Mahallet Minouf, were spread over the tiled floor of the hall. Right down the middle was set a row of low, narrow tables on which were placed small kerosene lamps, Iraqi's candles, and little braziers containing burning coals covered with incense. Clouds of smoke billowed up, and the intoxicating fragrance of the incense filled the room. The dervishes sat in two rows on either side of the low tables. Every now and then the door would swing open and a peasant would step in and greet those present. Looking around gingerly, he would take off his shoes and sit down at the end of one of the rows. Finally, when the time came, the big chest was brought out from an inner room—the chest in which were kept the copies of *The Tokens of His Blessings,* El-Busiri's *Mantle, The Intercession,* and a number of other awe-inspiring books.

Abdel-Aziz kept his eyes on the chest as one of the dervishes bore it in on his shoulder and set it down on the matting at the head of the two rows of men. That wondrous chest! When the older people had gone out to the fields for the toil of the day and the streets were quiet with few passersby, Abdel-Aziz, oppressed by the stillness, would sneak into the inner room where that big chest was kept. When he tugged on the lid it would come sliding off and reveal piles of yellow-paged books filled with tiny lines of print. The sight of those books always struck fear in his heart, but summoning all his courage he would pull one out of the chest and open it in front of him. Tiny lines with hardly any space between them went on and on, filling page after page. He would stare at the writing, unable to fathom its secrets. He went to school and had his own books, small, cheerful books with big print that told nice stories about little boys with clean clothes and little girls with braids and ribbons. But it was this mysterious writing that fascinated him. It disclosed to him only meaningless letters and words. How was it, then, that these yellow pages could be transformed into the magic that spread through the gatherings of the brothers, while Hagg Karim sat cross-legged in his place on the bench, slapping the bottom of his left foot with the palm of his hand.

"The lamps of God, Sheikh Ahmed! Light our gathering with the lamps of God, with *The Deeds of the Righteous.*"

The book entitled *The Deeds of the Righteous* was handed to Ahmed Bedawi, who read from it in a rhythmic, chanting voice. Misty images burst into the mind, images of men not like other men, stirring in the four corners of the inhabited world. Nails were hammered into their hands and feet, and their backs were lashed with whips. But there was something uncommon in these men, something that remained above the torture and did not bleed. As the tears rose in Hagg Karim's eyes, Abdel-Aziz tried with all his heart to capture the fabulous secret—the dark, coarse bread, the bitter salt, the turbid water, the tattered shreds, the eyes like strange birds, alighting nowhere. Men not like other men. Their legs were not like other legs, but like pointers moving over a map, covering huge distances in an instant, and their hands were not like other hands, but like the needles of instruments ordaining destinies.

Abdel-Aziz dared the chest again, pulling out other books and examining their covers. Some of the volumes had pictures on them from which he could determine their contents.

This one, without any doubt, was *The Romance of the Banu Hilal,* and the men shown on the cover were Hassan ibn el-Rabî', Abu Zeid, and Diyab ibn Ghanem in the council of the Arabs. How Abdel-Aziz loved Hassan ibn el-Rabî'. He was a wise, quiet, and sorrowful man who could foresee the misfortunes that were to unfold in the days ahead. As Ahmed Bedawi intoned the poetry that told of his wisdom, the men's heads would begin to sway with joy and contentment.

But Maryam, the skillful Christian woman in *The Thousand and One Nights* who devoted herself to needlework, aroused a feeling of special sympathy in Abdel-Aziz. She was borne about on ships that plowed the billowing waves and was sold in the slave markets. By the skill of her hands and by her needlework she would bring good fortune into the house of the man who bought her.

And there was that monkey who would turn every now and then into a handsome prince. How funny it was. One day, after Abdel-Aziz had grown older and gone to school, he had taken one of those books and read aloud from it to the brothers as if he were in class. But his father Hagg Karim had stopped him.

"That's not how poetry should be read, my boy. It has to be chanted."

Everything written on those yellow pages was poetry to them, and reading was always chanting or singing. It was the box of joys and sorrows, that big chest.

The copies of *The Tokens of His Blessings* were distributed among the dervishes. Everyone sitting on the shiny mats facing the low tables was a dervish.

A kind of silence came over the gathering. Nothing could be heard except the sucking of lips, the clearing of throats, and then the clap of Hagg Karim's hands.

"Begin, Sheikh Mohammed Kamel."

Mohammed Kamel was the oldest and most dignified of the dervishes and the paladin of the *zikr* on meeting nights. He began with his deep voice, and the chorus of dervishes echoed him. The recitation flowed with a smooth, calm rhythm, and countless blessings on the Prophet came one after another, as abundant as the grains of sand and the waves of the sea, as profuse as all that has been written by pens and all that has yet to be written. The voices grew warmer and stronger until the recitation of *The Tokens of His Blessings* was complete, leaving the dervishes with an even greater longing to continue their recitations and chants. Hagg Karim clapped his hands again and swayed with contentment.

"Begin the recitation of El-Busiri's *Mantle,* Sheikh Ahmed Bedawi."

Ahmed Bedawi, the intelligent young man with the beautiful voice who read books to the brothers in their gatherings, was the right person to lead the dervishes in the recitation of El-Busiri's poetry. For *The Mantle* was full of music, and his voice was full of color. He was the one who could carry the reading to the peak of exaltation.

"Help us, Lord Busiri!"

His eyes clung to the pale rays of light that floated on the ceiling of the big hall.

"*The Intercession,* Sheikh Ahmed! *The Intercession,* my son."

A soul full of longing for which there was no cure but these recitations was borne on the wings of the men's blessed voices to the clarity and splendor of the heavens, and a heart cauterized by fire responded.

"May God bless us through his saints!"

Then Ahmed Bedawi went on to lead the dervishes in the recitation of *The Intercession.* How Abdel-Aziz loved *The Intercession,* and how he loved to hear his father, Hagg Karim, say:

"While those whose hearts are empty sleep, the noble-hearted stay awake. They draw near to God through the remembrance of his saints."

"There was no fear on them, nor did they grieve." They were the breath of God in his creation, taken from the loins of the Prophet, his seed through Fatima in every generation. They were few in number, but they were the nearest of God's creatures to God himself. They were set apart from other men by their green turbans. Hagg Karim loved these men as had his father, who had even married the daughter of one of them from Sharqiya province. After her death, as they were carrying her to her grave, her coffin had risen abruptly into the air, almost wrenching the pallbearers' arms from their sockets. She desired to be buried next to her pious family, but Abdel-Aziz's grandfather had stood next to the coffin weeping and pleading with her to stay. The coffin did not come to rest, however, until he promised to build a shrine with a dome and a crescent over her tomb, and that shrine still stood in the village cemetery. From that day his grandfather had adopted the sheikh who had fathered his wife as his own sheikh and had become his disciple, and afterward Hagg Karim had become the disciple of the great sheikh's son.

The verses of *The Intercession* enumerated the saints of God and their miracles. The hearts of the dervishes were filled with humility and hope as they pleaded for God's favor through the merits of his saints. Abdel-Aziz waited impatiently for the verses that mentioned their present sheikh:

Through Mohammed ibn el-Fadl the exalted,
Lion of the noble and glorious, and of bounty.
O Lord, illumine his heart and his Path,
And may he avail us on the Day of Reckoning.

Abdel-Aziz's heart pounded as he thought of the sheikh, of

his gracefulness, the serenity of his features, and his calm and dignified bearing.

When Ahmed Bedawi came to the end of the recitation his head remained bowed and little beads of sweat glistened on his forehead. Hagg Karim continued to move his head to the same rhythm, as if the echo of the recitation were still in his ears. A long silence fell over the gathering. No sound could be heard except the men wiping their foreheads with the hems of their galabiyas. Then Hagg Karim announced with a clap of his hands:

"The Openings, Sheikh Mohammed Kamel!"

The repeated recitation of the first chapter of the Koran was an awesome ceremony with which every gathering was brought to an end. It was led by Mohammed Kamel with closed eyes. He began with his resonant voice, gesturing with his hand and naming those for whom the Opening was to be recited.

"The Four Poles! The Four Archangels! The Four Caliphs, Vicars of the Prophet! The Opening for them!"

The seated men recited the Opening in vague, barely audible whispers.

In the name of God, the Merciful, the Compassionate.
Praise be to God, Lord of the Worlds,
the Merciful, the Compassionate,
Master of the Day of Doom.
Thee alone we worship, thee alone we ask for aid.
Guide us on the straight path,
the path of those whom thou hast blessed,
not of those who have earned thy anger,
nor of those who have gone astray.
Amen.

"The Opening for the indulgent ones!"

"The Opening!"

"The Opening!"

"The Opening for our brothers in the Path, those present and those who are absent."

Some evenings a timid, hesitant voice would add:

"The Opening, Brothers, for . . . , may God remove his affliction."

Perhaps the brother in question was ill or in distress, confined to his house or on a trip for some business he had to attend to. Mohammed Kamel, closing his eyes, would repeat the request and call for the Opening.

Then came the dead, brothers who had been the flowers of these evening gatherings. Death had taken them, but the dervishes had not forgotten them. Mohammed Kamel called for the Opening for each one of them. Theirs was the abode of permanence, while ours was the abode of decay. How fortunate they were. God had brought their lives to a good end and had chosen them to be near him.

The burial ground was in the minds of all the brothers, the abode of permanence with its gray mud gravemarkers standing silently one after the other. On the morning of the feast the clear voice of the cantor would echo in the main mosque.

And when the preacher climbs the steps to the pulpit,
and praises God and proclaims his unity and his greatness,
then those who are present
must listen to what is said.

They would listen until the preacher, a small, pale, blessed man, finished his sermon and came down from the pulpit and the prayer of the feast came to an end. Then Hagg Karim, dressed in his most splendid attire, would walk out of the mosque, with the brothers in the Path and crowds of villagers following silently behind him. No one would utter a word. They were walking to the burial ground. There were no handshakes and no greetings, not one word before they had greeted the departed. When they reached the burial ground, Hagg Karim, the folk of the village behind him, would stand facing the tombs with sublime dignity.

"Peace be upon you and the mercy of God, household of believers. You have gone before us and we shall follow after you."

When Hagg Karim and the villagers appeared at the tombs, the women in mourning would begin to slip away from the cemetery to return to their homes. Each of them had spent the night before the feast by the tomb of a child or husband who slept in the dust. She had kept him company on the blessed night. The more fortunate women had spent the night in the village with their children, or on their husbands' breasts.

The men would disperse along the paths of the burial ground, greeting the dead and praying for them. The prayers of the living for the dead illumined their graves and made them spacious. They would pay their respects, spread green palm fronds over the graves, and water the aloe plants. In the end they would meet together in the tomb of Grandfather Mohammed's wife. There they would hold a morning recitation and offer its merits for the dead. After they had greeted the dead in this fashion, they would be free to greet each other, to talk, and to exchange their best wishes for the feast.

The dervishes recited Openings for the near at hand and the far away, for the living and the dead, until at last Mohammed Kamel's voice rang out:

"The closing recitation for the Prophet!"

This time the Opening was rendered with strong, loud tones, full of reverence and awe. At its conclusion the observance came to an end. Now the brothers could discard the serious air they had taken on for the recitations. They relaxed and began to chat. Little jars and old pill boxes filled with chewing tobacco were slapped into palms to loosen their contents, cigarettes were rolled, and puffs of smoke rose into the air, while eyes glanced here and there searching for shoes.

In this manner, every Sunday and Thursday evening, they held a blessed observance in which they recited *The Tokens of His Blessings,* El-Busiri's *Mantle, The Intercession,* and then the Opening many times over at the end.

But tonight was not like other nights. On a recent afternoon, while Hagg Karim was sitting on the porch of the guesthouse drinking coffee, Selim Sherkasi the Carpenter had come up to him. He was wearing his satin galabiya, his white felt cap, and his ankle-high orange shoes. On his face could be seen traces of dust from the road and that touch of joy one recognized in the features of those who were returning home from a journey.

Selim Sherkasi was not the kind of carpenter who made irrigation wheels and threshing sledges. His profession was making the leaves of doors and windows, knife handles, and sliding bolts. That was why his tools were always so brightly polished, his clothes so smart, and his temperament so high-strung and nervous. There was something frightening about him, too. Perhaps it was his furtive glances, or perhaps it was the stories they told about the ancestor of the Sherkasis, how he was of unsound mind and addicted to *manzoul* and how he used to do and say the most outrageous things. Perhaps a trace of the madness of this man flowed in the veins of his children and grandchildren, something you could not put your finger on, but something you felt and feared.

Sherkasi the Carpenter's wife was a tall, slender, fair-skinned woman who had borne him six daughters, and the man's longing for a son from his own loins had made him even more high-strung and added a disheartened tone to his voice. But after he had been drawn to the Path, his wife had given birth to a son whom they had named Shahhat, or "Beggar." Were we not all beggars? The good things of this life were few, scattered morsels here and there.

The carpenter climbed the steps, the traces of dust and the touch of joy still on his face. Hagg Karim never waited to be greeted. He was always the first to greet any arrival.

"Two welcomes, Sherkasi."

"And two greetings, Uncle Hagg Karim, one from me and one from our friends."

Hagg Karim echoed the joy of the meeting, slapping the bottom of his foot with the palm of his hand:

"Hey! Hey! Hey!"

He wanted to get to the heart of the matter quickly. But Sherkasi took his time, carefully gathering the hem of his satin galabiya. He had been wearing that white, flowing garment winter and summer ever since Abdel-Aziz could remember. He wore it on trips, feast days, and for the celebrations held by the brotherhood. He took out his box of chewing tobacco. Sherkasi did not break up the tobacco with a stick from the ground like the others. He used a sharp new nail. He offered some to Hagg Karim.

"I recited the Opening for you in the Sultan's tomb."

"Help us, O Lord Sayyid Bedawi!"

The words were spoken with a humility that went straight to the heart.

"I called on Sheikh Ali, too. 'When is the moulid?' I asked him. He told me the Big Night was one week from today."

Hagg Karim called out the name of God in joy, as if he had seen the crescent moon at the beginning of the lunar month.

"Help us, O Lord Sayyid Bedawi! Help us! You have called us, O Abu Farrag, and we are coming."

The blessed news spread through the village, stirring feelings of longing and devotion. Abdel-Aziz's heart fluttered in his breast like a caged bird. At times Sayyid Bedawi called his children through someone's passing remark. But they were impatient. If they were in Tanta on a trip, they would go to the great mosque, perform their ablutions, and go in, tracking still more water on the wet tiled floors. Perhaps the attendants would be able to tell them when the big celebration was to take place. But somehow the days would pass, and finally an announcement would be published in the papers establishing the exact date.

That night Iraqi the Deaf-Mute climbed the stairs to the porch hastily and excitedly. Before greeting anyone he thrust a folded newspaper into the hand of Hagg Karim. Abdel-Aziz's whole body shook with laughter. Ahmed Bedawi poked Iraqi in the ribs.

"Greet us first, son of a dog."

Iraqi looked at Ahmed Bedawi's lips and knew that he had insulted him. He responded with splintered words:

"Just don't say 'son of a dog.'"

They all laughed, and Iraqi joined in. Then he ran into the hall, came out again with a chair, and sat down in front of Hagg Karim. He was still laughing. Hagg Karim folded the newspaper and set it beside him on the bench. From the movement of his lips and the gestures of his hands Iraqi knew that he had already read the announcement in the afternoon.

As Hagg Karim was pouring his coffee from the brass *kanaka* into the big painted china cup, he had been surprised by Sheikh Ibrahim el-Gamal, a clerk at the government experimental farm. Sheikh Ibrahim was wearing his poplin galabiya with the western-style collar and his white calico skullcap. His amber prayer beads rotated between the fingers of his hand with amazing speed. Abdel-Aziz politely gathered the edges of his galabiya. Sheikh Ibrahim el-Gamal was his teacher who had taught him the fundamentals of reading and arithmetic. Perhaps the milky film over one of the clerk's eyes had frightened him a little too. People always wondered how Sheikh Ibrahim el-Gamal could possibly manage to say the words of praise as fast as the beads of his rosary slipped through his fingers. Maybe he mixed up the words so that they became meaningless sounds that did not spring from his heart. Hagg Karim would say that only God knows the secrets of the heart. But people went on wondering.

Hagg Karim offered his guest the first cup of the afternoon's coffee, full to the brim and covered with froth. The clerk responded by unfolding a newspaper he held in his hand.

"Uncle Hagg Karim, God has proclaimed the moulid of the Sultan."

He thrust his finger against the spot on the page where the announcement was printed.

"Read it to me! Read it to me! Reading the paper hurts my eyes."

"The Big Night is to be held . . ."

When he had finished reading, Hagg Karim took the newspaper and held it close to his eyes. Then he held it out at arms length and read the announcement for himself, moving his lips. He put the paper down beside him and gave a loud clap with his hands.

"You have commanded and we shall obey, O Sultan."

Then he intoned joyously:

O you who journey toward him
with firm intention,
you left longing in my heart
the day you departed.

This was the way Sayyid Bedawi called his children. It was different with the Dweller in the Wilderness, beyond El-Qurein in Sharqiya province, Sidi Selim Abu Misallim Iraqi, who had come from Iraq to the good earth of Egypt surrounded by his banners and his men and had then decided to live in seclusion in the wasteland. Still now he seemed to be present in the midst of his followers. He had a low tomb with walls that were falling down. Around it stood other tombs where his companions lay. Here and there were scattered a few rustic huts, as though they were the attendants of the saint and his men in their evening gatherings. In the vast space around the tombs nothing broke the force of the powerful winds. But when the moulid came, the empty space was filled with people, tents, drums, horses, and cuts of goat meat. Thieves and murderers repented, and the whole area echoed with chants. How marvelous this saint was, and how strange the way he called his children.

"Before Iraqi's moulid, Abu Garida, the man with the palm-stick, always comes, doesn't he?"

He was as black as if he had been made out of rubber tires, and his muscles were as sinewy as those of a black colt prancing about on its hind legs. He came barefoot, almost running, carrying in his hand a long stripped palm branch. To the end of this branch was attached a piece of paper with the date of the moulid written on it and bearing the seal of the sheikh of the Misallimiya order. Abu Garida made the rounds of the seven provinces announcing Iraqi's moulid.

When the dates began to ripen, Abdel-Aziz would wait for his arrival. One day in the forenoon he would appear on the road, careening through the village like a phaeton. He would stop before the guesthouse and proclaim the moulid. Then, at Hagg Karim's invitation, he would leap up the stairs to the porch, and, after devouring the food he was offered and drinking the curdled milk right from the rim of the bowl, he would jump up to go. Hagg Karim would try to keep him a while longer.

"Rest a little, man."

"I can't, Uncle Hagg Karim. There are four provinces left."

And so he would disappear down the road, carrying with him the heart of little Abdel-Aziz. Hagg Karim would be glowing with contentment.

"Help us, Sidi Selim Iraqi! Help us, O Daughter of Hussein, Sayyida Nafisa, Pearl of the Two Abodes!"

Abdel-Aziz had been small and thin, and his hand had been like a newly hatched bird resting in the moist, warm palm of his father the day they stood before the tomb of Sayyida Nafisa in her great mosque in Cairo. He had peered through the brass grill and the clear polished glass at the gauze draped over the head of the tomb—a bride's apparel on her wedding night. Abdel-Aziz loved her and the sweet fragrance of her perfume.

It was always a festive morning when the postman came. He would get off his donkey and greet Hagg Karim politely. The letter was always from Hassan Effendi, who lived on Commander-in-Chief Street in Cairo with his fair-skinned, kind-hearted wife. She was still nursing her baby daughter, whose body was covered with tiny sores. Abdel-Aziz's heart would leap in his breast as his father handed the letter to Ahmed Bedawi.

Greeting one's fellows was always the great joy of the brothers, and the time was now at hand. The apartment was a big one in a block of the old style. Love itself was the bed of good friends and their pillow, and we all lived in the bounteous presence of the Bride of the Saints Sayyida Nafisa. Hagg Karim could barely restrain his tears.

"O God, Generous Lord, do not let us stray from thy Path!"

What would the world be without these lamps?

Hagg Karim sat cross-legged in his place on the bench, while the dervishes sat in two rows on the shiny white mats facing the low tables with the kerosene lamps and the incense burners. In their hands were copies of *The Tokens of His Blessings.*

"My sons, next week we will hold our gathering in the sacred presence of the Sultan."

The men's faces beamed with pleasure. "Help us, O Lord Sayyid Bedawi! Help us, O Abu Farrag!"

Tobacco-boxes slapped in their palms. The coming days promised many delights. Their yearning had ripened in the heat of the midday sun over long days of uninterrupted toil. O Sultan, comfort of heart and soul!

"The money is not there, Hagg Karim."

Ahmed Bedawi was the boldest of the dervishes with Hagg Karim. He slapped his hands with his copy of *The Tokens* and thought. He had hidden fifty piastres in a box somewhere, but his wife had come across them and taken them. What could he say to his pampered wife?

"It will work out. Things will get better."

The anxiety that came over the men's faces like a cloud was dispelled only by Hagg Karim's deep, trusting voice.

"Things will get better, my son. Things will get better."

Things were always going to get better. One crisis followed another, and the men's money drained off into bottomless pits. But at the appointed time they set out for the tombs of the saints. Hagg Karim lowered his head for a moment in silence, creating in those present an intense longing for conversation.

"By God, . . . By the one who willed his death, . . ."

It was the grand sheikh he was thinking of. They were coming back from the moulid of Sidi Ibrahim Disouqi. They had got off one train and were waiting for another. A mat was spread on the station platform for the sheikh, and he lay down on it.

"Hagg Mohammed."

"What is it, Uncle?"

"I want a soda."

"I'm out of money. God is my witness, Uncle. I just have enough for the tickets home."

"Hagg Mohammed, I want a soda."

The sheikh ordered the soda and drank it.

"Pay for it, Hagg Mohammed."

"With what?"

The sheikh went into a fit of rage and hurled the empty bottle into the air. It flew as though it had sprouted wings, and when it came down it bounced up again and landed upright on one of the rails, without a crack or a chip. The dervishes praised God at the sight of the miracle, and people began to gather around. As the news spread, the crowd grew larger and larger, and silver coins piled up on the mat of the sheikh. People with special needs kissed his hand and begged him to pray for them.

"Pay the price of the soda, Hagg Mohammed."

This had happened when Hagg Karim was still a young boy and a novice in the Path. Abdel-Aziz had never seen anything extraordinary of this sort. The present sheikh was a good-looking and holy young man, but he had performed no great miracles such as this. If only Abdel-Aziz had seen the great sheikhs of the past with his own eyes as Hagg Karim had. The present sheikh was the descendant of those poles of the Path, but people's hearts hardened with time, and in every age God diminished his favor in the world by a measure. There was no refuge but the Path. It was good, all good. Take up your provisions, your cane, and your tent, and set out to visit the Sultan. This is what that godly man and his follower did. When they reached the holy grounds he struck his tent pole into the earth and set up his tent. Then he lit a fire and put the pot on. His follower said to him:

"Uncle, the lentils are few and the hungry are many."

The godly man replied:

"My son, if the Sultan has sent us his children but has sent us no lentils for soup, then soak the bread in water."

The follower poured water into the pot without any lentils, but when the bread was added it made a dish more delicious than any they had ever tasted. How then could a disciple abandon the gate to linger idly by the walls? The money was not there indeed, but things would get better.

His father would send him to call Mitwalli Saroukh, and the man would come and sit on the bench beside Hagg Karim. Saroukh was a thin, somewhat gloomy peasant, unpolished perhaps, but reserved. Abdel-Aziz's heart pounded with fear.

"I need a few piastres, Saroukh."

"Right away, Hagg Karim. Anything you want."

The village scribe would come next. His hands and body were soft and he had very bad breath. His glasses hung down on his nose. He was a strange man who was always peering around people's houses and going in and out of them. He would sit down cross-legged, resting his papers on his knee, and write squintingly. As he wrote, land and animals were transferred from one person to another, while the people themselves looked on. Where had he been? Where was he going next? Who had sold, and who had bought? The thin slice of land Saroukh owned next to Hagg Karim's property kept getting wider and wider every year.

The anxiety that was building up in Abdel-Aziz's heart could only be eased by his father's deep voice and trusting words.

"We own nothing ourselves. We are merely guardians of what we have."

Everything in their houses belonged to the poles of God's Path. The cow that had given birth, the newly weaned calf, whatever their eyes fell upon was slaughtered without hesitation. If any good fortune befell one of the brothers, he would come to Hagg Karim with the news.

"Uncle Hagg Karim!"

The man would stand before Hagg Karim with bashful joy.

"My buffalo gave birth."

"God be praised, my son."

How Hagg Karim rejoiced at the good fortune of the brothers.

"The milk is enough for me. The calf is for the chosen of God."

"May God reward you many times over, my son."

There would be an evening of celebration at the brother's

house, but it would be put off until the sheikh's annual visit to the village. Those were blessed nights, the most splendid nights in the year.

All the brothers would go out to meet the sheikh at the train station, and they would come back by the road in a glorious procession. The sheikh led the way with Hagg Karim at his side, two men joined by kinship and the Path. The procession followed them. Each brother would welcome the guest who was closest to his heart. The Dandy had Mistikawi in stitches. Ali Khalil was clinging to every word Hassan Effendi said. Sheikh Abbas was off to one side with Sherkasi the Carpenter, while the coffee brewer was hanging on to Mohammed Kamel. The charm writer, his eyes wandering, ambled along muttering endless expressions of praise. The way was strewn with words of welcome and affection.

Those were blessed nights, the most splendid nights in the year. Every evening the sheikh and his men would be invited to the house of one of the brothers or aspirants. Animals promised as offerings would be slaughtered, and recitations and *zikrs* held. The walls would tremble with the festivities. But the most splendid night of all was when the celebration was held at Ali Khalil's house. You had hardly stepped across the threshold going down toward the courtyard when you saw a mud stairway leading up to the flat roof. You would rush toward the stairway, hardly noticing a cavernous opening beside the door. Perhaps it was a storeroom, or perhaps it held a heating oven, a refuge for the children on winter nights. Perhaps. Abdel-Aziz had never been inside it. But Ali Khalil's sickly children would come bursting out of it, followed by his youthful wife, a tall woman with rosy cheeks who looked like a strip of rich, fertile land.

The sheikh's procession advanced toward Ali Khalil's house. Before the door to his house was a small square surrounded by tiny, low houses unlike the taller ones on the main street. Out of these tiny, low houses women and children clambered up to the street level to watch the sheikh's procession as it moved toward Ali Khalil's door.

The sheikh, followed by the brothers, climbed the mud stairway to the room on the roof. It was a delightful place, spread with white reed mats and freshened by a cool northerly wind. In the window, on a round brass tray, were arranged new clay water jars with red, green, and yellow plastic covers that Ali Khalil had brought back from Tanta. How elegant he was, and what fine utensils he had. Every now and then a man or woman would climb the steps bearing a small child. Ali Khalil would take the child in his arms and go over to the sheikh. His house was in a poor quarter, and the people there loved him. He himself had been poor, but God had been generous to him. The others could not afford to hold such splendid evening celebrations or to invite the sheikh.

From the minute the sheikh arrived at Ali Khalil's house, people would begin to come with their children to seek blessing. Ali Khalil carried the children to the sheikh, who would stroke their heads and spit in their mouths. The charm writer was busy writing out spells and making amulets for women who were barren or whose children died in infancy. The sheikh's visit to Ali Khalil's house was a festival for the whole quarter. Ali Khalil remained standing, constantly looking around to see whether any of his guests wanted anything. The sheikh called out to him with his Sharqiya accent:

"Sit down, man. Rest a while. We're fine. We don't need a thing."

Ali Khalil gave a timid smile and then went down to the central enclosure. There Hagg Karim was slaughtering the sacrificial animal, which writhed and twisted in its bonds with extraordinary force. The men surrounding it, in awe of the beast, pulled on the ropes with all their might. Hagg Karim pressed his knee against its neck. His face was like this only when he was slaughtering, or plowing, or disciplining a wife or a child. His knife slit the throat just below the back of the jaws, and the blood spurted out, splattering the ground and the hems of the men's galabiyas. The girls stomped their heels in the blood of the slaughtered animal, pulling their long dresses up their legs. The body quivered on the ground, and Hagg Karim and the men around him smiled. Then Hagg Karim slapped the flat side of his knife against the quivering carcass. He could not wait. He grabbed one of its hind legs, pierced it with his knife just above the joint, and opened several passages beneath the skin with an iron skewer. He put his mouth to the hole and began to blow the animal up like a giant balloon to separate the hide from the flesh. After the carcass had been blown up it would be hung from the roof and Hagg Karim would skin it and cut it up. He knew everything, he was skilled at every task, Abdel-Aziz's incomparable father.

The little square before the door of the house was ablaze with light. Children filled the street, while the roofs of the surrounding houses were crowded with women and girls. The Dandy, in his fine turban and his resplendent caftan, looked just like a pasha, except for the needle for cleaning lanterns stuck behind his ear. He wandered around staring grimly at the mantle lanterns. If the eye of one of them grew sleepy, he would rush over to it with the big ladder, scramble up like a monkey, and clean and adjust it, all the while glowering as though he were reprimanding it or pinching its ear. Then the bright light and loud hiss would return.

The white mats were spread out, a huge expanse of mats. Every man and woman had brought something from his home to help cover the ground. These people loved Ali Khalil. They stood around him talking and laughing. His face was pale in the white light. He was a good, tender man. With a gentle hand he would move along the children who were milling about and kept getting in the way.

The wide stretch of mats was divided down the middle by a line of low tables and two long rows of seated dervishes. There were many of them on this night, very many, men with kindness and sincerity in their faces who had left their houses to come to Ali Khalil's. Each man took off his shoes and, placing them together sole to sole in front of him, sat humbly and reverently on the matting. The two rows kept growing longer and longer, while the line of tables seemed to shrink and grow shorter as the number of men increased.

Iraqi, anticipating the joys of the evening, came wearing his red turban and his belt with the shoulder strap that came down across his chest. In his hand he carried an incense burner. He was crying at the top of his voice for help from the Sultan. Then he put his incense burner on the floor and broke into a violent dance, throwing himself right and left to the rhythm of his voice.

"Allah hayy! Allah hayy! God lives!"

When he discovered he was dancing alone, he burst out laughing. Everyone laughed with him, men, women, and children. Then he began to run about the square with his incense burner, laughing and calling out for help from the Sultan.

The smaller boys, off to the sides, were holding their own *zikrs,* little imitations of the men's dances, which lasted for a few moments and then broke up, only to start again somewhere else. They were laughing, running about, tugging at each other, and tossing back and forth whatever they could get their hands on. The older boys sat in row after row behind the dervishes. The rows covered all the mats and extended beyond them onto the earth, which was still moist from the evening dew. The women kept to the edges of the square where the light was dim, or they remained scattered about on the rooftops. The faint glint of their eyes and their cheap jewelry, their whispers and their laughter, gave an obscure frame to the evening's gathering.

Hagg Karim came out, and everyone fell silent. Dressed in his great cloak and holding his cane in his hand, he walked unhurriedly into the midst of the gathering. The only sounds were here and there a whispered request for quiet. He stood still for a moment, without saying a word. Abdel-Aziz's heart almost stopped beating. Then Hagg Karim's voice rang out loud and clear, as if God himself were speaking:

"Pitchers of light are pouring down from heaven over your house, Ali Khalil."

Ali Khalil's face froze as though it were made of wax. The ear-splitting trills of the women filled the air. Hagg Karim spoke again in a low but audible voice:

"Begin, Sheikh Mohammed Kamel."

Tonight Mohammed Kamel was dressed in his most splendid attire. He had wrapped a white shawl around his cap of rust-red wool and draped a long muffler over his shoulders. His face was shaven, and, with his broad shoulders, he looked just like one of the saints of God whose pictures were sold in the market. He closed his eyes, and his face took on a sublime dignity. His deep voice intoned the beginning of the recitation, and the chorus of dervishes followed him in a calm, steady flow. "I seek refuge in God from Satan the accursed. In the name of God the Merciful and Compassionate. O God, bestow thy most excellent blessings on the most fortunate of thy creatures, Our Lord Muhammad, and on his family, blessings in the number of all things thou knowest and in the measure of the ink with which are written all the words thou hast spoken." It was an immense world, deserts and sands, seas and rivers, trees, clouds, and tiny specks, and in the breast of every creature, however small, even in the particles of dust floating in a ray of sunlight, there was a warm, throbbing heart that praised the name of God and blessed the most fortunate of his creatures. In this strange journey through the regions of the universe, through the heavenly spheres and the bottomless depths, the men's hearts were kindled with longing, and the recitation raged like an uncontrollable fire. The women's trills split the air.

Ahmed Bedawi's shrill, piercing voice stood out among the others. Little by little he began to impose himself on the river of flowing voices, carrying them toward a provocative, swaying rhythm full of shades and color. The words became progressively clearer and seemed to take on flesh. Letters wept, syllables danced, and words implored humbly amid the profusion of dazzling meanings. When the reading of *The Tokens of His Blessings* came to an end, the men's hearts had become so light that they seemed to soar away with their bodies into the blinding light.

He was shrewd, by God, that Ahmed Bedawi. When he took over, the dervishes were hoarse and sweating from the recitation of *The Tokens.* But he would lead them on to the infinite realms of *The Mantle.* The women followed intoxicated on the rooftops, while the men swayed in the two rows like branches in the wind. The sheikh looked down on them from the window.

"Again, Bedawi! Again, my beloved! The strains of your music are from God himself."

His arms were swinging in the air, and in one hand he held a copy of *The Mantle.* His body would bend and rise.

Despair not, my soul, over sin that is great.
Mortal sin is paltry, if God forgive me.

Abdel-Aziz felt that same thrill he had experienced when he had seen those words glittering with life as the red and green light fell on them through the stained glass in the windows of the mosque. Hagg Karim had held his little son's hand and pointed to the inscription.

"See, Son. Read it. The whole *Mantle* is written around the walls of the mosque."

El-Busiri's mosque in Alexandria. A salty sea breeze was blowing through the sanctuary, and the letters seemed alive in the colored light.

O you who blame my innocent passion,
If you were just you would not reprove me.

Ahmed Bedawi's voice had all the hoarseness of the minstrels who sang the praises of the Prophet. On the evenings when those minstrels presided over the meetings in the guesthouse, a great crowd of people would gather at their feet and the beating of the big tambourines would shake the walls. Abdel-Aziz felt a tension greater than that of a drum skin tautened over fire. What was special about this night? Were these minstrels singing tonight, or was it just an ordinary *zikr* being held in front of Ali Khalil's house? Was it perhaps the way the lamps glowed with joy at the approaching festival of the Sultan?

The low tables were removed, and when Mohammed Kamel stood up everyone in the two rows stood up with him. The children crawled or pushed their way through legs and bodies and sat down on the mats between the two rows of standing men. The mantle lanterns were brighter than ever, and the rooftops were crowded with girls. Scattered trills anticipated the approaching joy of the *zikr.*

At the head of the two rows stood Sanhouti, the flute player and leader of the *zars,* the women's exorcism rites, in the village. He was so thin that his robe seemed to be draped over two swaying canes of bamboo. He was as pale as a corpse, standing there with his sunken eyes, and he never shook off the effects of opium any longer than was necessary to blow a few notes on his flute. How had Sanhouti happened to marry that enormous black woman who stood beside him holding a huge tambourine and baring her dazzling white teeth in laughter?

Mohammed Kamel stood between the two rows, and lifting up his hands, sighed a prolonged "Allah . . . !"

At the end of that deep sigh he gave a loud clap of his hands, and the rhythm began with the slow, regular repetition of the name Allah to the accompaniment of little solos blown by Sanhouti on his flute and the jingling of the disks on the rim of the tambourine. Two thin, hairy arms showed out of the flowing white sleeves of Sanhouti's galabiya. His wife's eyes, tranquilized by the rhythm, remained closed. These two, Sanhouti and his wife, his flute which was no more than a handbreadth long and her big tambourine, took hold of women from faraway villages. They would come wearing black, hesitant and wary, and wend their way through the twisting lanes until they reached Sanhouti's house, where the *zar* was held every Monday and Friday of the week.

The *zikr* became a mad frenzy. Mohammed Kamel in the middle, swaying and clapping his hands loudly above him, set a fast, feverish rhythm. Sanhouti breathed a maniacal spirit into his flute. His cap flew off and his black hair waved back and forth over his temples and forehead as his slender body shook with the rhythm. Barking sounds erupted to the same rhythm from the hearts of dozens of dancers at once and echoed off the walls of the houses. The pounding of the men's feet on the ground seemed to shake the whole village. The two rows of bodies were drenched with sweat. They leaned together, twisted together, and came up together. They bent forward and rose together in one convulsive sequence. Sanhouti's wife was beating the skin of her tambourine—the skin that had been tautened over the fire—with her fat, black hand. There was nothing left in the world but the sound of the tambourine and the flute and the barking from the breasts of the dancers and the pounding of their feet. It was an overpowering noise that crushed the hardness in every heart.

Abdel-Aziz felt fear, but it was a glorious fear, like the feeling he had had at his paternal aunt's house in that faraway village. His father had married her off there into a big house with many long, dark passageways. The ancestor of the people of the household was buried in the central enclosure. They kept a lamp on the tomb that never went out, and whenever they passed by, they would look warily toward the spot where their ancestor lay. They were not ordinary folk. The elder daughter was a spinster and her body was full of spirits. They had brought her huge tambourines and pounded on them fiercely. That was when he had felt that glorious fear. His aunt had held him close to her breast and had taken the hem of his galabiya and tied a knot in it. That would protect him from the spirits, she had said. If only someone would tie a knot in the hem of his galabiya now to protect him from the fierce beating of the tambourine.

Mohammed Kamel raised his arms over his head and cried out to close the *zikr:*

"Allah . . . !"

The disks of the tambourine trembled until his voice became still, the sound of the flute trailed away, and storms of trills burst forth from the rooftops. The dancers could hardly stand from exhaustion. Omar Farhoud had been drawn by God, and no one was able to get him back on his feet or to control him. The Dandy remarked maliciously:

"Leave him alone. He won't stop until his wife sees him. He

tells her that God draws him in the *zikr,* but she doesn't believe him."

He laughed and all one could see was his black teeth. Sanhouti used a white handkerchief to wipe his short flute, which was dripping with saliva. Iraqi the Deaf-Mute was still absorbed in the *zikr.* He had not heard it end. Someone tugged at his arm to let him know. When he realized what had happened he started to scurry about, here, there, and everywhere, insulting people to hide his shame.

The walls of the big hall in the guesthouse bore the traces of many such nights. Ahmed Bedawi's voice possessed the fragrance of the nights of joy, the fragrance of the Path.

"May we gather next in the sanctuary at Mecca!"

"God was manifest here tonight!"

"The gifts of the Sultan, his breath!"

"May the Lord never deprive us of his bounty!"

They took out their handkerchiefs to wipe the beads of sweat from their faces. In strained whispers they recited Openings for brothers far and near, living and dead. The brothers were one's companions through the short journey of life. Without them the world had the taste of dust.

Those who were in a hurry to find their beds left after the Openings. But the beloved few stayed on with Hagg Karim. Out came the packets of tobacco, the cigarette papers, and the boxes of chewing tobacco. They stretched their legs out on the mats. Why should they be bound by the rules of decorum now that the evening gathering had come to an end? They spoke plainly but dreamily.

"We set out on Sunday, God willing."

They would set out to visit the Sultan—the trip, Tanta, the lodgings, meeting the brothers, the moulid, and the Big Night. Their conversation sparkled as the dream of the coming days was fashioned in the light of the dimming lamp and its burnt, sleepy wick.

The last to leave was always Ahmed Bedawi. He smiled.

"Good night, Uncle."

When the big door closed behind him, loneliness filled the hall. Hagg Karim returned to the house carrying the lamp and his cane. Abdel-Aziz walked behind him. Night was a terrifying stillness that led to the day, the day with its grim faces and shouting voices. If only the evening gathering would never end.

2

The Baking

The breath of the sleepers choked the room. The lamp, its scant light stifled by ghostly shadows, was a drowsy eye on the wall. The four tall posts of the brass bed were cast across the walls and ceiling. Sounds of breathing rose and fell spasmodically, as though an enormous animal lay beneath the heavy layers of slumber. Beads of sweat on brown foreheads, bodies bare in the closeness and heat. The dim world of shadow and gloom and the acrid stench of the chamber pot crept into the brain of Abdel-Aziz as he slept, unsettling his dreams. A bloated, hairy thing reached out to strangle him. He awoke. His father's woolly hand, moist with sweat, stretched heavily across his face. He pushed it away and looked around. Praise God, it was only a dream. He shut his eyes again but now he was wide awake. Hagg Karim stirred next to his son on the bed. He sat up, smoothed his nightshirt down over his naked thighs, and got up. On the floor the children lay close together on a reed mat. He made his way cautiously through the bodies to the clothes hook and pulled off his nightshirt. He stood completely naked, his back to Abdel-Aziz. The boy opened his eyes. His father naked. Folds of flesh sagging over his haunches. Abdel-Aziz shut his eyes again. The man put on his clothes and went out to the mosque.

Abdel-Aziz tossed uneasily. His sisters were twisting and turning on the mat, and he kept his eyes tightly closed to avoid seeing their nakedness. He buried his face in the pillow, terrified by a sense of guilt. He heard his mother's voice.

"Wake up, girls. Daybreak is here. We've got baking to do."

They sat up, straightening out their shifts and rubbing the sleep from their eyes. Then they covered the smaller children again with the sheets. Abdel-Aziz got down out of the bed. Putting on his skullcap and buttoning up the collar of his gal-abiya, he went out to the central enclosure of the house. The glow of the kerosene lamp was steady, undisturbed by any breath of air. Outside this small circle of light there was only darkness and silence and the stars of the morning clustering in the bare unroofed square over the central enclosure. He sat on the mud bench next to the wall. Obscure sounds reached him from the distance. Near the roof pigeons were rustling in their nesting holes. The animals were chewing their cud and the black donkey snorted peacefully. Over the house, supported by wooden beams, was a cover of corn and cotton stalks, where many birds had their nests. Perhaps their young were dreaming. The males and the females were nestled together, and their chirping was calm and restful. There were snakes in that cover too. A snake could swallow a bird whole without chewing it up. He would slither up to it and seize it in his jaws, and afterward you could see it inside him, bulging out of his long, sleek body like a ball.

Abdel-Aziz's mother came out with her headcloth tightly wrapped and warming her hands beneath her armpits. She took a kerosene lamp from a mud shelf on the wall and lit it from the one that was already burning. Holding the flaming lamp she brought out her keys—she was never without those keys—opened the storeroom door, and disappeared inside.

Just at the head of the mud bench a second door swung open. From it emerged Hagg Karim's other wife, carrying a black earthenware pitcher in her hand. As soon as she appeared in the doorway, her eyes met those of Abdel-Aziz.

"Good morning."

"Good morning."

She had dark skin, a deeply lined face, and big, wide eyes. Abdel-Aziz could see those eyes in his half sisters. But her cheeks were faded. She carried her black pitcher to the corner where the big clay water jar stood. Her breasts were enormous, her legs thin and bowed. She walked hurriedly. Drops of water could be heard falling one after the other into a receptacle beneath the water jar. She began to scoop water into her pitcher with the can they used for a dipper, and the water splashed in the belly of the pitcher. Her back was slender. She turned around, showing her large eyes and faded cheeks. Abdel-Aziz's mother said that she bought blusher soap to redden her cheeks and make herself prettier in the eyes of Hagg Karim. Once they had found a bar of red blusher soap in her room, wrapped up in a piece of paper, the kind used to irritate the skin of the face and make it look rosy. Every day she would make up her eyes with kohl and her face would shine. Then she would sit on her doorstep. But Hagg Karim would come in and go out without looking in her direction. In the evening she would polish the chimney of her lamp and sit on her spotless bed resting her chin in her hand. When he was little, Abdel-Aziz used to creep into her room, and she would hug him and kiss him and tell him those old stories about ghouls—the one about the ghoul and the eggplant seller and many others. She took her pitcher and walked toward the privy. Her clothes were spotlessly clean. Afterward she would pray. She knew nothing about the business of housekeeping. She was assigned the jobs that needed no skill or special care. Even Abdel-Aziz no longer looked in her direction when she sat on her doorstep. He sensed her helpless glances, but he did not look at her.

Without a word she carried her pitcher back into the house. The only sounds to be heard now were the clatter his mother was making in the storeroom, the monotonous recitations of his father's other wife at prayer, the murmur of the pigeons in their nests, and the dripping of the water from the water jar. He listened for something, turning his head like an eager hen. Vague, meaningless whisperings on the edge of the hush and the gloom produced in his veins a kind of numbness that progressed to his heart and formed there in a heavy lump, damming his chest and his throat and hindering his breath. He stared for a long moment at the flame of the lamp. Words welled up within him like tears. If only he were able, he would write many sad words, like those lines the heroine of the novel had sent to her beloved, accompanied by locks of her hair that had fallen out because of the agony she had suffered in her love for him. But he could not. The words in his breast were like wisps of cloud he could not grasp. Yet his imagination was filled with tense, sorrowful images, like the face of the lady journeying to meet her beloved, as she looked out of the window of the carriage, unable to bear the distance, her heart rent with anguish.

On the windowsill of the room Abdel-Aziz had a few books with dust clinging to their covers. How he would have liked to live somewhere alone, alone and far away from everything. But he remembered her—her two pigtails, her eyes, and her clear smile. A long time ago, when he was still very little, he used to wait impatiently for the feast, and on the evening before it came he would remain silent, isolating himself from the noise the children were making, and listen. Then all of a sudden he would hear the horn of the automobile and dart out to open the big gate.

She would get out of the automobile with her father and mother, small and dainty and looking just like one of those dolls you saw in the shop windows. For the whole vacation he would be with her and play with her and try to please her. When she left he would be sad and wait for them to come back for the next feast. Then her father fell ill and died, and now she lived in their lane. They went to school together every day in Tanta. But somehow strangely he still longed for her.

When he stood waiting at the beginning of the lane his breast would almost explode with anticipation. He would keep his eyes glued to the bend where the lane turned away and disappeared, staring with tortured longing. Then suddenly she would appear, like the miracle of a prophet, her skirt fluttering around her legs.

A smile came to Abdel-Aziz's face as he sat daydreaming on the bench. He thought of her as a butterfly with her fluttering skirt. He thought about her and his dusty books in the window, and the little pieces of paper that contained the fragments of his heart. How he would like to live alone somewhere, but he still loved everything here, the black donkey and that good-hearted woman his father had married before his mother.

Now the girls were coming out of the two rooms and going into the storeroom. A jumble of noises and still sleepy voices could be heard from there, cut through by the terse commands of his mother and the girls' muffled titters. Every now and then one of the girls would come back out carrying a lantern in her hand, do something or other in the courtyard, and then disappear again into the storeroom.

Abdel-Aziz's mother came out and started up the staircase, a wooden structure with a turned banister and steps of rough-hewn sycamore fig. She was short and stout and she pounded the steps with her feet. She had to carry her lantern on her head, since she had loaded herself down with all kinds of objects, some in her hands and others under her arms. If she had had ten arms, she would still have needed more.

The boy thought about his father Hagg Karim. Perhaps when he got back last night from his meeting with the brothers in the guest house he had asked her to bake the Sultan's Provisions. And perhaps she had burst out in anger, swearing that the bins were empty of grain and flour and that there was not a trace of butterfat left in the storage jars and that the few drops of milk that trickled from the teats of the water buffalo were not even enough to damp the thirst of the children and that the time had come for Hagg Karim to stop scattering the sustenance of his children on moulids and guests and that it ought to be enough for him to fill one basket and carry it in his hand to Tanta like everybody else and that those two great chests would keep draining the household until not a single morsel would remain for the children.

Hagg Karim, undoubtedly, had sat down cross-legged on the big brass bed and talked to her for hours about baking for the Sultan, about the children and the house, and about the special blessing by means of which these frail vessels, weighed down with burdens, move on the river of life, catching in their tattered sails the breath of the saints of God. She must have heard those soft and persuasive words as she sat squatting on the reed mat at the foot of the bed. But she had surely remained stubborn and unyielding, breaking in with blunt comments about the rabble in Tanta and those strange types into whose mouths he was thrusting the children's bread.

In the past he used to rage at her if she opposed his will. Their fighting had terrified Abdel-Aziz, and he would scream with fright and have to be taken away until the air was clear. The marks of that fear were still in him, like the scars of an old wound. He was somewhat sad for his father, who no longer raged at her as he used to do. There was little left of the old fierceness with which he used to confront her obstinacy, or her grudging compliance that was constantly waiting for the chance to say no.

Years had passed without the two worlds ever meeting—Hagg Karim's world, which soared on the wings of miracles and the power of divine blessing, in which sacrifice for the brothers was the best way to increase the little they had and to bless it, and her world, limited to jars and pots and stores of grain. She would mind her own business if the jars and pots were full, but grumble all day long if they were ever empty or only partly full.

She was engaged in an unending struggle. With all the sturdiness of her short build, the glower of her round, white face, and the narrowness of her two eyes, which were always staring at the ground, she was struggling to fight something off, to thwart the certain ruin she sensed was on its way. She showed it in what she said, in her strict orders to the girls and her warnings to them against carelessness and clutter and dropping bread crumbs on the ground. She showed it in her quick, flashing glances, which scrutinized every corner of the house, searching for some error or oversight. She would constantly be warning Hagg Karim about the future, and thrusting her worries in his face. But he would smile and shake his head, completely at ease about what was to come. The hand that gave would never be empty, and the house in which guests ate would never know ruin. Two separate worlds. They were a strange pair to be joined together. How was it that they could steal moments alone, in this house teeming with children and animals, to lie together and pile up more children year after year?

Abdel-Aziz stood in the door of the storeroom. Inside, the dim light of a kerosene lamp created small gaps of light between the shadows cast by the objects that crowded the room. Lengths of twine with bunches of onions and garlic tied to them hung from the ceiling, and palm-leaf baskets were hooked over pegs hammered into the walls. Large clay containers filled with flour stood next to the walls, and every inch of the floor seemed to be covered with clay jars and pots and jugs and bowls and dishes. The room was dark day and night. None of the men ever went into it. It contained the stores for the whole household, and Abdel-Aziz's mother never let go of the key for a moment. How could the girls move around in there without stumbling over something?

From the lamp a straight line of smoke rose to collide with the ceiling. A pale yellow light fell on the jars and jugs, and long shadows reached up the walls. His mother was shuffling about with a menacing look on her face, while the girls stood around her waiting for her instructions. Some were her daughters, and some were the daughters of the other wife. But they all obeyed her. The daughters of the other wife paid hardly any attention to their own mother. Perhaps they hated his mother, but they were tied to her. She taught them. If she burst out at them in a fit of rage, they would grumble for a while, but they always came back to her. Their eyes were sleepy, and in the shadows and the dim light they seemed even sleepier. His mother's orders were given in a muffled whisper, but they were obeyed. The girls were bustling about in every direction, moving through the crowded heaps of stores. It was like a frightening dream. They were busy sticking their hands into storage jars or lifting jugs to their heads to go and fetch water.

The preparations for baking always began before dawn. When Abdel-Aziz was little he used to hear stories about how the girls would get up with his mother to get ready for the baking. They were scurrying about the dark house amid a confusion of spheres of lantern light, still trying to fasten their headcloths around their heads and laughing in faint titters. Each one encouraged the other.

"Get to work! Maybe you'll get a piece of candy from the moulid."

"Candy! What do you mean candy, Sister? By the Prophet if they don't take me with them I'll never lay my hand to another job in this house."

Abdel-Aziz's mother broke in with a firm but mocking voice:

"Just be careful with what you're carrying. You'll go. The whole family is going to get up on the camel and go to Tanta. Just get busy, sweetheart."

His mother sat down in the middle of the storeroom among the milk bowls, the tapered vessels of clay that caught the milk as it streamed from the teats of the animals. She chose the bowls that had milk from two or three days before, the ones with a thick, sealed layer of cream on the surface. She tested them with her hand to make sure they were ready, and then she put them to one side. There were other bowls that had been used for milking yesterday evening or before dawn that morning. The milk in them was still fresh, and the froth on the surface was soft and had not sealed.

With a nimble hand and an uncommon skill she began to gather the cream from the surface of the sealed bowls and put it into pots of clay. Abdel-Aziz was sitting on an upside-down crate holding his face in his hands. The girls were in a circle around his mother, watching her and learning from her. She was the daughter of a government employee and had been brought up in the city. When Hagg Karim married her she had known nothing about life in the country. She was fair-skinned and beautiful, and the traces of that charm were still there in her plump white face. The women of the household of Hagg

Mohammed, Hagg Karim's father, had surrounded her and upbraided her for her ignorance of the day-to-day chores of housekeeping and cookery. Now the women came to her to learn the mysteries of running a house and the secrets of milk and cooking.

Her hand was filled with a huge gob of cream, which she waved in the face of Abdel-Aziz.

"See our buffalo's cream, Abdel-Aziz. Bless the Prophet! In the name of God the Merciful and Compassionate. Say 'In the name of God,' Abdel-Aziz, say 'In the name of God,' and bless the Prophet."

She was proud of her beast, but she worried about her, fearing the influence of envious eyes. When this buffalo first came to the house, she would not let the men bring her across the threshold until she had whitened the animal's forehead with flour. At first the cream on the surface of the buffalo's milk was no thicker than a cigarette paper. But his mother did not sit still. She kept on experimenting, trying to discover the trick that worked for her buffalo. It was a useless woman who could not find the right trick for her animal. She tried everything until she discovered the trick that worked.

She gave the girls firm, clear instructions. The milk bowls were to be washed in the water of the irrigation canal with a corn husk and the water used thrown out next to a wall. It was not to be thrown out in the middle of the lane. People would tread on it with their feet, and it had what was left over from the previous milking in it. This was wrong and unlawful and would bring harm to the buffalo. Next the bowls were to be turned over on their sides facing the east to dry. Then they were to be placed in an oven fired with bean straw and dried buffalo dung. When a bowl was taken out of the oven it was to be used for milking right away before it was spoiled by anything unclean.

The milk would spurt from the buffalo's teats into the bowl in a steady stream, and froth would form on the surface, bubbly, warm, and white. Slowly the froth would thicken, and the bowl would be covered with stiff, heavy cream. If the buffalo were to get sick or give less milk, or if her cream were to spoil, his mother would get up before daybreak and go out and choose seven doors facing east on which she would smear some of the cream from her animal. When the sun began to shine and the thick cream melted and ran, the buffalo's milk would flow like a river, God willing. In her own world this little woman had become a priestess who knew all the mysteries. But that was not what had attracted Hagg Karim when he married her. What had won him was a young girl sitting on a sofa doing needlework in the living room of her father's house in the city.

A great quantity of cream had been collected in the clay pots. The curdled milk from the bowls was poured together into one big jug, while the fresh milk was poured into another, which one of the girls took to the fireplace to be boiled over the fire. A large number of milking bowls were put outside the storeroom to be returned to their owners later on in the morning. The news of the baking for the moulid had plainly spread, for each of the women had brought her animal's milk to share in preparing the Provisions for Sayyid Bedawi's feast.

No doubt Zeinab, the pious daughter of the village marriage registrar, had learned the time of the baking from Abdel-Aziz's mother and had then made the rounds of all the houses, happy to have something to tell. She was a spinster and an incurable talker. She never stopped. Abdel-Aziz would laugh when he remembered how she used to come to visit his mother and sit next to her on the bench against the courtyard wall. She would start talking and just not let up. His mother would fall asleep where she sat and the girls would escape into the rooms. Even when the whole house had become silent, she would keep on talking. What would she do if she had no one to talk to? They had not taught her anything about household affairs. They had said she would never get married. She had only one eye, she was scrawny, she was too dark-skinned, and she was ugly. It was strange with girls. The daughter of a woman like Oum Sabah, who was so poor, was growing like an early planting. Her shape was filling out, her cheeks were rosy, and her ripening breasts pointed impertinently up. But this Zeinab, the registrar's daughter, was as scrawny as a severed sprout.

They had said she would never get married. So they had her devote herself to the study of the Koran until she had memorized it. Then she began to go around and intone it for the women at funeral receptions. But how long the days were between the death of one man and another! What could she do? She would go around and visit people in their houses, gathering up her long dress to keep it from touching anything unclean. When she sat down she would start to talk, and nothing could make her stop. Her brothers had grown up and married, and each of them now had a house of his own. All her sisters had also grown up, got married, and left the house. But she still lived in her little room with her rabbit hutch. They bred a lot, those rabbits. She had a small cloth pouch she kept in her bosom that was always full of money. Once Abdel-Aziz had borrowed fifteen piastres from her to go to Tanta to see a film. A scandal almost erupted when she asked him to pay it back and he could not. His sisters mocked him until they were sick. Had it not been for the indulgence of Hagg Karim, who smiled and paid her the money, who knows what might have happened.

Yes, it was certainly Zeinab who had gone from house to house spreading the news about the time of the baking.

Ahmed Bedawi's wife was putting seeds in the bottom of the furrow that her husband was digging with his short hoe and covering them with handfuls of earth. He raised his hoe and looked at her with a smile. A bashful blush came over her face.

"Tonight I'm taking the buffalo's milk to Hagg Karim's house, for the baking."

He smiled at her again.

"God bless the animal for you."

That same evening she came, carrying her buffalo's milk on her head and her little son in one arm. God had given her that son in place of her two small children who had died in the cholera epidemic. She had rosy cheeks and straight teeth. Abdel-Aziz kissed her child on both cheeks. How many times, when she was still nursing him, she had brought this child to his mother. She would be crying, and the child would be whining. His mother would put him in her lap and run her hands over his body under his clothes, moving his limbs about and fingering his flesh. Then she would ask for an egg and break it in her hand, letting the white flow between her fingers and keeping the yolk in her palm. With the child stripped completely naked, she would put the yolk on his body and start to roll it over the entire surface of his flushed skin. At some spot the yolk would break, and she would press it onto that spot, together with some bran, and bandage it. In the morning he would be well.

Ahmed Bedawi's wife handed his mother the milk shyly and hurried off.

One of his sisters laughed to him:

"Do you know whose bowl of milk *this* is? Rawayih's."

The girls all laughed with delight, as if they had found a treasure chest filled with finery. Rawayih's ways could keep them entertained all through the night. Surely the milk was unlawful. She could hardly steal a bowl of milk, but last night she had certainly fed her buffalo with food stolen from the fields of the neighbors. But Sayyid Bedawi had a huge belly and did not mind eating what was unlawful. Once a woman had stolen a hen and killed it for her children. But when she went to look at it on the fire she did not find the dead hen. She found the "Bald One," as the womenfolk called Sayyid Bedawi, squatting and looking at her. When she asked about the hen, he simply opened his mouth. She looked inside and saw a boundless sea with the dead hen floating on the surface. He had swallowed it so the children would not grow fat on unlawful food and turn out to be mean and naughty.

"Can anybody have a sea in his stomach?"

"Of course! Don't they say, 'O overflowing sea, O Sayyid Bedawi.'"

Abdel-Aziz tried to explain.

"Overflowing sea means . . . it means . . ."

"Don't sit there trying to tell us what it means. That's the way it is and that's all there is to it."

Anyway, in Tanta there were people who ate gravel. They would eat these cookies even if the dough were made with kerosene. They laughed at this, and they laughed at the people who lived in the same lane as Rawayih. They were holding onto their hearts with their hands these days. The Dandy's trip to Tanta was going to cost them more than a little. They told about the two sons of Tarawa, who lived together in the same house and had a huge drake with red wattles. Whenever it came out in front of the house, it would strut about proudly and hiss. They would call to it fondly, dreaming of the meal to come.

"Come back in the house, you wonderful animal. The blessing of the Prophet preserve you from the evil eye."

"The night we eat you will be like jasmine."

Many long days the precious drake was force-fed. Corn and beans were stuffed into his craw until he got so fat he went blind. And then suddenly he disappeared. They looked for him everywhere. They could guess where he was, naturally, but they went on looking just in case. Then one day, when the two brothers were sitting on the mud bench in front of their house, the drake came strutting and hissing out of Rawayih's door. They would have liked to take him back to their own place and to have killed Rawayih. But who could do it? There was not a single man in the village who dared go near her. She would grab him by the testicles and force him down on his knees, making a spectacle of him for all the passers-by to see. They said she would die one day and feathers would grow on her face because of all the birds she had stolen. It had happened to her mother, who was a thousand times cleverer and more dangerous a thief than Rawayih.

But when the girls talked about Showk—the milk of Hagga Showk's buffalo filled a huge bowl and was sealed with a thick layer of cream—when they talked about Hagga Showk they would be wide-eyed with admiration, though a smile of mischievous delight would come to their lips.

"What a bowl of milk, Hagga Showk."

"Her buffalo is monstrous!"

Everything was plentiful in her big house. Her husband was dead and she took care of the housework and the fields as well, just like a man. To her children she was both mother and father.

When Hagg Karim went to see her he would call out, "O Coverer of Sins," as was customary to give women the chance to cover themselves, and Hagga Showk would come out to meet him. She was a tall woman with high, firm breasts, as if she had never given birth and never suckled a child. She had big eyes, dark skin, and a fresh, smiling face.

"Welcome to our friends. Welcome Hagg Karim. Your foot is welcome on our threshold."

He would let her have his hand, which she would kiss two or three times, and he would stroke her shoulder and kiss her on the head. Then he would sit down on the mud bench by the door in the courtyard, while she squatted on the ground in front of him, scraping the dust with a stick and talking. Her words were calm and even, and when Hagg Karim spoke to her, she would look at him with bright, smiling eyes.

Sometimes Abdel-Aziz wished that Hagga Showk were his mother. When he was little he used to go with his father to her house and she would hold him close to her. He still felt the tenderness with which she used to hug him. He could not recall his mother hugging him or coddling him as a child. She was always frowning, always wholly taken up with her housework, and at night she slept like a rock, she was so tired.

When Hagg Karim came home, Abdel-Aziz could sense that he longed for loving words. But his wife would just annoy him, going on frantically about the certain ruin in store for them. Showk, with her flashing eyes, spoke to him in an altogether different way. They had gone to the Hejaz together, two young people who undertook to serve the other pilgrims out of love and respect. They never stopped talking about that trip, and Hagg Karim would nod and say amen when she said to him:

"God will never bring on you the scandal of poverty, Hagg

Karim. God willing, your house will always be open to guests."

The girls knew about Hagg Karim's fondness for Hagga Showk, and so did Abdel-Aziz. They smiled at one another with a look of mischief and collusion on their faces. Sternly, his mother ordered them to stop their chatter and get back to the work at hand.

A large metal basin was filled with sifted white flour, heaped up soft and fine. Abdel-Aziz's mother went over to the salt jar, pushed her hand in, and drew out the yeast. This was where she kept it. She never wasted it. She would put it in the dough and then take out a lump to replace it, which she would put back in the salt jar. And so this blessed leaven had been carried over from the dough of one baking to that of another, for how long no one knew. She never lent any of it to anyone, and she kept it surrounded with secrecy and mystery. She dissolved it in warm water in a small bowl. Then she dug a deep hole in the white flour, and with a deliberate, reverent look and a trembling hand she poured the warm leaven into the hole, murmuring over and over again, "In the name of God the Merciful and Compassionate."

The girls were sitting around the basin of flour in a circle, their faces betraying an uncommon concern. They repeated the phrase with quivering lips as the warm liquid flowed into the hole in the flour. Even Abdel-Aziz found himself uneasily reciting the same words. A girl standing with a pitcher of boiled milk in her hands poured it out. Steam rose from the milk as it streamed into the hole. When the hole was full of milk they began to knead the dough with their hands. Arms were driven in up to the elbow and then pulled out with effort. They were all working. Each of the girls was proud of her skill and found fault with the others. High-pitched giggles, rapid breathing, the sound of arms getting stuck in the dough, loose shifts revealing small breasts and little brown nipples. The fever of kneading the dough had them in an unremitting fit of laughter.

"That's enough, all of you."

They pulled their arms out of the dough and wiped them off. Abdel-Aziz's mother smoothed over the surface of the dough with her hands, again repeating, "In the name of God the Merciful and Compassionate." The girls were exhausted and breathing hard. They covered the basins of dough they had made and lined them up one next to the other, first the dough for the bread and then the dough for the biscuits, which took longer to rise. When the baking was done, the two big chests would be filled up and loaded onto Omar Farhoud's camel to be sent to the lodgings in Tanta.

Now there was nothing to do but wait for the dough to rise. Each of the girls took a place amid the heaps of things in the storeroom and sat quietly. The lantern cast a dim light and faint shadows on their faces. Abdel-Aziz's mother went out, perhaps to check on the younger children who were sleeping in the other room or perhaps for some other reason. She could never sit still in one place and wait. The basins of dough were covered with clean pieces of cloth cut from old clothing. Millions of tiny organisms were doing their work in the dough now, or maybe it was the secret of his mother's leaven. The mysterious life hidden inside the dough created an unnatural air in the room. The girls sat bent over, supporting their heads with their hands and talking with muffled voices like chickens in the henhouse at night.

What made them bring up the wife of Omar Farhoud the camel driver, that gentle-hearted woman with the slight build and soft voice? Her father was a village Koran reciter who died and left her a quarter of an acre of land in the fields and the word of God in her heart. And he left her the book of Abu Ma'shar.

That strange book contained between its covers all kinds of sorcery and magic. Whoever was able to fathom its secrets and decipher its symbols became master over the spirits and could do whatever he wished. He could make people hallucinate, he could make men hate their women or render them impotent with their brides, he could heal the sick or cure the fright of children and stop them from screaming in the night. Abdel-Aziz had seen the book, and he had seen in its yellow pages the checkered diagrams with strange shapes and symbols in the different squares. He had read in it about substances to be mixed, things to be burnt, and nails to be driven; about pieces of paper cut in the shape of men and women and how the eyes were to be pierced with needles; about packets of all kinds of things, bones of the dead, bird feathers, and snake skins, that were to be slipped under doorsills so that those toward whom one intended good or evil would walk over them. He had read all this and had not believed a thing, but now he was stricken with fear. One of his sisters spoke up, wide-eyed with fright in the shadows and the pale light:

"But that woman never works any evil."

All that really happened was that the women would go to her with a piece of their children's clothing when they were ill and she would measure it in spans and fingerbreadths and tie knots in it. Then she would measure the distance between the knots and recite formulas of refuge and praise until she knew exactly what was wrong with the child. She would prescribe amulets and incense and what the child was to drink and what his body was to be rubbed with. So she never wove spells that harmed anyone. One of the girls laughed:

"Haven't you ever heard about what happened to Omar Farhoud?"

All the girls wanted to know.

Once when he was alone with Abu Ma'shar's book he had decided to try out the magic in it. He started to read the spells without any idea of what he was doing. He was only a simple camel driver and knew nothing about the mysteries of books. It happened that he read spells to summon the serving genies, and they appeared before him and waited for him to give them a command or to dismiss them. But he became confused, and God did not provide him with the words he had to say. So it seems the genies got very angry and turned him upside down. They planted his head on the earth and turned his feet up toward the ceiling, letting his clothing fall down and uncover his private parts. The girls shrieked with laughter as their sister told how his wife had come in and found him, and how she had quickly dismissed the genies and saved her husband. He was always committing some kind of blunder, and she always took pity on him when he came running to her like a helpless child.

But one of the girls had remained speechless and had not joined in the laughter of her sisters. Pale as death and with a faltering voice she blurted out:

"I'm scared."

They all fell silent. Abdel-Aziz sat waiting to hear something. He did not believe in demons, but fear crept into his heart. Outside the storeroom, outside the small circle of light, darkness squatted on the earth, and the stillness was filled with strange whisperings. Trying to subdue his fear, he shouted out to his sister:

"What are you afraid of?"

But the girl, her eyes wandering, whined like a sick kitten.

"I'm scared."

Abdel-Aziz's voice grew even louder, as he attempted to thwart the feeling of dread.

"Nonsense, all this talk about demons and such."

One of the girls broke in boldly, although with trembling in her voice:

"It's people who are the real demons."

Another of the girls started to speak in a whisper that could scarcely be heard:

"They've cast a spell on Mohammed Kamel's wife."

No one made a sound.

"They wrote out the spell on the shoulder blade of a child who drowned . . ."

She caught her breath:

". . . and was buried in an unknown grave."

Abdel-Aziz felt his fear returning as the girl spoke.

"Every night she gets up and walks around among the graves."

He yelled to make the girl shut up:

"Stop these silly stories. You've always been a liar."

The girl insisted:

"By the Prophet, it's what they say."

His mother could be heard coming down the steps, and the sound dispelled their fears. She came into the room and uncovered the dough, which had risen and spread over the rims of the basins.

"The Bald One has already puffed it up with his breath."

"He's in a hurry for the Provisions."

The woman spoke firmly:

"Come on, girls. The day's here. We've got to get busy."

Abdel-Aziz went out. The courtyard was still dark, but daylight filled the sky. Pigeons, chickens, and ducks left their nests and coops and started to peck and nibble at the grain Hagg Karim's other wife was throwing to them. Abdel-Aziz smiled. She was always given the least important jobs in the house. His mother spoke to her:

"After they drink, shut them up again so they don't get in our way while we're baking."

She gave no answer, but she would obey. Later on she would sweep the house slowly and quietly. Abdel-Aziz looked at her and laughed when he recalled what had happened the last time she went to visit her family. They had given her a male duck, which she stewed over a blazing fire from morning until evening. When the evening came, the reed mat was spread out in the courtyard and a low table was set out. Hagg Karim sat down with his children and his field hands. The rice and *fatta* and the stew were brought out, but the drake was not yet done. The woman was humiliated. Hagg Karim himself went over to the fireplace and felt the meat. But it resisted his finger as if it were rubber. He took the knife and cut it into pieces, ordering that it be put on the fire for another day from early in the morning. Abdel-Aziz laughed at her. She was never successful in anything she did. But she was good-hearted, gentle, and affectionate. Hagg Karim had married her after the death of Rashida's mother, his first cousin on his father's side and the wife he had loved the most. After she died Hagg Karim had gone to see his maternal uncles, and they had married this one off to him. But he loved Rashida's mother more than anyone else. After she was gone he found no happiness in marriage.

Abdel-Aziz's mother screamed to the littlest of the girls:

"Go and call Oum Sabah."

"Rashida too?"

"Rashida too."

Oum Sabah was the woman they paid to sit before the oven during the baking. Her slim daughter with the high breasts would be there with her. She aroused Abdel-Aziz, and she would not escape him today. Rashida would come too and make them laugh themselves to death with her sarcasm and the way she made fun of people. It was going to be a strange day, full of noise and laughter led by Rashida. She was plagued with a chronic eye disease, and when she used to live with them she had always been excused from housework. She would spend the whole day by herself in a room on the roof. Her clothes were spotless and her hands were smooth. No, Rashida had not had to work. But she had traveled a lot to Tanta to treat her eyes, and she had spent many long days there with her mother's relatives. She had learned quite a few things from the city girls. She wore city clothes and dreamed of marrying an effendi who would take her away from the village. Once she had found him, she would only come back on holidays. She would get out of the cab and call to her clean, well-bred children:

"Kiss your aunt's hand, Son. Kiss your aunt's hand, Daughter."

But she had married a huge peasant who wove wool and made his own galabiyas and skullcaps and mufflers from it. Before her, he had been married to a woman who died leaving behind a whole brood of dirty children with scabby heads. On the day of Rashida's wedding the enormous bridegroom had lumbered in wearing a woolen galabiya that hung as stiffly about his body as if it had been made of wood. When Abdel-Aziz, who was still only a little child, saw him, he had screamed with fright.

Now Rashida hardly ever had a chance to get away from her housework, and when she did find a moment's respite from her daily chores she would start mocking everything in sight, making everyone around her howl with laughter.

One of the girls was sitting in front of the oven raking out the ashes left from previous baking days. During the night this oven with its two huge openings had had the appearance of some dark and threatening mass crouching at the far end of the courtyard. In just a short while a fire would be blazing inside it and the women would be working feverishly and noisily around it.

The low, round table was placed in front of the oven, and pieces of old reed mats and gunnysacks were spread around it. A basin of dough was put next to the table, and Abdel-Aziz's mother sat down where she could reach them both. After they had covered the table with bran, she began to scoop out lumps of dough and arrange them one next to the other on top of it.

Oum Sabah pushed open the door and came in, with her willowy daughter Sabah behind her. Abdel-Aziz's heart leaped in his breast. He sat down warily on the bench and waited in silence. Oum Sabah called out:

"Bless the Prophet. In the name of God the Merciful and Compassionate."

Then she went straight to the oven and sat down cross-legged in front of it. Abdel-Aziz's mother spoke to her:

"Say 'In the name of God,' Oum Sabah, and light the oven."

The girls and Hagg Karim's other wife were sitting around the table. Each was holding in her hand a big round wooden paddle. For a time they were all silent. But then their lips began to quiver, invoking the name of God, as Oum Sabah held a cornstalk over the wick of the lamp and said in a loud voice:

"In the name of God the Merciful and Compassionate. O Guide! O Lord!"

She threw the flaming stalk into the firebox and began putting one stalk after another on top of it to feed the fire. Each of the girls took a lump of dough and patted it on the table with her hand to flatten it a bit. Next she shifted it to her paddle, which was covered with bran, and continued to hit the lump with the palm of her hand and to roll it around so that it spread out wider and wider until it almost covered the surface of the paddle. Then tossing it up into the air and blowing off the bran, she flipped it over onto the other side and repeated the operation, patting the flattened dough with her hand until it spread beyond the edges of the paddle.

There was now a hot fire going in the oven. Oum Sabah took the girls' flattened disks of dough on her long-handled paddle and shoved them into the oven. There they lay, thin and white, and then suddenly they were filled with life, puffing up and twitching in the oven until they were baked through and browned on top. When they were done, she took them out again with a long hooked rod of iron.

Thick smoke lingered in the courtyard and almost hid the pigeons in their nesting holes in the wall. They cowered and then flew away from the smoke to the roof. The sparrows in the covering of stalks over the courtyard were hopping about from spot to spot and twittering incessantly. Particles of flour were flying in the air, warmed by the heat of the thin, flat loaves coming out of the oven. The slapping of paddles, the hissing of burning corn and cotton stalks, and the chatter of the girls forced Abdel-Aziz's mother to raise her voice when she wanted to give an order. She almost had to scream to be heard. Every now and then the street door would open and a woman or young girl would come in and shout at the top of her voice:

"In the name of God the Merciful and Compassionate! Good baking, children, and many happy returns of the day."

The girls would return her greeting in a loud chorus of laughter and invite her to join in.

"Lend a hand, by the Prophet, so the baking will be blessed."

The visitor would reply politely:

"It will be blessed because of you and the one it's going to. Look down on us, O Sayyid! God keep our uncle Hagg Karim and preserve his customs always."

Then she would take off her sandals, choose a paddle, and sit down next to the low table. Her voice would mingle with the general confusion, the noise, the laughter, and the prattle. She had probably come to get fire.

"My children are alone at home. I have worlds of work to do. I don't have any time now."

But the girls would keep urging her on, and she would be caught up in the fever of the baking.

"Come on, Sister. Just bake two loaves. This is the baking for Our Lord Sayyid Bedawi."

She would bake one loaf and then another until she nearly forgot what she had come for. Then she would jump up, shake the flour from her lap, light her lamp, and run off, with the cries and laughter of the girls following behind her.

Abdel-Aziz could not take his eyes off Sabah as her hands steadily worked the dough on her paddle. Her breasts were trembling underneath her thin dress, and her cheeks, through the white particles of flour that had gathered on her face and lashes, were blood red from the effort. A blazing fire raged in the oven, and Oum Sabah offered it loaf after loaf. The girls were lost in their chatter and laughter. They were like an ear-splitting machine with tireless arms throwing off flour dust in the air around it. His mother sat frowning and silent, still scooping out lumps of dough and arranging them on the big round table.

The door opened with a push, and Hagga Showk came in, tall, smiling, and radiant in her black satin dress.

"In the name of God the Merciful and Compassionate! Bless the Prophet!"

The noise Hagg Karim's daughters and their friends were making grew louder. Abdel-Aziz stood up from his seat on the bench by the door. Hagga Showk gave him a big hug. Her face and her clothes were soft and smooth, and she smelled of perfumed bath soap. He freed himself from her embrace, frightened by an uncertain but powerful feeling running through his veins.

"How are you, little darling? God keep you for your father."

With that she strode proudly in the direction of the oven and the girls.

"Greetings, girls. Good baking, and many happy returns of the day."

The shrieks and the squeals could have wakened the dead.

"By the Prophet, Aunt Hagga Showk, since daybreak we've been wondering why you hadn't come. Come sit beside me and help with the baking, so it will be blessed."

"I'm no good at this any more. Greetings, Oum Abdel-Aziz."

His mother had to answer her.

"Welcome, Sister. God keep you in health."

They exchanged greetings without a kiss. Showk went on talking in the direction of the girls:

"It's all up to the girls now. We're finished. Our days are over."

The girls cried back that it was not so. His mother remained silent. She had not missed the subtle arrogance in the woman's voice.

"Oh my! Your days over! You're cleverer than anyone, Hagga Showk."

She laughed, pleased with the compliment, and sat down by the table in her satin dress. Taking one of the paddles, she started to flatten her loaf. Abdel-Aziz kept his eyes on the outline of her shoulders and her arms. There was no woman like her anywhere.

"I wouldn't let Sayyid Bedawi's baking pass me by. I have to bake a loaf or two. If they turn out bad, I'll eat them myself."

As she sat there laughing cheerfully, Abdel-Aziz compared her with Sabah. She was ripeness and maturity, the splendid culmination, while Sabah was a blossoming beginning. He heard the girls' voices.

"Turn out bad? Your bread never turns out bad. All right, we'll put a mark on your loaf and see. Oum Sabah, here's the hagga's loaf. Be careful with it."

Everyone's eyes followed her loaf as it was laid on the metal floor of the oven, thin and white. After a while it began to twitch, and then it puffed up as big as a strutting rooster. The girls cried out in amazement, and the hagga laughed jokingly:

"Pure chance, girls. The Lord didn't want to shame me."

But she undid her headcloth, and her dark blue kerchief stood out against her shining hair, which fell in two thick braids down her back. Tied in those braids was the key to the chest in which she kept her finest things. She pulled up her sleeves and lost herself in the excitement of the baking.

The door creaked again and Rashida came in.

"You thoughtless creatures!"

"Ah! Little Karim's mother is here."

She discovered Abdel-Aziz on the bench.

"Darling!"

She hugged him tight. She loved him in a special way. He held her tightly too, her small frame and her narrow shoulders.

"How are you, Abdel-Aziz? Those sisters of yours are inconsiderate. Couldn't you girls have told me last night so I would have known to come early? I heard your voice from a long way off, Hagga Showk. How is my aunt?"

Before she did another thing she turned to greet Abdel-Aziz's mother and kissed her hand. Rashida never neglected the rules of etiquette. Then she turned back to Showk.

"I heard your voice from a long way off, Hagga Showk. I said, 'Is there any real baking without Hagga Showk?'"

"God keep you, light of my eye, and that sweet tongue of yours too. You really are your father's daughter."

Everyone said the same thing about Rashida. She was her father's favorite. She took off her headcloth and joined in the excitement of the baking. Any gathering that included both Rashida and Hagga Showk was going to be a delight. And this was Sayyid Bedawi's baking, with the moulid only a few days off.

One of the girls begged:

"Rashida, by the Prophet, make your father take us with him, Rashida. I'll help you cook at the moulid. Please, Rashida. I'll do anything you want."

"Of course I will, little sister. Of course I will."

"And me, Rashida."

"All right, you too, sweetheart."

"And me!"

Hagga Showk broke in laughing:

"All of you will go. Why not? It's a great feast, and it only comes once a year. Look down on us, Abu Farrag."

The girls were delighted and completely let go of themselves. The paddles seemed to be flying in the air, and the disks of dough flipped over lightly on top of them. In the heat and the effort and the merriment Hagga Showk took off her black dress and worked in her long pink shift. Rashida and the girls followed her example—baby blue shifts and pink shifts with wide necks and short sleeves. What need was there for modesty? There were no strangers, and Abdel-Aziz was harmless. Nevertheless, Sabah's mother cast a suspicious glance in his direction and recalled a proverbial warning:

"Never trust a young man, no matter how small."

Abdel-Aziz lowered his head with embarrassment, and his sisters laughed at him. When he raised his eyes he saw Hagga Showk—her bosom, her throat, her laugh, and the deep dimple in her chin. He looked at Sabah. Her threadbare shift was torn at the neck and revealed the tip of a brown breast and a delicate brown nipple. He turned his gaze quickly away, but his heart was about to leap out of his chest. He looked back, and his eyes met Sabah's. Her hand flashed toward the tear to close it over her breast and then back to her lump of dough, letting the tear open and the breast pop out again through the tattered cloth. Abdel-Aziz could not take his eyes off her. And so the game went on, amid the noise and the heat of the flames, the slapping of the paddles, the hot particles of flour flying in the air, the ceaseless chatter and the convulsions of laughter. The game went on. Her hand would close the tear and then dart back to the lump of dough, and out would pop the breast again. Abdel-Aziz sat there gasping, unable to catch his breath. He could have died right on the spot.

"You would really look fine in city clothes, Rashida."

Rashida scrutinized her arms as they stretched down toward

her paddle. Mock pride was on her face. Her eyebrows played over her ailing eyes, and she sucked her lips in feigned admiration of her beauty. The girls were in stitches. She yelled out, pretending to scold them:

"What are you laughing at? We're as pretty as roses. We just don't have any luck."

They all laughed. Cheap earrings were tinkling, and carnelian necklaces made a clattering sound. Virgin breasts and erect little nipples rubbed against thin cotton cloth. Abdel-Aziz, his heart pounding in his chest, was still gaping at Sabah, and the impertinent breast that kept popping out of her shift.

"If our men would only dress us up and give us a little chance to rest, we'd be far prettier than the women in Tanta."

Hagga Showk replied:

"Those women have their own way of teasing a man and turning his head. They don't have anything else to do."

As she spoke she pushed one shoulder forward and made her breast quiver and shake in a way that startled Abdel-Aziz. The girls shrieked with delight. How could Hagga Showk hide all this flirtatiousness behind her usual facade of dignity and poise? It was the madness of the baking. The day was a strange one. Abdel-Aziz could hardly keep from springing on Sabah and gorging himself on her breasts and lips. When would they send her to fetch something so he could be alone with her and seize his prey?

Rashida protested, gesturing with her hand in Hagga Showk's face:

"To hell with those thick-witted women with their puffy cheeks and fat bottoms."

Hagga Showk answered in her new and shameless manner:

"Do men like anything else, my dear?"

Abdel-Aziz could not believe what he was seeing and hearing. Hagg Karim's other wife was wide-eyed with astonishment. But Abdel-Aziz's mother had a singular ability to isolate herself from everything. She was watching the bread with the eye of a hawk. Not a morsel would be wasted or lost.

Rashida replied gloatingly:

"Let them like what they please. They can go to Tanta if they want, but they have to come back to us here anyway. We'll be behind them until they drop. There's no use in their trying. Looking at women outside the house won't get them anywhere."

The girls split their sides at Rashida's boldness. One of them exclaimed recklessly:

"The women in the city are good-looking, and the men are good-looking too!"

Amid a new burst of laughter Rashida commented:

"You took the words right out of my mouth. What I need is a regular town gentleman to bring me back to life."

Like a cat, Abdel-Aziz scanned the frenzied circle of women and girls, taking stock of every movement. Now Sabah would be sent to the dark storeroom to get more flour. He slipped away and waited in the darkness behind the door. As soon as she came in he pushed the door nearly all the way shut with his foot. The two of them were together in the dark, breathless and hearts pounding. Snatching her shift by the hem, he quickly pulled it up over her back and threw his arm around her naked waist. He hugged her so hard that her head and arms were flung back and the flour jar fell from her outstretched hand. Her breasts were right beneath his nose. He pulled her shift the rest of the way up, and she twisted her head to free it from the collar. The shift fell in a crumpled heap on the floor. Her head still flung back and both his arms around her naked torso, he began to rub his face in the cool moisture of her breasts. She was as slippery as a fish as she squirmed in his grasp. He squeezed her tighter and tighter until her knees bent. Then he lowered her body onto the crumpled shift and lay down on top of her. He went on rubbing his face against her breasts and biting her on her lips and neck and nipples like a rabid cat, while she wriggled and squirmed beneath him. She gasped:

"No, Abdel-Aziz. No!"

He reached down to take off her pants. But she pushed

against him with extraordinary force and almost threw him off her.

"By God, I'll call your mother right now."

He let her go and jumped up. That threat frightened him. In his confusion he tripped over a pot and almost fell flat on his face. She cried out with concern, standing totally naked in front of him except for her pants:

"The Prophet's name protect you!"

He answered in a low voice:

"It's nothing."

She put on her shift, filled the jar with flour, and went out. Abdel-Aziz sat down on an overturned crate, trying to catch his breath.

When he came out he found her caught up again in the excitement of the baking and tossing her flat loaf into the air. She had forgotten everything. He felt angry. But he sat down quietly on the bench and watched them as they baked. The fever of their work took hold of him again, as Sabah's nipple bounced up and down before his eyes. Nothing would ever satisfy his hunger. He would forever long for one kiss and one embrace, one moment that would absorb his whole life. He leaned his head against the wall and shut his eyes.

Samira was coming down the steps, her dress fluttering about her legs. Her sparkling laughter brightened the way before her.

"Abdel-Aziz!"

The girls shrieked.

"Samira! Samira!"

Rashida called out a cheerful reproach:

"Join in, Samira. But you shouldn't forget to greet us first, my little brother's bride."

Samira turned red. Everyone said that she and Abdel-Aziz were going to be married when they grew up. When he stood up to meet her, she handed him a book she had borrowed from him and fled. She stirred a very special feeling in him, a very special sadness. He went into the bedroom to put back the book. Here were the dusty covers, his novels and his other books, his little private sorrow set aside in a corner, folded up and covered with dust. And here were those little pieces of paper on which he wrote down his thoughts—Samira, Sabah, Hagga Showk. In his heart there was a dryness that no river could water.

He came out and stood by the door of the bedroom. Now Sabah's back was to him. The main door opened and Ahmed Bedawi's wife came in together with Saddiqa, Mohammed Kamel's wife—two faces, one bright with rosy cheeks and a smile that revealed regular, white teeth, and one dark and lusterless with big, sad eyes.

"God grant you a child soon, Sister."

Saddiqa accepted their wishes with her head bowed. She baked without turning to anyone. Abdel-Aziz knew that she was suffering from their sympathy. If only they would worry about the baking and leave her alone. She threw herself into the work, praying that the excitement of the baking would make them forget her. She had only come to bake two loaves of Sayyid Bedawi's bread in the hope that the blessing of the saints might make her barren womb fertile. They were torturing her with their expressions of pity, the sucking of their lips, their wishes and prayers, and their suggestions about sheikhs to see and remedies to try.

"He made up a ball of wool for one woman, for her to wear. By the Prophet! She never had her period again, I swear, bless the Prophet. She has three children now."

Ahmed Bedawi's wife, her face flushed with embarrassment, kept her head down and went on baking.

Then suddenly Rawayih burst into the courtyard, towering like the roc. She had long limbs and green eyes that flashed like the eyes of a kite. She was exactly like a kite. There was excitement in her voice.

"I don't know whether to trill, or sing, or what to say, Sisters. May Hagg Karim's house flourish a thousand years. O Lord God!"

Then she pounced on Abdel-Aziz, snatching his hand in hers and raising her other hand to give notice to the world.

"God willing, you'll have a big government job when you grow up."

The girls broke out laughing. They were not afraid of her. She stole from everyone, except from Hagg Karim and his house.

"Sit down and bake a couple of loaves, Aunt Rawayih."

"I don't have time. I'm baking for your uncle Mohammed the Dandy. The Provisions for the moulid. Biscuits dripping with butterfat. There are no men like our men anywhere. They're the light of our village. Without them it would hardly be a hamlet."

Rashida and Showk laughed and said to her in the same breath:

"Sit down, sit down, Rawayih."

The door opened wide. Hagg Karim came in along with Ahmed Bedawi, the Dandy, and Iraqi the Deaf-Mute. The laughter and chatter broke off. The women and the girls scrambled for their headcloths to cover their heads and shoulders.

"Many happy returns of the day, children."

"Welcome, welcome, light of my eye!"

Rawayih shrieked, waving her hands toward the Dandy and Hagg Karim:

"Welcome! Welcome!"

Then she started to leap and dance in front of them, and the Dandy burst out laughing:

"That's enough, wench."

She snatched her milk bowl and ran out without further ado. Everyone was happy to see Hagg Karim. Rashida's face was beaming.

"Many happy returns of the day, Papa. God keep you and keep your men."

Hagga Showk had regained her composure, and her face was glowing with a strange light. She lost no time.

"God preserve your house and your customs always, my brother."

Hagg Karim beamed at her.

"Many happy returns of the day. Welcome!"

Ahmed Bedawi's eyes were on his timid wife, who was hiding

her face with her headcloth. The Dandy was roaring with laughter. Iraqi was beside himself with delight. He cupped his hands around his mouth and shouted out for help from the Sultan. The house was full of noise and laughter. Rashida, with the girls squealing after her, begged Hagg Karim to take them to the Sultan's feast. Hagg Karim laughed.

"God willing. God willing."

Then he went out, and the dervishes followed behind him.

The dimly lit storeroom was full of the smell of freshly baked bread and biscuits. The flame of the lamp cast a pale light and faint shadows. Abdel-Aziz's mother was sitting amid the bowls and the jars. Overhead the bunches of onions and garlic were hanging from the ceiling. The girls sat around his mother, bleary-eyed and drooping with fatigue. She sorted the loaves of bread one by one, dusting the flour off them with a rag and setting aside whatever was broken or burnt. No one would eat that. She would have to live off it herself. Nothing was ever thrown away, and no one else was willing to eat it.

Hagg Karim came in again and looked with delight at the piles of bread and biscuits. Then he nodded his head with satisfaction and smiled at the girls.

"Many happy returns of the day."

Abdel-Aziz's mother answered him:

"We put all the butterfat we had in it. The rest of the year we'll eat bricks."

The girls looked at the two of them and froze, anticipating the coming storm. But Hagg Karim just shook his head in despair and went out to the courtyard. He turned to Abdel-Aziz.

"Take the lamp to the guest house, Abdel-Aziz."

Then he walked out slowly, to his friends and the evening gathering.

3

The Journey

He could not sleep. He would close his eyes only to be attacked by strange waking dreams. The sound of a diving mosquito buzzed in his ear, and fleas marched across his body under the old galabiya he kept for sleeping. The pillow gave out puffs of dust that stifled his breathing. Then more of the strange, disturbing dreams.

He slept alone now, up in this room on the roof. He had found a rusty old bed in some forgotten corner of the house and brought it up here. His mother had warned him:

"You're going to sleep alone? Something might get you."

From Hagg Karim's room, which was directly beneath his, he could hear the clatter of copper vessels. His father was taking a bath. Today he would travel to Tanta. Abdel-Aziz shut his eyes again, trying to sleep, but the dreams came back. The images grew huge and gigantic, taking on incredible size and frightening shapes. Repugnant mouths with fangs dripping poison and pus spoke the ugliest and most blasphemous words. He grasped the slender rusty bedpost and opened his eyes. But the room was totally and hopelessly dark.

The sound of clattering copper from the room below brought to his mind images of his early childhood—Hagg Karim completely naked, standing on a wooden stool in the middle of the shallow copper basin, the hot water pouring over his body from the black clay pitcher in his wife's hand. He would blow the water out of his nostrils with violent snorts and shout exuberant, resolute invocations. Abdel-Aziz himself seemed so small you could hold him in the palm of your hand, as he snuggled up in the bedclothes on the towering brass bed. Steam rose from the water splattering down from the black pitcher. His mother's hair was disheveled, and the neck of the thin shift she had over her body was wide open. The children were piled on the floor in a heap of nakedness, sweat, and strong smells.

Abdel-Aziz tried to lose himself in sleep, but the shapes kept twisting themselves and posing in horrible postures, their mouths screeching and dripping poison and pus. He opened his eyes, hoping to cling to wakefulness just long enough to put things in their place and then go back to sleep.

He sat up in bed and lit his lamp to drive away the perils of the darkness. In the corner was his pile of books with their dusty covers—his illness and his cure. Their words led him into mysterious labyrinths. Nothing remained fixed in his world any longer. The relentless pickaxes of knowledge were demolishing his fantasies one after the other, both emboldening and embittering him. He was addicted to their biting pain.

He went slowly down the staircase. The sparrows were twittering in the tangle of corn and cotton stalks on the roof, the hens were greedy for their morning grain, and downy little squabs were stirring in the pigeon nests. The day was awake and had just washed its face. The dreams were gone. But somewhere in a corner of his brain there was an unresolved question and a feeling of uneasiness that would not go away.

Hagg Karim was sitting on the mud bench in the central enclosure, his face freshly shaven and still moist after his bath. He was wearing his striped satin vest, and his silver watch chain hung across the front of it from the button loop to the pocket. Abdel-Aziz could feel the softness of the satin and the coolness of the silver from where he stood. He would have liked to rest his head on his father's breast, but that was out of the question now.

He kissed his father's hand and sat down on the edge of the reed mat, guarded and ill at ease. Hagg Karim was just finishing his morning devotions. He spoke the final words of praise, prayed for his brothers in the Path, and brushed his hands down over his face as he said amen. Then he called out:

"Well, children, bring me a bite to eat."

A piece of bread and a pinch of salt. He stuffed his mouth and handed the rest to Abdel-Aziz. It was a wonderful taste.

The light in the courtyard was bright and clear, fading only a bit in the corners. There were some late sparrows whose eyes still twinkled in their nests.

"Now my coffee."

Out came the shiny brass *kanaka* and the big painted china cup. He began to sip his coffee with enjoyment.

He had often talked to Abdel-Aziz about coffee, telling him how it was the drink of the Sufis and how they drank it black without sugar to help them stay up all night remembering God, repeating his name, and praising him. If such men wept, it was at the sweetness of the bond of love and fellowship, not at festering apparitions and frightening words of blasphemy and unbelief. Abdel-Aziz no longer knew the sweetness of that bond. Inside him things were out of balance. He hated the night and fled from it to the clear light of day. If only he could rub his face in Hagg Karim's hand and cry.

"Have some coffee, Abdel-Aziz."

Hagg Karim handed a cup of coffee to the boy. He took it quickly, but with diffidence. This was the first time he had been invited to share his father's coffee. He kept his eyes on the ground and did not move them. It tasted good. The drink of the Sufis who remember God.

His mother brought out the tarboosh and the winding cloth of his father's turban. Hagg Karim, still sitting, bent one leg up in front of him and pressed the tarboosh down on his knee. Then he spread out the cloth, long and diaphanous, between himself and Abdel-Aziz's mother and began to make successive lengthwise folds in it until it became a long, elegant band. When Abdel-Aziz was little he would run ahead of his mother to spread the cloth out in front of his father. He would never get it right, and his father would laugh at the absurdly contorted movements of his hands. But he would try again. There was delight in everything then.

Hagg Karim began to wrap the cloth carefully around the tarboosh. Abdel-Aziz followed his father's meticulous movements distractedly.

Hagg Karim's other wife was sitting quietly in front of the door of her room, resting her chin in her hand. The girls were doing various morning chores in silence. Hagg Karim handed the turban to Abdel-Aziz's mother and walked unhurriedly to his room. Standing in front of the wardrobe mirror, he put on his open-fronted caftan of striped satin and tightened it around his waist with an embroidered sash. Next he donned his big cashmere galabiya. Then, taking his turban, he twisted it down on his forehead and looked at himself in the mirror. With the flat of his hand he smoothed the front of his galabiya against his chest. His lips were closed and he looked awesome. Everything about him was elegant. There was not a single flaw.

"Abu Zeid performed the ablution and prayed two rakaas to God. Then he took his equipment, his sword, his helmet, and his veil, having resolved to set out for the land of Tunis. The folk of the Banu Hilal gathered to bid him farewell and to pray that his journey might be safe. Abu Zeid turned his eyes toward the barren sands and the wastelands. Then he looked at the elders around him and composed these verses: Bless Taha the Prophet. . . ." Abdel-Aziz had forgotten the poetry. He had even forgotten the inflection of Ahmed Bedawi's voice as he chanted these verses. But the yearning he had felt at the time had mingled with his soul and become something almost tangible. He was engulfed by a desire to travel, to leave.

Hagg Karim stood a while in the courtyard without speaking, his brown eyes not fixing on any object. There was not a sound. Even the pigeons in their nests were silent. It was as though he were standing there about to pray. No one would have dared walk in front of him.

"Good. Let's go."

He held out his hand and Abdel-Aziz's mother handed him

his cloak. He threw it over his shoulder and pressed it to his chest with his left hand. Next she gave him his cane, which he hung on his right arm. When he moved in the direction of the door, she followed him, and he held out his hand to her. She kissed it without a word. His other wife, and then the girls, did the same. Hagg Karim went out into the street, walking with slow deliberate steps. Beside him, with a confident stride, walked his son Abdel-Aziz.

The porch of the guesthouse was clean and recently swept, and the benches were spread with reed mats. The morning dew was still holding down the dust in the streets. Hagg Karim sat down in his accustomed place on the bench, put his cane aside, and laid his cloak next to him. Pulling out his tin of tobacco, he began to roll a cigarette. Before him the steps of the porch led down to the street. On the other side lay the threshing floor, with its few palm trees, and then the fields, stretching as far as one could see. Hagg Karim's longing brown eyes cut across the dull green expanse. His full brown face was beaming with contentment. The delights of the trip. The journey. The way to the Sultan. Nothing could create all this joy in his heart but a journey.

Mohammed Kamel climbed the stairs to the porch with a broad smile. He had on a freshly washed galabiya and had wrapped a white sash around his rust red woolen skullcap. A heavy muffler was thrown across his shoulder. Hagg Karim got up to welcome him, and they greeted each other with such longing that it seemed they had not seen each other in years. Yet they had been together the previous evening in the guesthouse. Mohammed Kamel kissed Hagg Karim on the shoulder, and Hagg Karim returned the kiss between his eyes. After turning to greet Abdel-Aziz and uttering a few good wishes, Mohammed Kamel sat down on the bench, his face beaming with happiness. He took out his tobacco-box and began scraping in it with a stick. Hagg Karim spoke to him:

"What was it the romance reciter used to say?"

Mohammed Kamel, smiling and with his eyes shut, nodded his head in anticipation of the verses.

"Yes. Go on. Go on."

"Well, sir, he used to say:

You Arabs who have called me, I stand at your door.
If you allow me, I will come in."

"Allah! Allah! Allah!"

Mohammed Kamel held out an open palm, offering Hagg Karim a little chewing tobacco.

"O Lord, never let us be deprived of thy Path. Give us love and fellowship, Abu Farrag, give us love and fellowship."

Mohammed Kamel had hardly settled in his place when Ahmed Bedawi came up, along with Iraqi the Deaf-Mute. They too were smiling and laughing happily. Iraqi put down his red turban and smoothed his beard. He gave no greeting but stood in the middle of the porch and, raising his voice, cried out for succor:

"Help us, O Lord Ahmed, O Bedawi, Help us!"

Ahmed Bedawi threw himself on Hagg Karim and embraced him. He had an elegant air in his new galabiya, his skullcap that held tight to his head, and his long muffler with its fringes that dragged on the ground because he was so short. As Iraqi bowed to put his lips to Hagg Karim's hand, Hagg Karim gave him a kiss on the head and said with a chanting voice:

"Let there be light on the Sultan's beloved. Help us, Uncle!"

People came from every direction and filled the porch with joyful faces. Packs of smoking tobacco were brought out and cigarettes exchanged. Tobacco-boxes were slapped into palms, and moist, finely crushed chewing tobacco was offered to the brothers. Abdel-Aziz sat quietly in the corner and smiled. Their collective joy had swept away his depression of the night, flooded it and washed it away.

What had brought them all here? Was it Iraqi's shrieking out for succor? Or was it the breath of the saint, manifest in the anticipation that had been in the air for days in the village, that had so suddenly kindled every heart with fire? Sitting on the mud benches by the doors of their houses, or on the heaps of topsoil, they had passed the moonlit summer nights speaking about the days of rejoicing. Those blessed days were few in the course of the year, and the time between them was filled with toil and hardship. But the moulid of the Sultan was unique among the days of rejoicing—the wonderful trip to Tanta, and the nights there bursting with light, music, and excitement.

"By God Almighty, if I have to steal, I'm going. Even if I have to fill my pockets with grain from the storage bins and sell it, I'm going."

The men sitting around looked at this youth who had been so carried away by longing. They pondered his excitement and his ironclad oaths and laughed. That longing was in every heart, but in their worn-out purses there might be a few piastres or there might not. Yet God was generous, and between now and the day of the journey he could raise seven heavens and unfold seven earths.

On that morning everyone was wearing freshly washed galabiyas. They had their canes hanging on their arms, and their faces were radiant with delight.

"What are we compared to the men of the old days? May God bless us through their merit and intercession!"

Hagg Karim slapped the palm of his hand on the arch of his stockinged foot, and a throng of eager faces turned toward him.

"Not one of them would ride an animal on his way to the Sultan. Never. To ride was unseemly."

From deep inside himself Mohammed Kamel called out:

"How great, how great is thy bounty, O Lord!"

And from the dozens of hearts crowded on the porch or pressing against the cement wall that enclosed it came a rumbling storm of dazzlement and faith. The faces splotched with white from malnutrition were flooded now with mystical contentment.

"Think about it, Uncle Mohammed Kamel. In the train we can sit down and travel comfortably."

Mohammed Kamel was so affected he almost wept.

"We're weak and frail, Uncle Hagg Karim."

Then he lowered his head and went on in his cracking voice:

"There was a man who lived near Mahalla el-Kubra who used to get up in the morning and say to his wife, 'Woman, bring me my cane. I want to go and visit Sidi Ahmed Rifa'i in Iraq.' She would give him his cane, and by the afternoon he would be back. He would give her Iraqi dates and say, 'God provided me with a few dates while I was sitting next to Rifa'i's mausoleum reading the Sura of Yâ Sîn.'"

Faith and belief hummed in their hearts like the droning of bees. They sucked their lips in astonishment and uttered words of prayer and supplication. Here and there voices were murmuring, "There is no strength nor might but in God!" Hagg Karim again slapped the arch of his foot, and with his eyes closed said:

"They have flown away on the back of the two letters of the word 'BE.'* Those were the Men of the Giant Stride, Mohammed Kamel, my old friend."

Hagg Karim opened his brown eyes. In them shone the longing Abdel-Aziz knew well, the longing that appeared in his eyes when he would stand on the porch of the guesthouse and gaze into the distance. The imprisonment of the day, the going nowhere and doing nothing, burdened his spirit. He would remain fidgeting in his place, with the deep pain of that longing showing in his eyes. At times the road would reveal one of them, one of the Travelers in Time, the Wanderers, those lean and tattered spirits who roamed through the countryside.

That particular man had a white face, a thin beard, and big, wide eyes. When he took off his turban, straight black hair fell down over his forehead. He took a piece of candy out of his sleeve and gave it to little Abdel-Aziz. The boy had never tasted

*This is the divine command of creation, cited among other places in the Koran in the next to the last verse of the Sura of Yâ Sîn just mentioned: "Verily, when he wills a thing, he commands it saying, 'Be,' and it is" (36:82). In several passages this command is repeated specifically in connection with the denial of the Christian belief that Jesus was begotten by God, as opposed to having been created by him (2:117, 3:59, 19:35).—Trans.

anything more delicious. He discovered that beneath his clothes the man weighed down his body with iron chains. Hagg Karim had asked him why.

"What's the reason, Uncle?"

Although the man was younger than Hagg Karim he called him Uncle.

"The sins of men. I carry them on my back."

In the evening when they held the *zikr,* he flew about between the two ranks like a white pigeon, and the men taking part were crazed with excitement.

The next morning Abdel-Aziz asked with concern:

"Where is the man, Father?"

Hagg Karim looked into the distance.

"He's gone, Son. He's gone."

Whenever Abdel-Aziz saw his father standing on the guest-house porch and gazing in that way, he would sit at his feet and watch his brown eyes as they seemed to take flight toward the horizon, helpless with longing. One day the silence uncovered an enfeebled specter creeping forward on his stick, one of the Travelers in Time. Beaming with joy, Hagg Karim went down the stairs to greet him.

"Welcome, Uncle."

He was a decrepit old man, with feeble vision and tattered clothes, who leaned constantly for support on a rough stick of acacia. He sat down on the bench, concerned only with himself, and kept muttering unintelligible sounds. He saw nothing around him. The brothers in the order, and the other villagers as well, flocked to see him, but the man remained completely unaware of what was happening. Taking out his tobacco-box and emptying its contents into his hand, he would put the tobacco in his mouth and chew it for a while. Then he would take it back out of his mouth and return it to the box. He twitched restlessly and stuttered a few fragments of speech.

Mahmoud Abu el-Yazid arrived carrying the big brass tray, loaded with food from Hagg Karim's house. Each man brought something from his own house. The place was crowded with people and things to eat. Hagg Karim was in a state of delight and could not hold still. Then suddenly, and without warning, the man took up his stick and made his way haltingly down the stairs. Eyes and hearts followed him as he went. When he came to the middle of the open space before the porch, as if a demon had mounted him, he was filled with an uncommon strength. He raised his stick into the air and began to yell. Hopping on one foot and turning in a circle, he danced a strange dance and shouted at the top of his voice. One or two turns and he was a fragile old man again, hobbling off with the aid of his stick. They all looked on in amazement as he disappeared around the bend in the road.

In the midst of this gathering of travelers, Abdel-Aziz's spirit soared. He would have liked to set out and wander from province to province, not asking where or why. But how could a man journey without a cane, without baring his feet, without performing his ablutions? He was ritually impure. His head was weighed down with intractable question marks, and his heart was burdened with constant misgivings.

Ahmed Bedawi burst out laughing as he reminded the brothers of their last trip to the moulid of Hussein. They had all packed into a truck. Hagg Karim had sat next to the driver, but the dervishes had spread out their long mufflers and sat next to their wives in the back of the truck, where they had bounced back and forth and laughed until they reached Cairo. They had arrived totally worn out from the strain of the trip and the laughter.

Mohammed Kamel broke in distractedly:

"The people from Sharqiya should be in Tanta tomorrow, God willing."

Hagg Karim smiled warmly. They themselves would leave now and get the house in Tanta ready. Tomorrow the people from Sharqiya would arrive and spend the period of the moulid as their guests.

Early tomorrow morning their sheikh in Sharqiya would step out of his house wearing his green turban and his big cashmere galabiya. He would go over to his guesthouse to sit and wait for the brothers to gather for their trip to Tanta. Perhaps there too, in front of the sheikh's guesthouse, there would be a gathering like this one, alive with conversation and overflowing with longing for the joys of the journey.

Abdel-Aziz imagined Sheikh Abbas appearing in the distance to join the assembly of the Sharqiya brothers in front of their sheikh's guesthouse. He had to feel his way with his cane. His vision was so feeble he could barely distinguish shapes. But as soon as he had managed to seat himself and had begun talking, no power in heaven or on earth could stop him. He had studied at Al-Azhar, but had abandoned his studies without acquiring a whit of knowledge. Nevertheless, he wore a sheikh's robe and turban, and he took the liberty of giving counsel to people in matters of morals and religious law. He would advise you however you liked, making religion easy for you, even if you deliberately broke the Ramadan fast.

"Never mind. Pray two *rakaas* to God and ask his forgiveness. He will forgive you. If you are a rigid Hanbalite, then give some food to a poor man. God is all-forgiving, my brother. Why all this harassment of his servants?"

Ahmed Bedawi practically rolled over with laughter.

"By the Prophet, Sheikh Abbas, you deserve to have a dome built over your tomb. Your belly can hold more than Sayyid Bedawi's."

But Mistikawi put on a ridiculous solemnity and asked in his Sharqiya dialect:

"Tell me, Sheikh Abbas, is stealing donkeys allowed or forbidden?"

The Dandy broke in, pretending to be serious:

"It's not forbidden, Mistikawi. It just makes the angels angry at you."

The whole gathering broke out laughing, and Sheikh Abbas cursed them all.

"Sons of bitches! Hashish-smokers!"

Mistikawi and the Dandy did indeed smoke hashish. They worshipped it. And they were in love with fine clothes, smooth material, and cologne. No one knew how Mistikawi managed to get hold of food for his children, and no one asked. Perhaps people did whisper among themselves that he stole donkeys. But one thing was sure; he had never stolen a single donkey during the moulid.

Maybe they were there now. But tomorrow morning at the latest they would be sitting in front of the sheikh's guesthouse and waiting until they were all together. They would wait for that black man who made their coffee to arrive, with all his gear packed in his little saddlebag, and for the *fiki* who wrote charms and made amulets, who never stopped mumbling words of praise, and who hardly ever spoke to anyone. Then, when they were all together, they would set off on the journey to the feast of the Sultan. It would be a delightful evening, when they all met in the lodgings in Tanta.

How the men yearned for the approaching journey and the reunion with brothers and friends. Whenever they thought of the trip, they would be overcome by a flood of fond memories. Hagg Karim leaned toward Ahmed Bedawi.

"I wonder if our letter reached Hassan Effendi and he knows the date of the moulid."

When the postman had handed Hassan Effendi the letter, he had read it with a beaming smile. The next day he would put his tarboosh on his head, button up his overcoat, and stand for a moment at the head of the dark staircase, uncertain and a bit ashamed. Then he would turn to his wife, who would be standing at his side and holding her baby in her arms.

"Take care of yourself."

And he would hurry down the stairs.

The Dandy showed up with his saddlebag over his shoulder and his watch in his hand.

"It's still early."

But Selim Sherkasi growled back angrily:

"If we start a little early, isn't it better?"

When the Dandy had greeted the brothers, he remained standing on the porch, talking and gesturing with his hands.

"It's still early, everybody."

Ahmed Bedawi cut in quickly:

"Early or late, never mind. What have you been doing all this time at home? Couldn't you get enough of Rawayih all night long?"

Everyone laughed. Even Hagg Karim had to suppress a chuckle.

Suddenly Rawayih herself appeared at a distance and called out to the Dandy. The laughter grew louder and louder, as the Dandy with his slight frame strode toward Rawayih and stood at her flank. She seemed huge, and her eyes were gleaming like the eyes of a kite. She spoke to him insistently, while he gestured helplessly. Every time he tried to get away, she pulled him back by the collar of his galabiya. Finally he managed to slip out of her hands and hurried back to the group. She stood where she was, following him with her eyes as if he were a child traveling for the first time on a road full of dangers. A storm of laughter and questions awaited him on the porch.

"What did she want with you?"

"Is everything all right, Dandy?"

"She brought me a packet of tobacco."

"You must have been a lion last night."

The Dandy chuckled and broke into a wide grin, showing stained teeth ruined by tobacco and tea.

"It was a beautiful night. A pair of pigeons and a little hashish."

Beyond all doubt no one there gave a thought to the hashish or the beautiful night. They were concerned about the pair of pigeons that had been cooked for the Dandy. Everyone thought about the pigeon nests at his own house. Whose pigeons had been slaughtered last night? Ahmed Bedawi let the moment of silence pass, and then asked the Dandy:

"Didn't you pass by El-Gazyeh to wish her well before leaving?"

"No!"

"You should have."

"Look, my friend."

"Yes?"

"Rawayih has the nights when I am going to travel the next morning, the nights before a holiday or a feast, and the nights after market days. The rest of the time I am free."

"Suppose you went to El-Gazyeh on one of Rawayih's nights?"

"If I dared go home the next morning, Rawayih would break my leg."

Everyone laughed, and someone remarked:

"So Rawayih must have poured soapy water in front of her door this morning."

The Dandy chuckled:

"Perfumed soap."

Hagg Karim rose and held his cloak over his shoulder with his left hand. With his right he gripped his cane. His face was calm and dignified. All the others stood up after him, and for a few seconds there was complete silence. Mohammed Kamel broke out in a voice that revealed the depth of his joy:

"The Opening for the righteous saints of God, so God may make all our affairs prosper, make our journeys easy, and open doors before us. The Opening!"

The Opening was recited in inaudible whispers. But Iraqi the Deaf-Mute understood what they were reciting. He held up his hands before him in supplication and began moving his lips until he perceived that they had completed the recitation. At the amen he passed his hands down over his face and breast and raised his voice, calling out for succor. No one commented. No one said a thing. Hagg Karim moved with deliberation toward the steps and started quietly down. They were all behind him, shuffling silently along in their freshly laundered galabiyas, their minds elsewhere. Now and then someone cleared his throat or sucked his lips. Today it was not allowed to wipe one's nose on one's sleeve or on the hem of one's galabiya. One had to have a handkerchief, or a clean and neatly folded piece of cloth.

Hagg Karim looked straight ahead. There was tenderness,

longing, and a solemn grandeur in his eyes. Abdel-Aziz had never seen that expression in the eyes of any other man. It was engraved in his mind—an unquenched longing for vague worlds flooded with clarity and light. When he was little, that look on Hagg Karim's face had filled him with fear or sadness. He would walk close to his father's side, silent, submissive, and withdrawn into his tiny self. He would walk with a heart full of awe, tripping on pebbles in the road. Today he was at the tail end of the procession, but he could still see those eyes, like birds fluttering forth to scout out the way and then coming back to alight on the procession. He could see the effect they produced on the people lining both sides of the road as they came forward and quietly bowed to kiss Hagg Karim's hand. Today he did not pull back his hand from anyone. They greeted him, and he would reply to them almost in a whisper:

"God willing, we will find you well when we return."

Someone raised his eyes to him pleadingly:

"Remember, I asked you to recite the Opening in his tomb."

It was one of the men who was not going. Empty hands and empty pockets perhaps, or maybe it was worries at home and work in the field. Or he may have lacked resolve, like a sailing vessel motionless in a feeble wind. Alas for the heavy ships that cling sluggishly to the shore, the anxieties of the soul, and the uncertainty of the night. Hagg Karim, indulgence and compassion showing in his features, nodded his head to reassure him.

"God willing. God willing."

When the procession of travelers passed in front of their own house, Abdel-Aziz noticed that the door was ajar. He caught sight of the eyes of all the girls crowded into that one little crack peering out. He laughed to himself at their eagerness. They worshipped their father Hagg Karim. Who in the village did not love him? They would leave the next day. But what a journey! They would leave wearing the plainest black clothing, and they would not walk on this road that went directly to the train station. Instead, they would take a path that led through the fields, avoiding the ways people usually took and stumbling over the dried manure piles. They would laugh, and would curse Sayyid Bedawi and his treacherous paths. Of course they would have Rashida with them, and a man too. But he was certain to be some hapless helper who had missed the chance to go with Hagg Karim.

That is the way they would leave. They would wish they were men. But the worst of trips was better than staying at home. They would have to brave whole oceans of perils—the train, the conductors, and the teasing and annoyance of the town boys.

The procession of travelers passed on beyond the house, and soon they were joined by the wives of Ahmed Bedawi, Mohammed Kamel, and Sherkasi the Carpenter, who were setting out with the men. They were carrying baskets of provisions, and the wives of Ahmed Bedawi and Sherkasi were each holding an infant. Mohammed Kamel's pitiful wife Saddiqa kept her head bent and her sorrowful eyes fixed to the ground as she walked.

If only Hagg Karim would call back to them to come along too, the girls must have been thinking. They would load the baskets on their heads and dash out to catch the procession of men. But Hagg Karim's provisions were not carried in baskets. They were borne in two great chests on the back of Omar Farhoud's camel. Abdel-Aziz looked over his shoulder to find the door shut. He laughed to himself again as he imagined how they must be rushing about here and there to get ready for their departure. He imagined his mother, totally unconcerned with the excitement of the girls, coming and going in the house, frowning, and determined to get things done, feeding the chickens, watering the animals, or preparing the bowls for the evening milking. All that was hidden now behind the door.

The procession of men passed on, greeted by the other villagers as they went. Lowered voices would ask for Openings to be recited in the mausoleum. The women looked out at the passing group from the doors of their homes. As happened from time to time, one of them rushed up to Hagg Karim carrying her little child.

"Please, by the Prophet, Hagg Karim, please recite the Opening in Sayyid Bedawi's tomb for my son."

Hagg Karim stopped for a moment, placed his hand on the child's head, and prayed. Then he patted the woman on the shoulder and moved on. Tears poured down the woman's cheeks, and as he continued on his way she cupped one hand over her mouth and let out a long trill. The procession responded with repeated sucking of lips. The Dandy straightened his saddlebag over his shoulder, and a strange glint appeared in his eyes.

"What's the matter, wench?"

Ahmed Bedawi struggled to overcome a smile as he scolded the Dandy.

"Mind your own business, you son of a dog. Do you have some kind of worm that never lets you alone?"

Abdel-Aziz, embarrassed, hid his own smile. He reminded himself of the solemnity of the occasion and walked on in the procession. Some distance ahead he saw Ali Khalil in front of the door of his shop. Dressed in a spotless galabiya and with a beaming smile on his newly shaven face, he was clearly ready to leave.

"Peace be upon you, and the mercy of God, Uncle Ali Khalil."

Ali Khalil bent over Hagg Karim's hand and kissed it. Hagg Karim returned the kiss on his forehead. Then the grocer went into his shop to fetch the mat to cover the bench. The shelves of the shop were jammed to the ceiling with cartons, cans, tin jugs, soap, sugar, rolls of cloth, lamp bowls, and all sorts of merchandise. The strings hanging from the ceiling held various kinds of long men's scarves and red and green shawls for girls. The boxes along the walls were filled with dried dates, lentils, and broad beans. On the floor were big earthenware jars of black molasses and sacks of rice and salt. Everything was piled up in disarray and covered with dust. When Abdel-Aziz was little, his mouth used to water when he saw the colored candy in that small glass window at the top of the counter. Now he liked to watch how Ali Khalil made his way with such ease through all these heaps of goods without ever stumbling over a thing, just the way his mother moved so deftly about in the cluttered storeroom at home. But when there were no customers, the grocer with the pale face would settle down on a sack full of something or other and open a book with yellow, oil-spattered pages, and become engrossed in his reading.

Ali Khalil spread the reed mat on the bench and wiped the dust off with his hand. Hagg Karim reassured him.

"That's fine, Ali, fine."

Then he sat down. Whoever managed to find a place sat down too, while the others stood in a circle around Hagg Karim. Ali Khalil brought out the hard candies and passed them around. Abdel-Aziz did not like them anymore. Ali Khalil hesitated to offer any to him. Effendis were cautious as a rule about accepting things from peasants. But Abdel-Aziz took them right away.

At every man's place they had a clean, pleasant spot to sit, and when they sat down to talk, there was no telling when they would stop. Cigarettes were passed around, and tobacco-boxes were slapped into palms. The Dandy's voice rose above the others in boisterous laughter. Iraqi looked around him, not understanding a thing, but smiling in response to the joy he saw on their faces.

Omar Farhoud came running up. His house, near which knelt his camel, was only a few steps from the shop. He kissed the hand of Hagg Karim, who returned the kiss on his forehead.

"Many happy returns, Farhoud."

Omar Farhoud replied in a humble voice cracked with emotion:

"Remember we asked you to pray for us, Uncle Hagg Karim."

"God willing. God willing."

Then he smiled at Farhoud, reminding him:

"The chests, Omar, early tomorrow morning. The Provisions of the Sultan, my son."

"With all my heart. It's my sacred duty. May God never forsake us."

"Amen."

Then Omar Farhoud saw Abdel-Aziz and greeted him with laughter in his voice.

"How are you, Master Abdel-Aziz? Don't you want to ride the camel this year?"

Everyone laughed, and Hagg Karim smiled at his son, pleased that the brothers were so fond of him. Abdel-Aziz replied in embarrassment:

"I'm too heavy for the camel now, Uncle Omar."

They all laughed again, and Farhoud went on:

"The thing he liked most was to ride on top of the chests."

In those days, when he was little, he would stand waiting in front of the house. From the distance Omar Farhoud's huge camel would approach, its hooves skimming the ground and its neck jerking back and forth. Omar Farhoud would be jumping around it with his big bamboo stick. When the camel reached their house, it would lower its enormous hulk to the ground and stay kneeling there with a perplexed look in its eyes, impatient, indignant, and complaining. Omar Farhoud would attempt to calm its ire with that special drawn out sound the camel drivers made.

"Hikh-kh-kh-kh."

The adolescent boys of the village came up shyly with downcast eyes, but their faces were flushed with excitement. Little Abdel-Aziz could hear the whine of excitement in their breasts, and he looked at them with fear and hostility. But the girls watching from the various corners of the house were wide-eyed and could hardly suppress their titters of delight. Their faces were blood red with the same agitation. Abdel-Aziz's mother acted with fixed purpose. She knew exactly what she wanted.

"Over here, you two. Two on each side. Easy does it."

The youths launched their attack on the two chests. Four of them, their arms bursting with manliness, carried each chest. They took them outside and put one on each side of the kneeling camel. Omar Farhoud was completely carried away. He darted back and forth from one side to the other.

"Careful, don't step in front of the camel. Hold it there. When I tell you, lift."

He bound the load onto the back of the camel with rope, while Abdel-Aziz's mother stood watching, her eyes on the two chests. The girls had their eyes on the boys. Abdel-Aziz could see the sparks flash back and forth between their eyes and it frightened him. But he turned his attention elsewhere and yelled to Omar Farhoud:

"Put me up, please, Omar."

"Right away, Master Abdel-Aziz."

The little boy was hoisted up on top of the chests and his mother tossed him a piece of white cloth.

"Put this on your head, boy, to protect you from the sun."

He caught the cloth without really understanding what she had said. All he could think about was the approaching moment of terror when the camel would stand up. He longed for that moment, but he was afraid of it. The loud and angry snorts of the camel complaining of the load on his back only made the boy's trembling increase. Everything he heard added to his dismay—his mother's warnings, the cries of Omar Farhoud, the shouts and laughter of the boys, and the giggles and shrieks of the girls. Then Omar Farhoud undid the rope that hobbled the camel, and the animal raised its breast, heaving its load to the rear. Abdel-Aziz would have gone flying to the ground had he not kept a firm grip on the handle running around the edge of one of the chests. Then the camel lifted its hind parts, thrusting the load forward, and Abdel-Aziz was almost thrown off again. Finally the animal stood all the way up, obviously taking pride in its unbelievable strength. Abdel-Aziz found himself a long way up in the air, sitting on this towering camel. He could almost touch the window of the room on the roof. He looked at his mother and his sisters down below and smiled with delight. Then the camel set off, moving his heavy hooves along the road. Omar Farhoud was pleased with his camel and always feared an envious eye.

"Let's hope for a safe trip. In the name of God the Merciful and Compassionate."

But why should he fear for his animal, when his wife had made an amulet to hang around its neck, an amulet of colored thread, beads, and bits of mirrors and glass?

The camel lurched forward. The load creaked, confined by the strong, thick ropes. Abdel-Aziz's body was jostled in rhythm with the monotonous movement of the chests, but he was happy. He could see the people's eyes. The children knew the camel's journey was to Tanta, and they laughed and smiled at him. Omar Farhoud was overjoyed at the privilege of carrying the Provisions to the moulid.

Abdel-Aziz found it truly beautiful to look around from this high place. By now the houses of the village were far off and were disappearing in the steadily increasing distance. This was the most direct way to Tanta. It went past the sister village and then the railroad station. Next it took you through the fields, turning somctimes right and sometimes left, or even going up a rise, but in the end it took you to the outskirts of Tanta. What joy!

From every village people were going to the moulid. Little paths led along the edges of the plots and fields like veins in a leaf, constantly feeding lines of travelers into the main road—men in freshly laundered galabiyas, girls in red, green, or lime-yellow shawls, and women carrying baskets and bundles of provisions on their heads. The groups kept coming, singing and clapping and shouting with joy.

Lord of the Green Threshold,
call us to you.
We have slaughtered our cow
and come to you.

The camel drivers were driving their beasts along too, but none of the camels was ever like Omar Farhoud's, none of the chests were ever bigger than the two huge chests of Hagg Karim, and none of the villages one passed ever had a guesthouse like his. Abdel-Aziz was so proud of his father he could hardly keep from shouting out a challenge.

There, in an open space before a big village, stood the cabs. The country folk were like whole nations standing around them, and the drivers were more ferocious than demons. They were punching people in the chest, pushing women and children, and screaming and demanding outrageous fares. Not only that, they insisted on taking the fare before starting the journey. Omar Farhoud shouted to Abdel-Aziz:

"Sons of dogs! Infidels! They want to be paid in advance. Maybe they won't make it. They'll have no right to that money. Help us, O Sayyid!"

The buses, so overloaded that they leaned to one side, stirred up whirling clouds of dust as they left. The cabs drove off with people sitting on the front fenders and the roof and hanging off both sides and the rear. Before a cab reached the traffic control point the extra passengers would get down, and the vehicle would pass by the policeman with only a few riders inside. Once out of his sight it would stop and wait for the passengers, who would swarm over it once again. The driver would punch and kick wildly, but the peasants would cling to the cab from all sides, totally concealing its iron body.

But Abdel-Aziz was secure in his place, and being up where he was he could see the fields stretching out for huge distances. He could see the villages and the hamlets and the narrow paths leading along the edges of the fields. The people were coming like swarms of bees, people who preferred to walk rather than to ride in those hellish vehicles with their demonic drivers. They preferred to walk and to talk. Talk was their entertainment on the way, and it flowed from a spring that never dried up. A youth was pressing his skullcap on his head, while the girl beside him was trying to straighten out her shawl and, at the same time, with an arm adorned with brightly colored bangles, to balance the bundle on her head. They were smiling and talking—another Ahmed Bedawi with his sweetheart on the way to Tanta. How delightful it was to hear Ahmed Bedawi talk of his trips to Tanta with the girl he used to love. But he hadn't married her. She had been married off to someone in a faraway village.

The acacia branches thrust their velvety yellow blossoms into Abdel-Aziz's lap and the thorns scratched against the rag he had wrapped around his head. Omar Farhoud led his camel toward the fountain to let it drink. People were crowded around the fountain, filling the spot with laughter and banter. One of the men shouted at them in a serious tone:

"Take your drink and bless the Prophet."

The fountain had a little dome over it, as if it were the tomb of a minor sheikh, a dome that sheltered two big clay jars of cool water from the sun. There was also a pump that spouted water into a trough for the animals to drink from. Once the water jars were empty, some good soul would fill them again. Omar Farhoud filled the dipper and hung it on his stick to hand it up to Abdel-Aziz.

"Drink, and pray for the man who built this fountain. You're still young and your breath is still pure."

Abdel-Aziz drank, and thought about the man who had built the fountain. Perhaps he had been a good man like his father Hagg Karim and had fed the folk who wandered through the land.

Omar Farhoud was giddy with delight. He struck his camel gently with his stick and cried:

"Heh! Heh! Let's go, my friend. We're almost there."

Only a short while later, indeed, the dome of Sayyid Bedawi's mosque appeared on the horizon. When Omar Farhoud saw it he let out a yell that split the heavens.

"Help us, O Abu Farrag, help us!"

Abdel-Aziz contemplated the great dome, and a kind of fear came over his heart.

Hagg Karim slapped the bottom of his stockinged foot with the palm of his hand as he sat on the bench in front of Ali Khalil's shop. The men who were going to Tanta were sitting or standing around him.

"The eye of a believer can see the Sultan's dome when he is miles and miles away."

The men sucked their lips in wonder, while Mohammed Kamel endorsed Hagg Karim's words:

"Yes indeed. Yes indeed."

Ali Khalil had finished getting ready now. He whispered to his wife, who was standing behind him in the shop, what had to be done while he was away, and then came out and joined the others. Hagg Karim stood up, followed by the others who had found seats, and the procession started on its way once again.

Some distance ahead, Rashida stood in front of her door, eagerly awaiting the arrival of her father. When he drew near she ran out to meet him, carrying her little son on her breast. Her face was beaming as she bent over to kiss her father's hand. He kissed her on the head and gave her son a caress, but the child put on an ugly face and began to cry. Hagg Karim laughed:

"You're crying, son of a dog, instead of offering us coffee!"

Rashida responded:

"With pleasure, Papa. Coffee? If only you would stop long enough to drink water from our water jar, just a little, for it to be blessed."

Hagg Karim walked on, and Rashida walked a few steps at his side.

"Everything depends on you, Daughter. Tomorrow morning early now, so the people will have something to eat."

The procession had now passed her house. What tenderness his father's eyes showed for Rashida, and what love hers showed for him.

"Go on back now, Daughter."

She stopped and bid them farewell as the procession left her behind.

"Good-bye. Safe journey and a safe return. May God never deprive us of you. You are the light of the village. Life would have no savor without you."

The procession moved ahead, out of the village and on toward the train station. Along the way peasants were working in the fields. Hagg Karim would raise his hand to greet each one of them. The man would stop his work and return the greeting with a cry and a wave of his hand. He would remain for a few moments looking at the travelers and then bend down to his hoe again. In the sister village there were men sitting on the benches by the doors of their houses. When Hagg Karim greeted them, they would stand and return the greeting at the top of their voices, inviting the men to stop a while. The procession would answer them with a clamorous litany of greetings and invocations.

The railroad station was a platform with a pole bearing a sign stating the name of the village. It was crowded with men who were going to Tanta. The few women remained off to one side with their baskets and bundles. Hagg Karim, his cloak folded over his shoulder, stood leaning on his cane and looking toward the distant horizon. The Dandy took his watch from his vest pocket.

"It's still early for the train, men."

Hagg Karim stretched out his arm to hold on to Ahmed Bedawi while he seated himself on the sand that covered the platform.

"God bless those who sit."

The dervishes formed a circle around him. He placed his cloak over his crossed legs and leaned on it with his elbows. He fixed his gaze straight ahead. Off in the distance, as though he could see it, was the dome of Sayyid Bedawi's mosque, and in a few hours they would meet their brothers from faraway provinces.

Abdel-Aziz looked at the faces in that circle one after the other. There was joy and there was fear. Travel was a perilous experience attended by many dangers. Dozens of tales were told in their gatherings by those who had returned from journeys. On the heaps of topsoil and on the mud benches in front of their houses the fears of this moment had been formed. They had washed their galabiyas and packed their provisions in baskets, and now they were about to board the train.

But the train had not yet come.

"Shall I roll you one, Hagg Karim?"

"Roll me one, Dandy."

The Dandy's clean, white fingers were not rough from work

in the fields. They were nimble and practiced. His face showed more vitality than those of the others. In it there was something that resembled the world they were about to plunge into, something bold and insolent. Everyone was looking at his face as he rolled the cigarette. It seemed as though he sensed their looks, and his face took on a brighter glow and greater scorn.

"Those townspeople are sons of whores."

The foul word collided with the sensibilities of the dervishes. Hagg Karim lowered his eyes as though he had not heard. But there was an air of general assent. The Dandy had traveled a lot. His daughters worked as maids in the houses of the townspeople. He would go to collect their wages and to carry off whatever the girls might have stolen for him from those houses full of nice things, so many nice things that their owners would not notice their absence or could do without them—clothes, spoons, socks, handkerchiefs, and more. They were traveling to a city of sons of whores. Yet it drew them toward it, despite all the trouble it promised. Was not the tomb of the Sultan there?

When they boarded the train they would find benches that faced each other. Hagg Karim would sit by the window, with Ahmed Bedawi next to him and Mohammed Kamel and Ali Khalil sitting opposite. The other men and the few women would scatter to seats on both sides of the car. Then there would be a moment of unfamiliar sensations and alarm as the train shook and rumbled, beginning to move. Next the conductor would come, scowling and shouting, passing from one end of the car to the other, striking the backs of the seats with his ticket punch and slapping people's shoulders. On the peasants' faces, already pale with apprehension, would appear confusion and bewilderment. But Hagg Karim's face would wear an intrepid mask. Or possibly it would grow dark with anger, and he would spring up to defend his men. As long as a man had his ticket in his hand, no one could say a thing to him. The train was there for whoever paid the price of a ticket.

When Abdel-Aziz was very little he used to sit with his heart throbbing, waiting for the moment when his father would take on the conductor. He would be overcome with delight when the effendi's fury would collide with his father's stubborn opposition and be forced to give way. He would listen to his father in wonder as he told of similar incidents with other people of high station. Not every trip he took was to visit the Sultan. Sometimes he might be called to meet the district officer. He would tell the story with a glowering face and with such indignation he could hardly keep his seat.

"I told the district officer to take it easy. Take it easy and you'll get what you want, I told him. We men are weak and have no control over our destinies."

Abdel-Aziz's heart nearly stopped beating. The district officer was on the point of leaping up from his seat to seize Hagg Karim and shake him through and through. Indeed he might have done so, if the medical officer, unaware of what was going on, had not come in and greeted Hagg Karim warmly.

"His Felicity the Bey doesn't know Hagg Karim? He's an extraordinary man."

The physician discovered they were in the middle of a battle and laughed.

"You two must have had a difference. It was the same with me. The first time I met Hagg Karim I had a quarrel with him. Afterward we became friends. He's an extraordinary man, Your Felicity. During the cholera epidemic he carried out the dead on his shoulders."

Then the three of them sat down together to have a friendly conversation, and the throbbing in Abdel-Aziz's small heart subsided.

"The district officer made his peace with me and patched things up between us. And he promised to come and have coffee in our lodgings in Tanta."

They were all transported with delight. Ahmed Bedawi remarked:

"Then we should tell Oum Talaat to leave the two couches in her living room so that if anyone comes he won't have to sit on the mat."

But Hagg Karim replied:

"Whoever is happy with our mat can come and visit us. Whoever isn't, we're better off without."

The men were delighted with their widely traveled leader, and here they were now traveling with him. The conductor left, and the tension died down. Groups began to strike up conversations on both sides of the car, while the train rumbled on its way through the fields.

At every station the train would stop, and more travelers, more dervishes with their leaders, would get on. There were the same baskets of provisions, and the same faces filled with wonder, concern, and a little fear. Ahmed Bedawi looked at their faces, their skullcaps, and the collars of their galabiyas. Each group had its particular way of dressing and talking. Hagg Karim would remember friends of his from various places and would talk of their generosity and their fervent devotion to the saints of God. Mohammed Kamel would speak of sheikhs who had their tombs in this village or that. And the train rolled on to the pole of poles.

The folk in some villages planted early, which showed wisdom on their part. What a terrible thing it was to delay, to have no determination or resolve. In some villages, too, they plowed their furrows from north to south. A peasant from one of the distant villages laughed:

"Well then, Uncle, your plant is never in the shade. The sun sees it as soon as it rises in the east."

The women listened with astonishment to the ways the women of other villages cooked, milked, or prepared charms for their children, and they learned who in their villages knew about books and magic and the varieties of spells.

This was the journey to the Sultan—longing and reunion, fear and wonder, and discovery.

The huge steel arm moved, and the platform trembled beneath Abdel-Aziz's feet. Fire exploded in the bowels of the black locomotive, and the train began to roll. Their faces in the windows smiled toward him as the train pulled out, taking with it something that had filled his heart. Now he was all alone. He stood there resigned, watching the train move off into the distance until it could hardly be seen.

Abdel-Aziz went down from the platform and made his way back to the village. He avoided the road his father's procession had taken an hour before. He took instead a little lane that twisted between the plots and fields where he could walk alone. With those men he had been part of a great body moving along, a throng of feet striking the earth and of legs rustling in galabiyas. He missed the reassurance he felt in their company. He could still hear the sound of the train as it dwindled into silence. The brown earth stretched to the horizon, bare except for a few thin, indistinct wheatstalks. He sat down on the bank of the irrigation canal. The still water was silver in the sun and brown in the shade. Nearby a weeping willow bathed its tresses in the canal.

His imagination was crowded with the images of their faces, thin faces with olive skin. There were few joys in their lives, few trips. But when these occasions came, their faces would beam with happiness. The Sultan's dome was a long way off, in the center of the world. Hagg Karim was heavyset, and his round face was full of serenity, but in his eyes was the glint of longing. In their gatherings the men would smile and reveal yellowed teeth. Abdel-Aziz felt in his heart the pangs of an unknown malady.

Once this strange and despondent feeling had taken him to her house. He had pushed the door open. He had had so many things to say that it must have been showing in his eyes. She was sitting there, scooping up water from a basin in front of her to wash her face. In her wide, limpid eyes there was both affection and curiosity. But he had found nothing to say. He had turned around and left, closing the door behind him.

He picked up a dried sow thistle stalk from the ground and began chewing it to rid himself of his agitation. The bitter taste spread through his mouth and through his whole being. Tears streamed down his cheeks; he could taste their saltiness in his mouth. He stood up like a man who was a thousand years old.

"I have to travel."

But where? The railroad track went perfectly straight, cutting through the countryside like a knife. Alongside it ran the line of telephone poles. Together the two went right to the horizon and disappeared, perhaps at the end of the world. Where he would go he did not know. But he had to travel. Nothing but a long journey could quench this strange burning thirst.

He thought of the man wrapped in iron chains with his serene, kindly face, of that old man Soliman, and of Abu Garida with his stripped palm frond—the Travelers in Time. They would hardly sit down before their eyes began to gleam with longing and they got up to go.

He thought of that godly man Sayyid from Mahallet Minouf. Perhaps it was that same longing that compelled him to roll up his mat and carry it all the way to their house, where he would throw it down with contentment in the presence of Hagg Karim.

"I love them! I love them!"

And the hot tears poured down his cheeks.

4

The Lodgings

In Mahalla el-Kubra there was a canal that cleft the heart of the city. He thought of it, and of the people like swarms of flies on both banks, washing their clothes and their cooking utensils—the voices of the women, their little battles, and the clattering of copper pots. He remembered his sister, surrounded by other women, talking with the local accent. His other sisters had been dumbfounded. She had become tender and soft brown like the city girls. He remembered how she took the clothes and the pots to the canal to wash them. The water of the river was never foul, even if you threw cadavers in it. But the water in pipes, who knew where it came from? He remembered those people, and their canal that stretched out like a filthy cow with an obliging udder, making room among its teats for those who came to milk.

Mahalla el-Kubra was nothing but an oversized village, with its dust and its flies and its canal. But this was Canal Street in Tanta, with geometrical promenades, trees with trimmed branches, and facades of apartments in tall buildings. There had been a canal here too. But it had been buried, and this splendid layout of pruned trees and tall buildings had replaced it. He could hear the echoes of the voices far beneath his feet, the women and their little battles along the banks of the Tanta canal. He laughed to himself. They were far away, sunken beneath the asphalt, along with the flies and the fleas and the mosquitoes. The village was a graveyard, day and night. Order and cleanliness, that was what he admired. The echo of those voices was a long way off, down beneath his feet, buried under the asphalt.

The memory of that young boy was distant too. He had sung with such agony. Abdel-Aziz laughed to himself again. The boy had been as thin as a rail, but his body was full of life that burst out in sad, mournful songs.

Farewell, canal of Tanta,
they've moved you away so far
Whoever wants to see you
has to ride in a railroad car.

He was begging in a train that made the rounds of the villages of the region to pick up passengers for Tanta. His sister stood behind him and accompanied his singing with her little tambourine. It was a far-off memory, like a bird way up in the sky. All you could see was a tiny brown dot.

Girls with cropped hair and sparkling laughter stood on the balconies. In front of the houses there were little walled gardens and children playing in swings. A clean, fresh breeze filled his breast as if it were a billowing, lighthearted sail skimming over the Nile. The hooves of horses clattered on the glistening asphalt, and the big wheels of carriages creaked incessantly as they moved along the street. There they were, the red flowers on the trees. He had seen them a thousand times and fallen in love with them a thousand times, bright, flaming red flowers.

Abdel-Aziz was walking alone. As he approached the center of the city, the bright, clean colors began to fade. Here they were overlaid with a film of dusty gray. The pedestrians walked more briskly, the carriages rattled along at greater speeds, and the automobiles roared through the streets, spewing smoke and steam from front and rear. The fronts of the buildings were covered with dust, and around the entrances plaques advertised doctors and lawyers. On either side were shops with big signs over their doors announcing a grocery store, a cigarette shop, or even an automobile mechanic's workshop. The promenades in the island in the middle of the street began to lose their self-respect, and the elegant little barriers that lined them were bent or broken. The feet of the pedestrians had ravaged them, and effaced forever all but the last traces of the grass that had grown there. People's clothes no longer seemed so splendid; often they were dirty. The faces grew paler. They were stubborn, oppressed faces. The laughter all around expressed the endurance of stone, no longer the lighthearted merriment of the balconies.

Then he began to see the faces of country folk. Peasants' caps and galabiyas were scattered here and there in the street in no particular order. The visitors ambled along wide-eyed and bewildered, looking warily about them. Abdel-Aziz recognized in their eyes the same yearning he felt in himself for that cleanliness, splendor, and immensity. Their eyes absorbed all the amazing sights around them. Why did they carry their bamboo sticks? Perhaps it was custom, or perhaps it was fear, the fear that country folk always took with them when they ventured into the city. A firm grip on a stick gave a feeling of confidence.

They scattered among the people of Tanta like alien seeds on a threshing floor covered with grain. They went along in little groups, and the city-born children would make fun of them, tugging at their galabiyas and snatching their caps.

"Your visitors, O Sayyid, every country bumpkin and his brother."

They were like frightened kites; they could scratch and flee to defend themselves. But they kept on walking and looking around, staring with eyes open wide and absorbing all the amazing sights.

Dilapidated automobiles plowed noisily through the streets, raising clouds of dust and spitting smoke and steam. Carriages rattled along behind galloping horses, and whips lashed the animals' backs. Bicycles sped by, swaying side to side with their riders. The bands of country folk would break and scatter to avoid these machines that tore along to the right and left of them, but they quickly regrouped in tight circles. They contemplated this strange world with bedazzled eyes and lively imaginations that would turn what they had seen into stories. On the mud benches or the heaps of topsoil in front of their houses they would sit and talk at night. The stories themselves were pleasant, but in the words there was a tinge of resentment and of ridicule, ridicule that would turn one inside out with laughter. These people had an uncanny ability to mock anything and everything, and their sharp eyes never missed the flaws or the ridiculous in what they saw.

Baladiya Square. The front of the municipal cinema had huge posters with writing the size of children and enormous pictures of the actors. Groups of people were crossing the square with their backs turned to the oncoming traffic. Their eyes were glued to the huge pictures on the posters. Every now and then someone would summon his courage and head for the ticket window to join the crowd of people waiting to get in.

Khan Street. A throng of people, endless displays of wares, and the distorted blare of loudspeakers. The vendors were doing their job with their hands and their mouths, like clusters of nerves addicted to movement and noise. He slipped through the crowd, twisting his shoulders right and left to avoid bumping into anyone. The merchants on the two sides of the street were clutching at the fringes of the crowd and coaxing those on the edge to buy. But the main mass flowed on between the two banks like a river.

The coppersmiths' market. The shops with the spacious interiors where they sold brides' trousseaux—wardrobes with big mirrors, chests covered with colored metal, shiny copper pots, mattresses and cushions, and bedspreads in various colors of silk that would steal your heart. The trousseau salesman was standing inside the shop with a big smile on his face. The man who sold things for brides always had a blissful countenance and serene features. He would congratulate his customers and generously lower his prices. In the end, his only profit was getting to know such fine people.

Where was Hagg Karim? How could any bride in the world get married without his being there? The salesman would be standing in front of him, while the families of the bride and the groom formed a circle around him. The merchant would swear he was taking a loss, and Hagg Karim would laugh:

"What you put in store with God is not lost. And never mind the coffee."

But that could not be. Tea would be served in narrow-waisted little glasses with gilt rims, arranged like dolls on a shiny brass tray. The sisters of the bride and groom would cover their faces with their shawls so that all that could be seen was their eyes staring at the things around them. What was it they saw in the city girls, their naughty sisters? They blinked their eyes in consternation or winked at each other and caught their breath with amazement.

The street became narrower as it led down a slight incline. It was still moist from the holy water the merchants had sprinkled in front of their shops that morning. The old houses, with their overhanging oriels of wooden latticework, were coated with dust and soot. Some of the buildings were new and had modern balconies. There were women with fat naked arms and men in thin white galabiyas who were reading the day's issue of *Al-Ahram* and sipping strong dark tea from a glass. He turned into Sidi Marzouq Street. Here the coffeehouses were beginning to do a brisk business with the country folk. Benches had been set out in rows on the sidewalks in anticipation of the hordes yet to come. Here and there, on both sides of the street, little circles of people had begun to gather. In the middle of each one there was no doubt a fat gold-toothed woman with a kerosene burner, a tea kettle, glasses, and a bucket filled with water pipes. A little laughter, sounds of people sipping tea, and a few puffs of hashish—the beginning of the storm.

Along the sides of the street, stone steps led up to square courtyards around which stood houses and small apartment buildings. Suddenly he had come to the house where they had their lodgings. The fronts of these buildings were all windows, full of women. The women of Tanta never left their windows. In the village, when you quit the street and went down through the door into the interior of the house, you would find women as sluggish as cows. But here they shouted loudly back and forth to each other and broke into long, provocative shrieks of laughter. The necklines of their thin shifts left uncovered the upper halves of their heavy breasts, and their hair shone beneath kerchiefs with little gold or silver coins sewn to the edges.

"They're fat from eating beans with oil instead of butterfat."

That was what Rashida said. Abdel-Aziz laughed to himself. Hagga Showk answered her:

"They don't have a thing in the world to worry about."

One of Rashida's sisters broke in:

"Just let one of them come and try to bake a few bushels of flour or spread new dirt under the animals in the pen. Then we'll see how fat she'll be."

Rashida teased her.

"You're just jealous because you're as skinny as a rail."

Abdel-Aziz smiled as he looked at the obese women in the windows. He remembered Hagg Karim walking slowly up those steps. Leaning on his cane and pulling his cloak, which lay folded over his shoulder, to his chest, he had looked up toward the windows and said:

"Good day, ladies."

He did not say "God grant you health." That was what he said to the women of the village. Here he took on another manner of speech, courteous and eloquent. Laughter answered him from the windows. One of the women shouted to the others:

"Well, Sisters, it looks like we have a bunch here for the moulid. Ha-ha! 'Something for God,' O Sayyid."

When the clamor died down so he could be heard, Hagg Karim spoke:

"We're here for the moulid, ladies. Dervishes of the Sultan. We hope you can put us up for the time of the moulid."

Here in this street they rented out apartments to those who came for the moulid. The Dandy's lean frame was twitching with excitement as he stood gripping the handle of his basket and eyeing the women with lust.

They had wandered through a number of streets and

knocked on a great many doors. A plump face would look out.

"We've come for the moulid, madam."

"Welcome, Brother. By the Prophet, I wish I could help you. But come in and rest a while anyhow."

The men were away at work for the day. Cool, dark rooms furnished with comfortable Arab couches would be opened. Hagg Karim would sit down with the Dandy next to him. There would be coffee and conversation. Pleasant conversation was Hagg Karim's specialty. His friendly words were like a cushion on which a woman could lean back and relax. She would no longer be so tense, nor would she attempt to hide the cleavage between her heavy, white breasts. She would no longer clasp her arms to conceal their untanned flesh with her hands. She would become uninhibited, listening and responding. And so the dialogue would begin, time and people, villages and cities. The city was a tree with its roots in the countryside. Who could tell? Perhaps they were related by blood or marriage. Believers were all brothers, and we were all descended from Adam.

"By the Prophet, I really wish I could. You seem to be such fine people."

True, they had not been able to rent the apartment, but the bond of affection had been tied. During the period of the moulid the Dandy would come by from time to time, wearing a light galabiya, a cap, and slippers, and knock on the door.

"Madam, Oum So-and-So?"

She would come out in the dress she wore around the house, which always revealed more than it should. The Dandy would blush and laugh with embarrassment, showing his teeth ruined by tobacco and tea.

"We'd like to borrow your kerosene burner, please, may God reward you."

"Certainly. And give my greetings to Hagg Karim. Tell him not to forget my moulid biscuits and *duqqa*."

"We're saving your share for you. I'll bring it myself."

The day they had found the apartment which they still rented each year Hagg Karim had leaned over and said to the Dandy:

"This place will be just right. The space in front will hold the *zikr* on the Big Night."

The Dandy twitched with excitement as he and Hagg Karim stood waiting for the cries of the women to reveal some reply. They called to Oum Talaat. She had her apartment on the ground floor and had said she wanted to rent it to people coming for the moulid.

Oum Talaat came out to meet Hagg Karim. She had big, black, puzzling eyes.

"Welcome. Help us, O Sayyid. Come in, please, Hagg. By the Prophet, you seem to be a good man, and you look respectable."

Unrestrained and gushing, and with those strange eyes, she had said he looked respectable. And indeed he did. What other name could one give to that quality one saw in his strong body, his serene, joyful eyes, his newly ironed clothing, and his bright white turban set over his brown brow? He went into the entrance hall of the apartment, calmly but warily, feeling his way with his cane on the tiled floor.

"O Coverer of Sins!"

The Dandy laughed and came in behind him.

"May God grant us good fortune with you, madam."

Her husband's portrait—he was away at work now—was hanging on the wall in the entrance hall. They went into an adjoining room, half of which was taken up by a big bed covered with a clean, white sheet. The pillows had cases with colored patterns and looked soft and fresh. The pillows and Oum Talaat's ample breasts, the soft carpet and the restful couch, the dim light and the cool air, the room was full of everything soft. Outside in the street the heat was scorching. Oum Talaat brought in a pot of tea and some tumblers of cheap green glass on a shiny brass tray. She placed the tray on a hassock between her and Hagg Karim. A rosy tinge came over her face like a thin veil. Her smile was mischievous and flirtatious. The glow of her cheeks, the color of the bulging pillows, and the inviting gap between her glistening breasts met a sparkle in the eyes of Hagg Karim.

"You will have a sheikh with you too?"

"Of course."

"Ha-ha-ha! Does your sheikh work any miracles?"

The Dandy added his bit:

"Is there any sheikh, madam, who doesn't work miracles?"

But Hagg Karim became solemn and grave. A cloud of disapproval passed over his face because the woman had made fun of the sheikh. She was obviously uncomfortable at the sudden sternness in his look, and she turned her face away in confusion. She kept shifting the glass of hot tea from one hand to the other. Suddenly there was a slight cracking sound, and the glass shattered. The tea poured over her hand and into her lap. She jumped up in fright and the Dandy cried out:

"Praise to the living God!"

He stood up in the middle of the room and leaped about ecstatically, while Hagg Karim implored in a muffled voice:

"In the name of God, with the protection of whose name nothing in heaven or earth can suffer harm. He is the All-Hearing and the All-Knowing."

The woman was wailing.

"Your sheikh has a mean temper. My hand is burned all over."

She held out her hand hesitatingly to Hagg Karim, who took it in his fat, brown palm.

"It will be fine, God willing. There isn't a thing. The sheikh just wanted to pinch your ear."

He closed his eyes and began to recite:

"Lord, forgive us if we are neglectful or sin. Lord, do not burden us with the weight of our sins as thou hast burdened those who have gone before us."*

She lowered her eyelashes. The Dandy looked at her as he unconsciously licked the edge of a cigarette paper and rolled it around a few pinches of tobacco. Little Abdel-Aziz slipped over to Oum Talaat's bosom and kissed her on the cheek. He loved her more than he loved his own mother. She lowered her head

*Koran 2:286.—Trans.

and pressed him to her breast. It was too much for the Dandy, who came out with a stream of confused, muddled words.

"The Path is all good from beginning to end. We're all beggars at God's door. After we die nothing remains but our good deeds. If it weren't for the Path, . . . Kiss your aunt, boy. What's wrong with kissing her? By God, Hagg Karim is the best man in the world. See how generous the Lord has been. He said to me, 'Dandy, what do you think of this place?' I told him, 'Go on in, Sheikh. May God open the way before you.' We are all dervishes of the Sultan."

The silence of the others stood out against the monotonous background of the Dandy's voice. Hagg Karim slung his cloak over his shoulder and, supporting himself on his cane, stood up slowly to leave. With unhurried steps he made his way across the room, through the entrance hall with the tiled floor, and out the door.

The women were laughing in the windows.

"Ha-ha-ha! Anyhow, soon they'll be swaying in front of us, and we'll get to eat the bread and *duqqa* they've brought for the moulid."

They had called the *zikr* swaying, those women. Abdel-Aziz smiled as he cast his eye over the windows. What a street it was, Sidi Marzouq Street. From that day on, Hagg Karim had never rented any other place. Oum Talaat was a good woman. And there was a distant kinship too. Blood, the wombs of women, what strange power they had to create bonds of affection between people. They would have their own place in the city, just as if it belonged to them, and they would fill it with bread and cheese and moulid biscuits. The big clay water jar would be set up in the corner of the entrance hall. Faucets? Who could wait for water to flow out of a faucet? Water should be scooped out of a water jar and drunk in big draughts. The place would be full of men, women, and children from every village. They would go out and they would come back, and it would always be this place they were leaving or returning to. The people of Tanta were their neighbors, and they had nothing to fear. They would greet them, morning and night, like old friends. The men's heels looked shiny in their light slippers. There was no dust from the streets or mud from the fields. The Dandy served as the messenger from their lodgings to all the women. Could they borrow a knife or an onion? His skin was white and smooth. Who else could deliver these requests? When the women from the village were in Tanta they were full of contentment and purred like kittens, while the men were smiling and agreeable. Sometimes the men would even wash the dishes themselves.

Perhaps it was a childhood habit that had remained with him, to walk along reading the signs and looking at the sights. He let the streets lead him on without thinking where he was going. That was the way he had walked when he was little. He would give his hand to his father, who would lead him along, wandering through the streets and looking at all the things to see. Sidi Marzouq Street led into the street known as New Street, which continued down to the square where the railroad station was. His heart froze. He saw it all at once. At the gates of the station, where the crowds of country folk were streaming out, they had stationed fierce, machinelike policemen, some of them on horseback and some on foot. They had mean faces and held long sticks of bamboo in their hands. All that just to make sure everyone had a ticket. Good Lord! Who could believe it?

Abdel-Aziz's heart froze and his throat constricted, but he kept on walking unflinchingly toward the railroad station. All the gates in the high fence of iron and concrete surrounding the open space in front of the station were shut, except three, which were heavily guarded. At each gate there were several employees and a squad of policemen—a human machine set there to strike fear into the hearts of the peasants who kept pouring out of the station. They would swoop down on the people like kites, battering with their sticks whoever or whatever got in their way. Every attack created a circle of frightened eyes and shrieking voices. The people would scatter with their caps flying in the air, somehow managing to get away. A little farther on, beyond the gate, the groups would reassemble, pull themselves together, and catch their breath, laughing at their narrow escape. Then they would head into the streets, ready to meet the city and everything in it.

"Help us, O Sayyid! Help us! We have come, O Abu Farrag."

The cries of joy, the trills of the women, and even the wailing of the infants gave way to breathless amazement.

Abdel-Aziz walked on with deliberate steps, his eyes and ears alert. He held out his railway pass, and the employee pushed him through the gate and turned to the next person. He took the shove with silent resentment and went on toward the station, his heart full of pride and arrogance. There, in the middle of the open space, he saw them. Hagg Karim led them, holding his cloak over his shoulder with his left hand and leaning on his cane with his right. Ahead was that terrifying sieve at the gate.

He walked toward them. The Dandy was in the background having trouble with his basket. As for Iraqi the Deaf-Mute, what use were his beard and red turban now? He cast quick glances around him like a hunted sparrow. Ahmed Bedawi, Mohammed Kamel, Ali Khalil, Sherkasi the Carpenter, and many others were there. The women brought up the rear. They looked toward him anxiously. He approached Hagg Karim and kissed his hand with unusual concern, with an almost overpowering fear for him. The man kissed his son on the forehead. Abdel-Aziz noticed a broken look in his father's eyes. But he quickly stifled his feelings. He was caught in the arms of first one man and then another. Each one hugged him tightly, and he was engulfed in a display of love and affection deeper than any he had ever experienced. He had been with these people only yesterday beneath the lantern in the hall of the guesthouse.

"How are you, Abduh?"

Ahmed Bedawi was glowing with joy, and his short, sturdy body gushed with emotion. Ali Khalil gave a hesitant smile. His face was still pale, and in the middle of his forehead, just below the hairline, he had a large callus from his prostrations in prayer.

"Welcome, Master Abduh."

He restrained his delight behind the pained composure of his face.

"God grant you knowledge, Son."

Mohammed Kamel, with his deep voice, his chiseled features, and his sunken eyes, bore a sad smile. One couldn't think of his smile without that sadness. It rose and set with it. Iraqi was hopping about like a monkey with a basket in its hand. The Dandy just kept talking.

"Look at all those people. Whole nations. Help us, O Sultan! Yes, indeed. Really, instead of sitting here in the station wasting time, the train should make one or two more rounds and bring more people. But whom do you tell?"

But as he spoke, his eyes kept turning toward the gate.

These men, with their cheap clothes, their rust-colored wool caps, and their thin faces tanned by the sun and spotted by malnutrition, these poor frightened creatures, were Abdel-Aziz's parents and his kin, his heart and his eyes. They stood around him and looked at him. He wished they were cleaner, and bolder, not like this—poor, ignorant, and frightened. At school he boasted of being a peasant to the city boys. He boasted of it. But inside he was angry and resentful. If only they weren't like this.

They looked at him suspiciously, as if they sensed the struggle going on inside him. Ahmed Bedawi spoke.

"Suppose one of your schoolmates saw you with peasant folk like us. Just in case, why don't you stay off to one side. We won't lose sight of one another on the way."

They had stripped him naked with their sharp eyes. A moment of shame came over him like a sudden chill.

"What are you saying? I don't care about that."

But he quickly realized what he had said. His answer was an admission of how he really felt about them. He wanted to shout out at the top of his voice, "You are the finest people in the world!" But he did not do it. Perhaps he sensed in advance what a lame protest it would be and how false his voice would sound. But his reply, in any case, had given them a certain pleasure. Hagg Karim looked at his son in reproachful silence. If one of them caught the other's eye, they would both look away. He loved his father. He loved them all. But what could he do? Had he been able, he would have made everything easy for them in the city, and he would have dressed them differently. They stood around him looking at him. Every peasant who sent his son to school in the city looked at him with that same look full of hope and fear. This was the big city. Abdel-Aziz loved this city and he loved them. Why did they have to look at him that way?

"May the Lord make an important man out of you, Abduh. Then we'll all walk around as we please and not worry about a thing."

Inside he did not believe he would ever be anyone important in this city. He loved its noise, its cleanliness, and its girls. He loved the cinema and the books. He could drown his inner crisis in the city by yielding to it and giving himself wholly over to it. He never had any desire to control the city. All he wanted was that it should penetrate the pores of his being and banish that aching pain that lay hidden in him like a cancer.

He understood the harshness of this city. He understood it especially when he looked at those policemen, country faces spewing out anger on crowds of country folk. He understood the harshness of the city, but he turned a blind eye to it and tried to forget it. But at times a cruel thought assailed him mercilessly. Suppose this city were one day to turn him into a policeman with a country face, a stick, and a mouth full of curses in the language of the city people. Lord of All! The thought appalled him.

Hagg Karim pointed his cane before him. He looked ahead with sadness in his face, and his brown eyes quickly scanned the fierce, frenzied machine that had been set up at the gate. He was trying to feel it out with his glances without really seeing it, like a Magian about to walk through fire. He anticipated the harassment and the pain, but he would endure it. There had to be adversities in the Path. His poor father.

Hagg Karim walked at the head of the group and the other men followed, casting anxious glances about them. But they went ahead with firm steps as Mohammed Kamel prayed in his deep voice:

"O Lord, O Coverer of Sins, do not raise against us for our sins men who fear not thee and show us no mercy. O Lord of the Worlds!"

The man snatched Hagg Karim's ticket and gave him a ruthless shove on the shoulder. Perhaps Hagg Karim was just taking a step forward and so the shove did not affect him, or perhaps it was a miracle of the saints. In any case, his sure steps were undisturbed. The band pulled together behind him, but their eyes strayed in every direction and their faces grew pale. A little forest of hands was raised in the air—hands carrying tickets, hands snatching tickets, and hands holding menacing sticks.

Their bodies were pressed into a jumbled, frightened mass. There was no retreat. Abdel-Aziz was carried along by the haphazard wave until they made it through to the other side of the gate. Drops of sweat were glistening on their foreheads and smiles beamed on their faces. Iraqi was beside himself with maniacal joy. Hagg Karim turned around. His eyes, shining with the faint light of an early morning star, followed the others as they came out.

Abdel-Aziz was seized with a violent rage and his whole body quivered with resentment. He turned his face away. His body had lost all sense of unison with the group of men and he moved off tensely on his own. The men looked at him as they were straightening their galabiyas and adjusting their caps. They were perplexed and obviously a little ashamed.

"Never mind, Abdel-Aziz. That's the lot of us peasants. We were created to be abused."

The Dandy just kept on talking. The weight of the basket almost pulled his arm out of its socket.

"If we were serving a country dancing girl, she would have done a little something to salvage our dignity. Help us, O Sayyid! Here we are, coming to you, O Bald One!"

The people in the square were like a thick flight of pigeons coming down on a field. Rattling, blaring automobiles cut their way through the crowds, and fear of the unaccustomed noise created little eddies, clusters, and rifts.

"O Coverer of Sins, cover us! Sons of dogs, addicted to the bottle. The drivers are sons of whores, taking short cuts through flesh and blood. Isn't there any government? Oh, glory of the Prophet!"

Abdel-Aziz wished he could strangle that panic-stricken fool. Every day he traveled to one place or another to visit one of his daughters who worked as maids in the towns, and he would come back with a series of tales about his trips. Now here he was, scared out of his wits by the noise of the passing automobiles.

Abdel-Aziz felt his body grow rigid from the violence of his anger. He moved along out of step with the men and off to one side. But they kept looking at him with furtive glances. Hagg Karim walked with his usual deliberate steps as though he were going to the porch of the guesthouse. But there was something in the way he carried his shoulders, something bowed and broken. Why had all these fears, this anger, and these strange emotions allied against Abdel-Aziz today?

The beginning of New Street was bordered by dusty old buildings on both sides. A succession of awnings stretched from one side of the street to the other and formed a continuous roof of canvas, giving the effect of a dark subterranean vault. The looks in the men's eyes grew softer. They would not see the splendor of Bedawi's mosque until their apprehensions had subsided in the restful shade of this street.

Suddenly the shrine was before them. Abdel-Aziz recognized the hesitation in his father's steps when the Sultan's dome appeared. He had expected it. The men's hearts were one with the heart of Hagg Karim. They were distracted from every other thing as their eyes clung in awe to Bedawi's shrine.

Abdel-Aziz was alone. They were like flecks of iron drawn toward the pole of a magnet. But he was made of a different metal.

"Peace be upon you, O Lord Ahmed Bedawi. Peace be upon you, O Sultan."

Then Hagg Karim whispered, as though to a long lost friend:

"We have come to you weighed down with hardships, O burden-bearing camel, Abu Farrag."

He did not greet Abdel-Al and Mojahed until later. Their domes were part of the same mosque, to either side of the great dome of Sayyid Ahmed Bedawi. But Hagg Karim did not pay much attention to them. Abdel-Aziz laughed to himself. The women of his village were fascinated with Abdel-Al. Every wife in a polygamous marriage invoked his aid against her counterpart, as did every mother-in-law against her son's wife. They promised offerings to him and swept the floor of his shrine with their black headcloths. Perhaps Abdel-Al had been something like the Dandy, passionately fond of women. Even after his death he was mixed up in pronouncing judgments between them and settling their disputes.

When Abdel-Aziz was little he would hang like a doll from his father's hand and look at the faces of the brothers as they stood humbly before the dome of the Sultan. Hagg Karim would squeeze his wrist gently.

"The righteous see this dome when they are still miles and miles away."

Back in the village Abdel-Aziz used to climb up to the roof and try to see the dome. If only he had been able to see it just once. His eyes wandered aimlessly over the dome of the mosque and the crescent at the top. There were holes in the covering of the dome, which had once been green. The boys of Tanta kept darting by them on bicycles like arrows, balancing on their heads wide wooden trays piled high with loaves of bread, or holding in their hands incredible jumbles of mantle lanterns and kerosene torches to heat them up.

"Look out! Here we come with the kerosene! O Gate of Breath, O Air Valve, O Sayyid! Your visitors, O Sayyid, every bumpkin and his brother."

Whips would break their pride. Or better, he thought, these

good-for-nothings should be hanged by the neck. Hagg Karim turned toward his son. Perhaps he wanted to say to him:

"We are all under the protection of the Sultan, my son."

But he said nothing. Looking ahead, he set his cane to the pavement and walked on.

They continued up New Street. The stands and benches along the way were heaped with mountains of roasted chick-peas, and the windows of the shops were full of red and white candy. Hanging strings were covered with children's toys, and behind some of the glass panes were rings, bracelets, and ear-rings. The metal glittered and the bright colors of the glass stones dazzled the eye. Girls' shawls and men's scarves of silk or cotton swung in the wind. Noisy loudspeakers were hung on both sides of the streets, and the vendors were engaged in a constant effort to lure buyers—mechanical smiles from tired, flushed faces dripping with sweat. The river of peasants flowed on, casting cautious glances at them.

Hagg Karim looked at what he saw around him with delight. He touched people on the shoulder gently to make his way through the crowd. This was Tanta, decorated, clamorous, clean, and powerful.

"Excuse me, men, I'd like to go over and say hello to my friend."

They smiled. The Dandy left his basket with Mohammed Kamel, and Ahmed Bedawi left his with his wife. They went over with Hagg Karim, while the others continued on toward the lodgings.

Abdel-Aziz muffled his laughter. Hagg Karim's steps became suddenly light as he walked toward the shop of the woman who sold notions.

"Peace be upon you."

An enormous, full-fleshed and fair-skinned woman stood up behind the desk that served as a counter. She had wound around her head a diaphanous black scarf that showed off her white forehead, and her welcoming smile disclosed a row of bright gold teeth. That boldness in her eyes! How could any man ever make her yield? Hagg Karim seemed to possess an uncommon manliness. He was as restless as a thoroughbred horse. She swayed softly.

"Peace be upon you, Hagg Karim. Nothing ever brings you to see us except our dear beloved saint."

He gestured like an actor on the stage.

"It's true, by God. Our longing for the Sultan brings us running."

He sat down opposite her. Her white hands were delicately shaped and her wrists were hidden by gold bracelets. The shop—shelf after shelf of costume jewelry, scarves, and bottles of perfume—echoed with her laughter. The Dandy, nervous and ill at ease on his chair, looked on wide-eyed, and unconsciously licked his cigarette paper. Ahmed Bedawi smiled like a happy child, just as if the heroes of the Arab romances had stepped out of their books to contend in front of him.

"Come to town and I'll open a shop for you, Hagg Karim."

"Shopkeeping is not my business. My business is farming. I plow the black land and irrigate it. I make it green."

She broke into laughter, and the clear ring of her voice mingled with the whisper of the bracelets. However many adventures the Dandy may have had, he had never loved anyone like this. Hagg Karim was a mighty horseman and she was his pampered mare. The fire that raged in Abdel-Aziz's breast had not fallen out of the sky. It had come to him from this father of his. Hagg Karim did not speak to her the way he spoke to the women in the village. He had the twisted dialect of the townsfolk.

"Is it really possible to live in the country, Hagg Karim? Here we have all the fine things of life."

"You can live there. You can live in the country. The town is just to visit. Then we go back to our land."

The boy from the coffeehouse came in with obvious embarrassment and tapped on his tray with a teaspoon. He picked up the empty glasses and left.

Hagg Karim continued along New Street, followed by his

three companions. Then they all turned into Sidi Marzouq Street.

"Let's pay our respects to Hamouli, men."

They agreed without saying a word.

Some distance away they could see Hamouli scattering bran on the sidewalk in front of his shop for some newborn chicks. Hagg Karim looked at him with a smile and walked slowly over to him. Hamouli straightened up. He was tall and lank with long, dangling arms and huge hands. His red eyelids blinked as he recognized Hagg Karim.

"Welcome! Welcome! Welcome!"

His exaggerated frame shook with the rhythm of the greeting.

"You bring such light."

"Your light is enough for us, Hamouli. Peace be upon you and the mercy of God."

Hamouli greeted his guests and hastily turned over several wooden Coca-Cola crates to serve as seats for them. His wife stood up. She was short and fat. She too had inflamed red eyelids, perhaps because her husband gave her so little rest at night. Before she got up, she had been sitting with her feet arranged as a seat for her little child, who had been gleefully defecating on the pavement. Her other child, a little farther off, was making mud pies in his urine.

"Three hundred welcomes! Light shines on the Sayyid's men."

Hagg Karim rested his chin on his cane and began to scrutinize Hamouli, who sat in front of him, slapping his knees with his huge hands as he talked. Hagg Karim listened to every word he said. Hamouli had been a peasant and had lived the miserable, wretched life of the country. The midday sun had scorched his body, and the palms of his hands had become callused and cracked from gripping his short hoe. How many days he had lived on dry bread and old white cheese from clay jars. How often the years had let him down and his crops had failed. Each year came bringing with it days of weariness and want. Hamouli had lived the life of the village until distress and poverty had suffocated his spirit. Then one day he took his wife and children and left for Tanta. How had this peasant dared to plunge into the city? In any case, here he was, with a shop and with little children who defecated gleefully on the asphalt. His eyes, two red openings that looked like pigeon anuses, were none the less able to reflect a sense of triumph in front of these passing visitors to the city.

"Bring us something to drink, girl."

His wife's sore eyes blinked her assent. Abdel-Aziz dreaded the ordeal of the drink about to be served. It would be tea, and it would taste of kerosene or olibanum or something else among the contents of this filthy shop. How was Hagg Karim, who was so hard to please and whose coffee had to be made just right, going to drink anything like this?

"Is this tea fit to be drunk, Papa?"

"It was made with friendship and sincerity, Son. You'll drink it and lick the glass as well."

He would stop by Hamouli's shop whenever he was exhausted from his obligations at the lodgings, where he had to stand on his feet all day long, serving food, welcoming whoever happened to stop by, and bidding farewell to those who were leaving. He would sit on an overturned Coca-Cola crate and Hamouli would sit opposite him, slapping his knees with his huge hands and talking. Hagg Karim would listen delightedly, while Hamouli's wife sat on the floor blinking with contentment.

Sidi Marzouq Street again—the groups standing on the sidewalks around women with pots of tea, the coffeehouses, and the crowds. Sounds from radios and the cracked voices of singers from battered metal loudspeakers echoed off the buildings. Dozens of peasants filled the street with life. Two days earlier it had been as still as death. The moulid had begun.

Hagg Karim continued on along the street, his cane striking the pavement with a brisk rhythm.

"The joys of the Sultan, children."

He climbed the stone steps and the others followed him. Standing in the middle of the courtyard he looked up at the facades of the old buildings that rose on three sides. The windows were crowded with Tanta women.

"Good day to you, ladies."

Time and dust had made the contiguous facades of these poorly constructed buildings into something extraordinary. The women's galabiyas were brightly colored, and their black hair, oiled and parted, was wrapped in square kerchiefs with coins sewn to the borders. Their faces beamed with joy. On the dingy walls the closely set windows formed colorful squares spilling over with life. Hagg Karim moved his eyes slowly from one window to the other. The Dandy was restless, pricked by the longing and delight that smoldered inside him. Abdel-Aziz gaped with lust at the women's bosoms and the cleavages between all those white-skinned breasts.

These facades concealed secret places—dark stairways and back rooms that never saw the light of day. He would creep into them like a cat, hunting girls. In foggy, trembling moments that engulfed his whole being and passed away as quickly as a flash of lightning, he would snatch a kiss or an embrace. Then he would come back out to this courtyard, to the festival, the crowds, the tambourines, the sweat, and the cries, to drown his excitement in the deafening noise.

Greetings rained down on Hagg Karim from the windows.

"Welcome, Brother. Oum Talaat has been waiting for you since the morning."

"By the Prophet, Sister, light shines on them. They're good-hearted people, and God-fearing."

Hagg Karim smiled with pleasure and contentment.

"Many happy returns."

Inundated with all this tender concern, he turned around to find Oum Talaat standing at her door. Her fleshy arms hung from shoulders that seemed to droop a bit, but her eyes were the same. From the day of the broken cup, Abdel-Aziz remembered everything. He had pieced together from her careless moments images of her breasts, her round stomach, and her buttocks. He saw them in his sleep and could not get them out of his mind.

Hagg Karim walked over to her. She was a gentle woman, gentle and soft in every particle of her being—in her eyes, in the hand she held out, in her head, which tilted a little as though it were too heavy for her neck. A warm smile came over Hagg Karim's face. She kissed his hand, and he returned the kiss on her head. Abdel-Aziz was not sad, but he was filled with a tender emotion that almost brought tears to his eyes.

"You have brought light to Tanta, Hagg Karim."

"Your light is enough, Oum Talaat. Your light is enough, by God."

She went ahead of him into the empty house, stepping across the worn, chipped tiles with her honey-brown feet. He followed, his cane tapping randomly on the floor of the entrance hall.

"I've emptied the house for you. But everything I have is yours. Furniture, a couch, mattresses, anything you need. Just ask for it, Hagg Karim."

The men smiled as they gathered in a circle around the reunion of Oum Talaat and Hagg Karim. He smiled back and said:

"Peace be upon you. Welcome home!"

"Upon you be peace and the mercy of God!"

For a moment there was a silence. Then the laughter broke out spontaneously, pouring from hearts brimming over with contentment and joy.

Hagg Karim tapped his cane on the floor.

"Hey!"

Mohammed Kamel sighed:

"It's over. We're here."

Hagg Karim closed his eyes. His face was serene.

"Praise be to God. O God, do not allow our customs to pass away. O God, do not keep us from standing at thy door. O Lord Ahmed Bedawi, here we are in your bounteous presence. O Sultan!"

The others responded quietly:

"Amen."

Oum Talaat could not take her eyes off Hagg Karim. She asked politely:

"Don't you need anything? Anything at all?"

Hagg Karim looked at her with a pleased smile.

"May the Lord reward you, and may he never deprive us of you."

He would not see her again until the day they left. He would shake her hand just before he set out for the railway station.

The white reed mats were laid out on the floor of the room. The walls were splotched and of an uneven color. Nails had been driven into them to hang Koranic verses printed on cheap paper, children's drawings, and photographs of people standing mummylike in mindless poses. The men took off the galabiyas they had worn for the trip. Some relaxed in their ankle-length drawers, their vests, and their reddish wool caps, while others had on only light house galabiyas. Hagg Karim took off his turban and placed it on a piece of newspaper that had been spread out on the windowsill. Next he took off his big cashmere galabiya and then his striped satin caftan and hung them on a nail in the wall. In their place, he put on a light linen galabiya. He looked like a peacock without its tail feathers. But dressed in this manner he seemed simple, warm, and friendly.

He sat down on the mat, and the brothers seated themselves around him. Abdel-Aziz took off the suit he wore to school, hung it on one of the nails in the wall, and slipped into a striped galabiya with a European-style collar. Then he arranged his books beside his father's turban and sat down with the men.

In the other room the women had by now taken off their black headcloths and their outdoor garb and were wearing only their colored housedresses. Surrounded by the children, they would be laughing with fascination and delight. Without a doubt Samira was sitting with them, smiling. She would spend the time of the moulid here to save herself the bother of traveling daily and the annoyance of the crowds. She would be with him in the same house for seven days. But she no longer stirred his imagination. He felt a strange indifference toward her. She did not have the flare of the Tanta girls and she did not affect him in the same way they did. When she sat there like that with her eyes wide, the coolness he felt toward her turned gradually almost to loathing.

The next day the sheikh and his band would arrive. They would go to meet them at the station, and the longing of the past weeks would be fulfilled in a few confused moments of affectionate greetings and warm embraces.

Here in this spot they would lay the mattress for the sheikh. He would take off his green turban, and it would be placed in the window beside Hagg Karim's. Then they would start to talk. How long had it been since they had been together? There would be the laughter, the friendly conversation, and the joy of their reunion in the city of the Sultan.

And here Mistikawi would sit, knee to knee with the Dandy. He would pull out a piece of hashish from his vest pocket and toss it into his friend's lap. The Dandy would smile with surprise and lick his lips. Abdel-Aziz could see it all.

"Here, boy. Roll us a cigarette."

The Dandy caught the pinch of hashish and rolled it in his practiced fingers. By now he was in stitches with laughter. Hassan Effendi and Ali Khalil interrupted their amicable conversation and looked in the direction of the Dandy. Hassan Effendi complained:

"Can't you give up that filth, if only for the moulid, out of respect for the Sultan?"

Mistikawi glowered.

"I wasted my money on this damned hashish for the sake of the Sultan. When I'm doped up I'll think he's the grandest of all God's saints."

At this the Dandy went into convulsions of laughter and his eyes practically popped out of his head.

"You can even ask Sheikh Abbas!"

Sheikh Abbas stretched his giraffe's neck and said:

"We have never heard that anyone among the ancients or the moderns declared hashish to be unlawful. Wine, to be sure, is forbidden. But hashish is just a plant like any other plant."

When they heard this, Mistikawi and the Dandy were

absolutely beside themselves with laughter. But Ali Khalil grew pale, and Hassan Effendi turned his face away. Ahmed Bedawi giggled like a child, while the sheikh of the order and Hagg Karim smiled in silence. Mistikawi broke into a series of binding oaths.

"By God Almighty, if I were king I would make you mufti of all Egypt! You're a rose, Sheikh Abbas!"

The Dandy recovered from his convulsion and held out the cigarette filled with hashish to Sheikh Abbas.

"Take a puff, Sheikh Abbas, and tell us something about the Deeds of the Hashish-Smokers."

But Hagg Karim did not let matters get out of control. He gave a solemn clap of his hands and they held their tongues. After the night prayer there was to be a holy recitation. Every night of the moulid there was a recitation and a *zikr*. Their hearts might still be laughing, but the return to sobriety was inevitable.

Before the entrance to this room would sit the coffeemaker. He would clear for himself a quiet little space in the midst of the tumult. On the Big Night, when the house would seem to be nothing but crowds, noise, and food, the coffee maker would offer a refuge to those who sought a moment of peace and quiet. As soon as you sat down that kind-hearted man with the gentle smile would hand you a coffee. Next to the sheikh of the order would sit the charm writer. From time to time a woman would come in with her child and point to him, and he would scribble out a charm and fold it into an amulet. The sheikh would take it, bless it, and hang it around the child's neck. Abdel-Aziz, off in a corner, would smile contemptuously.

In these temporary quarters of theirs each man would be assigned precisely the same tasks as in previous years. Ali Khalil was in charge of their budget and their daily cash expenditures. Rashida would come to him.

"We need some onions, Papa Ali."

"For how much? A piastre?"

"No, that's not enough. We need five piastres' worth."

"Hold on, Rashida. I'll let you buy two piastres' worth. Here. That will have to do."

Rashida would make no objection. Her job was to cook with whatever was available. She knew what Hagg Karim would say.

"Ask your Papa Ali. Whatever he says, you do it."

She would go obediently into the kitchen and take charge of the women. She would sit there resolutely amid the big pots simmering on the kerosene burners, breathing in the smoke-filled air and the odors of cooking.

The Dandy would die one day, but his passion for pestering the womenfolk would survive. He could always find an occasion to drop into the kitchen.

"Those burners are doing fine, ladies."

"Yes they're fine, Papa Mohammed, thanks to you."

He was, after all, the messenger they sent to the local women.

"Dandy, go up to Habiba and borrow a mat and two pillows."

"Right away, Uncle."

He would return with his face flushed with effort and throw down his burden.

"She sends her greetings and says she wants to see you to make sure you're well."

Hagg Karim would smile tenderly.

"God reward her with his blessings."

Sherkasi the Carpenter fetched the water, one huge tin of it after the other. He was given this job, which kept him from mingling with the others, because he was nervous and quick-tempered. As for Mohammed Kamel and Ahmed Bedawi, they were the right-hand men of Hagg Karim. They would be constantly smiling, welcoming people and feeding them, and preparing places for them to sit or lie down. This was the way things would go on until the night prayer, which they all prayed together. Then the evening recitations would begin.

The Dandy began rolling a cigarette for himself. His delicate fingers smoothed out the pinch of tobacco in the paper. He licked the edges and rolled it with expertise. His thoughts were not with the others.

"I want to go out for a while."

Ahmed Bedawi feigned childish innocence.

"Where to?"

The Dandy replied uneasily:

"I'm going to adjust the kerosene burners."

He looked around, uncertain of what the others were thinking, and added:

"I'd better fix them tonight, while we're free. There's no telling what will happen tomorrow."

Most of the men paid no attention. They were relaxing right where they had sat down, stretching out their bodies exhausted by the effort of the journey. Ahmed Bedawi grinned slyly, and Abdel-Aziz returned his smile. They both knew, as did all the others, that the Dandy was going to meet El-Gazyeh. When he reached Tanta she would already be there ahead of him, staying with relatives. So he was constantly waiting for an opportunity to go and see her. Abdel-Aziz smiled to himself. It seemed strange to him that those two women, Rawayih and El-Gazyeh, would fight over the Dandy, that irresponsible, pampered child. Each one wanted him for herself. That morning Rawayih had seen him off at the station, and now El-Gazyeh was catching him in her lap. Abdel-Aziz laughed to himself as he observed the flush of excitement on the Dandy's face and the way he twitched nervously as he sat. Knowing smiles appeared on the faces of the men. But Sherkasi the Carpenter scowled.

"Sit right where you are, Dandy. Control yourself."

The Dandy blushed.

"It's my job, and I know how to do it."

Hagg Karim's smile was a bit weary now.

"It's a job that should be done in the morning or during the day, not at night."

But there was no way to thwart the Dandy's urge to leave. He was like a child who could not sit still any longer or remain another minute in the house. Ahmed Bedawi broke in laughing:

"He won't calm down until he's fixed those kerosene burners. Leave him alone."

They all laughed, even Iraqi, who did not understand a thing. The Dandy exploded:

"You can never be sure about kerosene burners. If they break down, you'll all say it's my fault."

There was a knock on the door, and the shouts and laughter of children could be heard from the courtyard. A little girl called out in a playful voice:

"By the Prophet, Uncle, won't you please give us a couple of moulid biscuits and a little *duqqa*."

The Dandy ran toward the door. They could hear him talking to the mischievous girl.

"Did you have to come so soon asking for *duqqa* and biscuits? We haven't had a chance to rest from our trip. Pillagers, all of you!"

He drove the children away, and they ran off screaming, pretending to be afraid, and leaving behind them a deluge of insults.

"Peasants! Animals!"

"Get out of here. May you be struck lame in the knees, vagabonds!"

The men's faces became dark and grim at the children's insults. The silence was broken by Ahmed Bedawi.

"Are we animals, Uncle Mohammed Kamel?"

The man bowed his head, rejecting the idea calmly.

"Our Lord says in his Book: 'We have honored the children of Adam.'"*

Ali Khalil's thin, pale face grew even paler.

"There is no strength nor might but in God!"

Sherkasi the Carpenter was in a rage.

"'Animals!' Who do they think they are?"

Ahmed Bedawi was off on a track of his own, pursuing an idea in his head.

"If we sleep in the same place as our animals, and if we go out together with them every morning to the fields in the mud and the dust, then what's the difference between us and the animals?"

*Koran 17:70.—Trans.

Some of the men smiled, while others sucked their lips in disapproval.

"Once I was riding the train. Sitting opposite me was an effendi and his wife. The effendi was saying there was nothing but good in a peasant's life. It was all cream and butter. I said to him, 'Is that what you think? All year long we eat bread and cheese and wild chicory.' The lady leaned over to her husband and said, 'Wild chicory, Hamdi? That's what we feed to the geese, what they pick out of the clover before they feed it to the animals!' 'Yes,' I told her, 'we take it right from in front of the animals and we eat it. There's no difference between us and the animals.'"

The men were silent. A feeling of sorrow moved through Abdel-Aziz's veins with the weight of quicksilver. He loved the city. Why did the city not love his people? The sorrow almost suffocated him. Despite everything, they were his people. That spirit that shone in their eyes and never went out, Abdel-Aziz bore its mark on his soul.

"We're the finest people in the world."

Smiles flickered in their eyes and at the edges of their mouths. Perhaps because he was speaking about them, he placed himself among them.

"I said we're the finest people in the world."

This show of pride gave him some comfort.

Here they were. They had set up a place to stay in the city. They would impose themselves, their breath, and the clattering of their sandals on this city for a week. He felt better when he thought about that, and he laughed at the Dandy, who was making fun of the lady on the train.

"'Wild chicory, Hamdi.' Yes, Sister, wild chicory. Whore! Her mouth was burnt from eating raw onions and she didn't know the taste of wild chicory. She was a peasant through and through. But God gave her some effendi whose mind was muddled by the sun. He took her and moved her up the ladder!"

Sherkasi the Carpenter interrupted in his irritable manner:

"When God honors the children of Adam they become cruel."

There were more knocks at the door, more children laughing, and more offensive remarks. The attack was on. The Dandy answered them.

"Get out of here, girl, may you catch a thorn in your elbow! By God, we ought to drag them to the police."

Abdel-Aziz remembered the police he had seen at the railway station and smiled a bitter smile. The Dandy, a prisoner in the apartment, kept moving back and forth. Suddenly he gathered up all the kerosene burners and went out. They exchanged knowing looks, and Mohammed Kamel sighed a saying of the Prophet:

"Everyone has his way made easy to whatever he was created for."

Ahmed Bedawi tried to change the subject.

"Isn't there some good film playing, Abdel-Aziz?"

Ahmed Bedawi looked around at the men's faces to see the effect of his question and hoping they would respond enthusiastically to the suggestion. He stopped at Hagg Karim.

"What do you say, Hagg Karim?"

A big smile on his face, Hagg Karim began to nod his head repeatedly, as though he were sitting on the bench in the hall of the guesthouse telling a story. Abdel-Aziz laughed to himself. Tonight was the night for the cinema. Ever since he had had any memory of the moulids of Sayyid Bedawi and their trips to Tanta, this night had been devoted to seeing a film in the one regular movie house in Tanta, Cinema Egypt. Ever since he could remember, those images had been confused in his mind—a woman with a beautiful face who was singing, but whose lips moved only after you heard her voice, or sometimes before you heard it, a man with a big mustache threatening a slender youth with long sideburns who was tortured by loneliness and the harshness of mankind.

Hagg Karim was seated at his usual place on the bench telling the story, and the faces of the brothers were serious and attentive beneath the light of the big lantern. Abdel-Aziz had already seen the film with his father, but he saw it over again as his father related the scenes. Perhaps he was more affected by the story than those who had not seen the film at all. He experienced the events and lived with the characters once more. Every time they went to Tanta, Hagg Karim would return to the village with the story of another film. Every time, after the preliminaries were over and they had visited the Sultan, Ahmed Bedawi would look toward Hagg Karim.

"We want to go to the movies, Uncle Hagg Karim."

In the evening, as the brothers sat together, Hagg Karim would narrate, while Ahmed Bedawi laughed and followed the story in detail. But this time a strange uneasiness came over Abdel-Aziz. These people saw something different from what he saw, or something beyond it.

"But she loved him, Uncle Ahmed."

"No, Son."

Ahmed Bedawi frowned, and his face took on a serious air.

"She didn't love him. She just wanted to get him after things got better for him and he made good."

Abdel-Aziz was totally perplexed. Mohammed Kamel sighed:

"The plantation overseer's son was actually elected to parliament."

Hagg Karim observed in his imposing manner:

"Yousef Wahby is truly a great man. His films go straight to the heart of the matter."

And Ahmed Bedawi added gloatingly:

"The pasha's son turned out a failure."

All the men laughed, but Abdel-Aziz insisted:

"But the pasha's daughter really loved him."

Ahmed Bedawi grew stubborn.

"She was a bitch who just wanted him after he made good. If he had been digging with a hoe, would she have married him?"

Ahmed Bedawi's logic won out among the men. Abdel-Aziz was astonished that they could look at things the way they did. He went often to Tanta and had spent a great deal of time there, but he would sit with them in the evenings when they came back from visiting the city and listen to what they had to say with amazement. How had they seen so many things, and how had the city filled them with so much excitement?

Abdel-Aziz interrupted his thoughts and smiled.

"Yes, there's a very good film playing."

Ahmed Bedawi was overjoyed. Even Ali Khalil beamed a thin smile. Abdel-Aziz turned to him.

"It's a sad film."

They all looked toward Hagg Karim. He smiled at them as he started to get up.

"Well, as long as you all want to go. The Prophet said, 'My community will never agree unanimously on an error.'"

The children's rapping at the door no longer disturbed their joy. It was Mohammed Kamel who said:

"Let's amuse ourselves a little. It's a custom of ours. May God never allow our customs to be broken. Help us, O Lord Ahmed Bedawi!"

Ahmed Bedawi helped Hagg Karim to his feet.

"Aren't you coming with us, Master Abduh?"

"No I'm not, Uncle Ahmed. I saw the film yesterday with my friends."

Ali Khalil reproached him in a low voice.

"Don't break your custom with us, Master Abduh."

Abdel-Aziz was embarrassed, but he had no intention of seeing a film he had seen the day before. Iraqi looked around him without any idea of what was happening. Ahmed Bedawi gestured to his wife to come along, and she came into the room, politely covering the lower half of her face with her head-cloth. Ahmed Bedawi was a kind, affectionate man, and he pampered his wife. But Mohammed Kamel's wife, poor, sad Saddiqa, was not going with them.

Hagg Karim went out, followed by the others. Abdel-Aziz heard their feet fall on the stone steps. Iraqi gave him a questioning look, and he gestured back to him to explain. Iraqi grew fidgety and wandered about the apartment muttering incomprehensible sounds. Finally he came back into the room, and went to sleep with his galabiya folded beneath his head. Sherkasi the Carpenter turned his eyes toward Abdel-Aziz.

"Sit down, Master Abduh. What's bothering you?"

Abdel-Aziz sensed that Sherkasi really wanted to talk to him. The man that no one in particular enjoyed listening to wanted to talk now, and he wanted to talk to *him*. Abdel-Aziz felt a desire to sit down and listen to him, but Tanta was outside—the neon lights, the coffeehouses, and the little candy and refreshment stands. Perhaps, after everyone was asleep and everything in the house was still, Samira would come to him and ask him to help her with a problem in her homework. He felt tenderness toward her. But she was so ordinary and quiet, and that bothered him. He wanted something different. He wanted to lose himself in the lights of the city.

5

The Big Night

Before him there were piles of shoes, slippers, and clogs, disorderly heaps of worn-out footwear—misshapen, twisted leather and warped soles. Abdel-Aziz sat squatting, hugging his legs and resting his chin on his knees. On the tiled floor that stretched out in front of him dozens of feet moved about, unencumbered by shoes or dragging along the strangest sort of slippers. The floor that extended under all these feet was covered with a coating of grease and dust, genuine filth. The tiles had come loose from the floor and shifted beneath the treading of the feet. Perhaps under the tiles there were eyes shining in the darkness, cockroaches and black beetles exploring with their feelers and waiting in fear. When would they begin their nightly rounds? Their kingdom was under attack. The heavy footsteps kept falling. At the far end of the hall was the toilet with its round hole in the floor, wet and stinking. A steady flow of cool air blew from the toilet and filled his lungs with the offensive odor. The stench, the crush, and the cries and the noise almost suffocated him.

The hall was jammed with people sitting shoulder to shoulder. Hagg Karim's face was glistening with sweat in the light of the mantle lanterns. His reddish wool cap had receded to the back of his head, and his untidy galabiya was creased around the collar and stained at the armpits with dust and sweat. From time to time he took a puff on the butt of the cigarette he held between his fingers or turned abruptly in one direction or another to issue an order.

"The lanterns are almost out, Dandy."

The Dandy shouted back that he would fix them. He had taken off his galabiya and was wearing his knee pants, which revealed his hairy white legs covered with dirt. He stood on a chair and cleared one lantern after another with his needle. He went around the whole hall slipping angrily through the crowd.

"Get out of the way and bless the Prophet. Let me get my work done."

A serious look came over his face as he contemplated his work. The lanterns were hissing loudly and shed a strong light. They could not burn any brighter.

The stubble of Mohammed Kamel's unshaven beard was wet with the sweat that streamed down his dark, gaunt face. But his eyes sparkled as he moved about unhampered by his galabiya. His knee-length shirt was soiled at the armpits and his back was stooped and wet with perspiration. In his hand he held a big pot into which he scooped water from the water jar to take to the kitchen. Ali Khalil was stacking the plates in the window and counting the spoons. He had isolated himself from all the din as if he were beneath a glass bell. He would make sure that not a single thing was lost. His galabiya was so dirty one would think he worked in an oil press. The Dandy shouted at him:

"You people give those dishes back to me just the way I gave them to you; I had to beg for them plate by plate—one from every woman."

The Dandy's shouting did not disturb Ali Khalil's concentration. He kept on counting the plates without taking any notice. Hagg Karim bellowed at the Dandy:

"Mind your own business, and stop jabbering."

Ahmed Bedawi guffawed.

"He's afraid of upsetting the ladies."

Sherkasi the Carpenter came in through the door carrying the water pails. He was shouting angrily.

"The crowd was so thick at the pump you had to fight your way through. God damn this town."

They laughed with amusement. Even when they were shouting with anger they were laughing. In this singular crowd, here in their lodgings, they were able to come and go with ease.

Iraqi looked around, casting quick glances here and there, hoping for an opportunity to break into calls for help from the Sultan. The crush and the din, and the complete lack of attention from anyone, stifled his urge. But he kept looking about, watching for the slightest sign of interest and the chance to cry out.

In the kitchen the kerosene burners were lined up one after the other. On top of each was a soot-blackened pot with something stewing inside. The odor of the cooking and the hot fat almost made Abdel-Aziz throw up. The burners were hissing persistently as if they were reciting the *Tokens,* but with no life and no tune. The burners bore the pots on their heads as if they had been created in the image of the black-clothed women in the village. The women bent over the pots, uncovered them, and stuck their heads in the steam. They thrust ladles into the pots and retrieved them full of broth and black bits of meat framed in limp fat. The room was dark—kerosene burners, heat, and the obscure movements of the women. They seemed to be moving in a womb. Saddiqa, who had been divorced by Mohammed Kamel the year before, seemed to be floating in the vapor of the fat stew and the smoke of the lamps and the kerosene burners. She had suffered a touch of madness and would say things or bless the Prophet or call out to the Sultan for no particular reason. Ahmed Bedawi's wife was stirring the liquid in the pot in front of her, but her eye was on Saddiqa. There was apprehension as well as sympathy in her look. Sherkasi's wife was sitting on the floor, completely engrossed in the task of cutting onions. Tears were streaming down her face. Hagg Karim's daughters were hiding their smiles in the thick smoke, the steam, and the darkness.

Abdel-Aziz looked at Rashida's face as she leaned over one of the steaming pots. Was this why she had come from the village? To be imprisoned in the kitchen and then to go straight back to the train? Was this the only joy she had? She looked his way. Her fading eyes betrayed the tenderness she felt toward him. She dipped her ladle into the pot and brought out a fatty piece of meat and offered it to him. He refused it with disgust, and she put it back in the pot with a hand that almost wept. When the women turned to Rashida for directions, she would not have to say a thing. A movement of her body, a look in their direction, and they understood what she wanted. She had even greater determination than Abdel-Aziz's mother. The heat covered the floor of the kitchen like a carpet—wet, dirty heat. There was no space for the women's bare feet to move. Perhaps their feet would broil right there on the floor, while they kept stubbornly at their work. The black smoke formed a dome over the dimly lit scene, over the pots and the women. From nails in the walls hung baskets and crates and bunches of onions and garlic. The smoke settled on them with invisible feet.

Hagg Karim's face appeared at the door of the kitchen. Rashida offered him a scoopful of stew.

"Try this, Papa."

"Delicious."

His voice could be heard even when he was talking to himself. Abdel-Aziz thought how his voice carried through their crowded gathering beneath the hissing mantle lanterns. All their mouths were watering now, and their stomachs were twisting with hunger. After the long days of hard work throughout the year, the toil under the scorching sun, the coarse food day after day, after all this their stomachs were aching for something soft, fat, and tender.

"Shall I make *fatta,* Papa?"

"Make lots of it. What else can we afford? Set out the trays."

His words were heard by everyone in the kitchen. The women's hands, under Rashida's watchful eye, set out the big, round trays. How they made space for them was impossible to say. The trays were filled with dishes of different shapes and liquids of different colors, red, green, and white. Eyes of melted fat swam on the surface of the broth.

Hagg Karim avoided looking at Abdel-Aziz, and so did the brothers. Their faces would smile, but the smiles would be cut short. Those leatherlike faces, tanned and weathered by the heat of the sun as they worked alone scattered in the fields, had come streaming along the paths and the roads in one huge, determined crowd to the city. Now here they were. What had brought them? What meaning was there to what they were doing?

"Many happy returns, Uncle."

The voices and the laughter—Abdel-Aziz wished the men would stop for just one second and say something to him that he understood. But they passed over him. Their truncated smiles passed over him too. Here and there laughter would break out like drops of sweat on the back of your hand, hot and sticky. Echoes filled the gaps. It was a hot, scorching joy.

"Help us, O Sultan!"

They were all connected by electric wires, and he was a section of insulation. If only he could take his father by the arms, stop him for a moment, and ask him:

"What does all this mean?"

But there was no place on their stage for a scene like this. The grinding movement crushed everything and swept it away.

"Whoever misses out on the meat will have to make do with the broth."

"Everything is for the love of the Sultan."

Abdel-Aziz kept looking for a quiet place in this beehive. The coffeemaker? He was absorbed in the hiss of the kerosene burner in front of him. Abdel-Aziz looked at the coffeepot and decided that he was exactly like that pot—full inside with something black and bitter. Strange shadows played on the face of the coffee maker. He sat beside him for a moment.

"A cup of coffee?"

"No."

There was no free space left in the mat-strewn rooms. People were piled on top of one another. They might be sitting on the mats, but inside they were standing up, craning their necks, grasping, and chewing irreverently. The stomach was the moving force of history. The history of those creatures that were born in the primeval slime—little quantities of sticky, quivering jelly that kept quaking, stretching out, and devouring, swelling and fermenting, billions and billions of microscopic mouths—that long epic of ugliness, greed, and voracity, was the history of man. The gelatinous creatures that had kept regenerating throughout the ages until they had become people were smiling now, but inside they still had the same stomachs. Their tanned, weathered faces were mirrors that reflected the painful spasms of their entrails. The rooms were choked with huddled hunger. Words were clipped off at the end. They sat crowded together, thighs pressing against thighs. At the doors were pile of shoes, like severed members of their bodies, thrown down in neglect.

"*Fatta* is the chief of the feast!"

"Rice is the sergeant of food!"

"Help us, O Sultan!"

Abdel-Aziz felt sick and heavy inside. He looked at the faces in the sheikh's room. They were older and fatter. The amulet maker was selling upside-down letters of the alphabet written on tattered squares of paper to mindless fools who came carrying sick children on their arms. His eyelids were drooping, but occasionally he would become restless and look around to see if the food tray had arrived. Abdel-Aziz wished he could choke him, choke him with the turban cloth of that liar and fraud Sheikh Abbas.

"'Make sopped bread, for bread wet with broth is a blessed dish.' This is what the first believers, may God be pleased with them, taught us to do. *Fatta* is a blessed dish."

Mistikawi was reclining. His eyes were bulging and he was coughing incessantly, spitting out the phlegm each time. Between coughs he would question Sheikh Abbas.

"Isn't there some saying of the Prophet about meat with gravy, Sheikh Abbas?"

But it was the sheikh of the order who was the magnet of the crowd. He was a small god, graceful, tranquil, and serene, toying mechanically with the beads of a rosary and reclining on a mattress. The scion of the Messenger of God was spitting in the mouths of children and stroking their foreheads. What a comedy!

The mantle lanterns were hot moons that stretched out fiery feelers like glowing cockroaches, scorching their faces. The pictures hanging from the nails in the walls were like pale eyeballs looking down in silent, witless questioning. He imagined the others hammering him to the wall with a nail and dancing beneath him the savage dance of the chewing jaws.

In a more remote room they had heaped the little children and the girls. They were laughing and playing and pinching each other. Samira was there. She had the same wide eyes with that cold, wearisome composure. He was ready to give her his heart. All she had to do was to stir something in it. But Samira just looked at him with unseeing eyes. He loathed her. He wished she would go away, far away. He felt he was suffocating.

The Wanderers, those mangy tomcats who roamed through the countryside with their exaggerated beards, their long hair, and their shining eyes. They wore chains of iron, immense rosaries, and all sorts of turbans decorated with everything imaginable, even tiny baby shoes, and they carried different kinds of sticks and wooden swords. Their laughter was as piercing as daggers, and their faces were as strange as the clothes they wore. This was the time of the great gathering of the Wanderers, of the faces created to arouse dread, of the faces that cut their way like skillfully piloted ships through men's senses to their most deep-seated fears.

Here he was, Abdel-Aziz's man with the chains of iron, the one who flew between the two rows of dervishes in the *zikr* like a clown, with that sickening foam spilling from his mouth.

"Good people, I beg at God's door. In the love of the Sultan."

Hagg Karim went up to him and greeted him with open arms.

"Welcome, welcome, welcome, Uncle."

He tried to lead him into the room, but the man refused and made himself a place in the corner of the entrance hall.

"My bite to eat and my coffee, and then I have to go. I can't stay. I never leave my rounds."

The plate was set before him. He got food all over his mouth and his beard and his clothes. Then he had his cup of bitter coffee and went out belching.

The trays were coming. There would be no room left in their mouths now, not even for invocations and prayers.

"Make a little room, friend. Take it easy, Brother. Hold on."

Men's stomachs were those same gelatinous creatures out of the depths of the past—voracious, destructive amoebas that had not evolved since the day they came into being. All that had happened was that they had grown legs to carry them about and arms to hand them food. Abdel-Aziz closed his eyes. He felt the same shudder he had experienced early one morning out in the cotton field, as he listened sad and helpless, a battered insecticide sprayer in his hand, to the gnawing of the cotton worms inside the fresh blossoms. He contemplated this human carpet as it gnawed its food.

The dinosaurs had ruled the world for a million years with their huge bodies, their tiny brains, and their gnashing teeth. They had crowded together like this without any order. Abdel-Aziz almost wept with regret at being the son of these people who fell upon their food like so many animals. He wished he could rise up and shout to them to stop and try to comprehend the world, to divide it into small compartments and reflect on it. But the oppressive crowding made thought impossible, banished it and crushed it.

The cigarette stub in Hagg Karim's hand was stained with grease. He stood in the middle of the hall watching the frightful feast with a strange, incomprehensible joy. He looked at Abdel-Aziz.

"Sit down and eat."

"I'm not hungry."

"Eat with everybody else."

"No."

He was not with them at all. What he wanted to do was to stand before them and stretch out his arms to stop them.

The dishes on the trays were empty now. Scattered bread crumbs, remnants of stew, and shiny bones were the only survivors of the battle. There was licking of lips, laughter, and what sounded like cries of victory. Then their hands reached out and gripped the trays around the edge, one fist next to the other, and raised them up. Their throats broke out in unison.

May God give health to those who have eaten.
May he reward those who have given.
By the blessing of the Prophet
And the Opening!

The Opening was recited with resounding but sated voices, accompanied by deep-toned belches. In the kitchen the tongues of flame still licked the bottoms of the black pots, and the women crouched in the corners as though they were offering themselves submissively to the savage din.

Suddenly Abdel-Aziz went out of the door of the lodgings. The buildings that stood on the sides of the courtyard were adorned with strands of lighted windows. He heard the women's cries and calls to one another, the tinkling of their jewelry, and the provocative sounds of their laughter as it trailed off in the darkness. He caught sight of the hem of the dress of the Tanta girl he knew, glowing in a splinter of light in the dark stairwell across the courtyard.

She stood in the corner breathing heavily, and the sound of her breath pulled him toward her. He had his arms out in front of him like the feelers of an insect, and his hands bumped into the rough wall. He pressed his body against the softness of her flesh as she leaned against the wall. He thrust his lips onto her open mouth, and his teeth grated against hers. Her lips, two small cushions, soft and fiery, danced in his mouth like serpents. He rubbed his face against hers. Their lips were polluted with saliva. He almost tore her hair out by the roots as he pulled her toward him, trying to possess her hot, erring body. But she slipped out from under him and fled.

His forehead was covered with blood. He had bumped into the wall when the girl slipped away from him. He wiped the blood off with his hand, but his hands were bleeding too. His eyes had become accustomed to the dark. Under the steps there was a man with a woman. He was pulling her by the hair and burying his face in her neck. Abdel-Aziz looked at them in astonishment. The Dandy and El-Gazyeh! He suppressed the cry that almost escaped from his throat. The Dandy jumped up and straightened out his clothes. Abdel-Aziz ran off before the Dandy could see him. They had been right next to each other like rabbits in a hutch. He burst into the courtyard running. He could hear the tinkling of bracelets and the cries and trailing laughter of the Tanta women calling to one another from their windows, from those squares of light hung on the walls in the darkness. From the window of the lodgings roared the voices of the men:

May God give health to those who have eaten.
May he reward those who have given.
By the blessing of the Prophet
And the Opening!

What sort of wedding could there be between the tinkling of the women's quivering jewelry and their provocative cries and the bellowing of these men? He leaped down the stone steps and escaped. He headed down Sidi Marzouq Street. Dozens of groups had rented lodgings here. The ground floor windows opened into halls jammed with people—faces and peasant caps, hands and shoulders, the smacking of lips, the clatter of spoons and dishes, and the laughter of sated appetites.

Abdel-Aziz walked quickly. The sidewalks on both sides were crowded with people sitting in little circles. The nucleus was always a corpulent woman whose wrists were heavy with gold bracelets and whose smile revealed two rows of gold-covered teeth. These women were the hashish sellers. Each had in front of her a kerosene burner, a tea kettle and some glasses, along with a pail of water in which she had cooling a number of water pipes.

The people were like a river flowing between the two banks of the street. Thousands of feet were treading the pavement in uninterrupted movement. The stubborn, persistent shuffling went on, the unhesitating feet fell heavily on the asphalt. The faces were cleft with smiles and laughter.

"Where are you going, my people? Where are you going?"

It was as though some animal of incredible size and strange shape were stretching its body through the streets of the city. It moved along without wavering, wide-eyed and weak-witted, asking nothing. A continuous lowing sound rose from uncertain depths and shook the whole area as the animal went on, pursuing an unknown goal.

The monotony of the dark facades of the buildings on either side of the street was relieved by the lighted squares of the windows, which were always crowded with women. Their laughter gave off such sensuality. He wished he could squeeze their tender necks and choke them to death—the women and their city with its painted face.

The street was covered with a dome of illuminated dust. He was swept along, lost in a moving forest of bodies—men, women, and children. The merchants on both sides stretched out their arms on the counters in front of them in despair. No one was buying. They were only walking in the streets and looking. They had bought yesterday evening and they would buy again tomorrow, but tonight was the Big Night. The shiny, colored surfaces of the articles of merchandise, with thousands of glistening eyes, struggled against the particles of dust that continued to settle on them. The crowd moved through the street like a drizzling rain that would not let up. The shuffling of the feet continued unmitigated. He kept on walking.

He followed the crowds beneath Seigar Bridge, a long, dark tunnel over which the trains rumbled like earthquakes. The way became narrow and the crowd grew dense. The loud, shrill whistles of the Tanta boys reverberated off the walls of the tunnel. The mounted policemen were skirmishing with the edges of the throng with their terrifying sticks of bamboo. The trains kept roaring overhead. But the shuffling of the feet did not stop. The moving crowd possessed the mightiness of the river; it was unaffected by any blows that rippled its surface. The tunnel came to an end, and the festival of light, dust, noise, and loudspeakers began.

Wide areas of agricultural land, where earlier that year wheat had grown, had been cleared for the moulid, and the huge expanse had been filled with tents. Every sheikh of an order, or of any branch of an order, had set up a tent for his followers. Most of the tents were completely open at one end—deep rectangles, often with brightly colored geometric designs. Over the entrance of each was a great sign or banner bearing the name of the sheikh, his order, and the village from which he came. In every tent there was a Koran chanter, a singer of pious narratives and sacred love songs, a reciter of the history of the Prophet, or a relater of the Banu Hilal romances. The loudspeakers set up on the frames of the tents were like preachers out of legend. Each one seemed to be trying to outshout the other.

Abdel-Aziz entered the tent. The girl was standing on a raised platform. Her face was like a dark moon, wrapped around with her white headcloth. The members of the band were sitting at her feet and the instruments buzzed in their hands like poisonous red hornets. They were old men who made their eyebrows dance beneath their turbans. Their faces wore forced smiles, and their frolicking eyes seemed unrelated to the hands that toyed with the instruments. The girl sang with a sad, hoarse voice:

> You who have done me wrong.

And the crowd standing in front of her thundered back:

> Yes, by God! "You who have done me wrong"!

The loudspeaker screamed, as if to split the cloud of lighted dust that hovered in the air.

If only you would come to me one night in a dream,
you who have done me wrong. . . .

A roar of admiration rose from the breasts of the people standing before the girl. She lowered her eyes submissively. Abdel-Aziz wanted to tear off her dress, bare her breasts, seize her by the hair, and look deep into her eyes.

The reciter of the history of the Prophet seemed crazed as he stood on the platform. He danced about and hopped up and down, struggling with an imaginary enemy.

The sword said to the Prophet,
To the battle lead me.
On the flesh and gore of infidels,
beloved, feed me.

The crowd sitting in front of him was filled with the same madness.

"Ah, Prophet! O Prophet!"

The singer of narratives and love songs was enchanted with himself. Tilting his fez to one side and placing his hand over his chest, he shook his shoulders haughtily to the rhythm.

The eyes of my beloved are honey,
and their black makeup is divine.

A thousand voices seemed to respond.

"May God grant you long life, Sheikh! Again!"

The man bowed his head, acknowledging their praise with pride.

In the middle of the wide field filled with tents passed a long street with games and rides and tents for dancing girls and entertainers set up on both sides. There were the cheats and swindlers, the "Three Cards" players, and that amazing man who rode his flying motorcycle around inside a huge iron hemisphere. There was the two-headed calf, the man without any head at all, the electric girl, who lit bulbs when she touched them, Madame Safia from Alexandria with her troupe, and Ahmed el-Kassar, the wonderful monologist. The tents were enormous constructions of canvas and wooden beams. In front of them high platforms were set up with samples of what was happening inside—drums and flutes, dancers in glaring dresses, and faces covered with paint. A fat black woman who ran one of the shows was sitting at a high stand and selling tickets. The drawer before her was stuffed with money. She looked at a young girl who was standing in front of her and moving like a dancer.

"Get up on the platform, girl. Take these twenty-five piastres. It's the week of the moulid. Make yourself some money. Get up on the platform and shake your hips for a couple of hours, and we'll be quits."

The cries of the barkers fell upon the people from loudspeakers on both sides.

"Come on over, friend. Take a look at the wild animal trainer."

The noise and the gaudy sights succeeded in attracting the edges of the moving crowd. People would stand in front of the high platforms and look. They would gather in large groups, and the huge tents would be filled with them. Inside, on the stages of these temporary theaters, characters dressed in every imaginable kind of costume hopped up and down before them—artless movements and nameless faces deformed by makeup. Lions, tamed and cowardly, mooed like cattle. The spectators would come out of these tents despondent and be reabsorbed in the movement that did not let up and did not stop. The policemen were there too, some mounted on the backs of the government's big English horses and others standing on both sides of the way—country faces in uniforms of khaki. They seemed to want to take off those uniforms and move with the crowd, but like puppets they were bound by unseen threads to the headquarters tent, to sullen old officers who contemplated in despair these masses they could not possibly control. Orders would be issued, and sticks would fall. Fear would create little eddies, but they would soon be absorbed again into the flow. The policemen would look on with agitated, perplexed faces. How was it possible to control this monster that spread over the ground and twisted its flesh through the streets like a worm?

Once more he passed through the dark tunnel to return to New Street. Before him was a procession of people from Mahalla el-Kubra, a forest of mantle lanterns, huge lanterns, some of which might fork into two or three separate lamps. The men walked along carrying these great lanterns. They were not reciting any words and they were not swaying to the rhythm of the *zikr*. They just walked on carrying their lanterns.

Without noticing, he wandered into the midst of them—into the hissing of the mantle lanterns and the blinding white light, into the midst of the thin bodies dressed in shining satin galabiyas and the heads wrapped with glistening scarves wound to leave one end trailing over the neck. The workers at the spinning and weaving mills did not hold their procession by day. They worked in factory halls darkened by cotton dust and lit only by electricity day and night. The light of the sun was unknown to them. In their faces was fierceness and determination. They walked along in that forest of hissing lanterns, swishing in their galabiyas and puffing on cigarettes of hashish. The fragrance of the hashish filled Abdel-Aziz's nostrils. His legs were heavy, but he continued to walk, no longer possessing a will of his own. The procession left him behind and moved on like a galaxy of hot moons. He watched it, lost in the crowd around him.

Then he found himself in the midst of another procession—two lines of dancers, each of whom held in his hand a little drum which he whipped with a strap of leather. The sounds were high-pitched, cutting through the hoarse, crazed barking rising from the dancers' breasts. Two lines of peasants, dancing wildly and sweating profusely. The sheikh, a wily-faced man, was riding a frail, emaciated mare, and was surrounded by colored banners held high by his men. The wild beating reverberated in Abdel-Aziz's head and almost made him vomit. The dregs of his consciousness clung to that sheikh towering on his poor, frail mare. It seemed that every imposing being had a humble mount. This mare and the preacher's undersized, aged donkey had the same abject, brutish eyes. Abdel-Aziz felt his head about to explode. But his senses were numbed, and he was drawn on by this tempestuous din as it moved through the city.

Tomorrow, Friday morning, was the procession of the vicar of Sayyid Bedawi, his living successor. In it would be gathered all the people, all the banners, and all the drums. The throng would move along a fixed route in the heat of the sun. With them would ride the vicar, wearing his robe and holding on to his turban to keep it from flying off. New Street, with its roof of awnings, would be too narrow for this great multitude. The buildings on both sides of the way would be practically swaying with the burden of people who had come to watch. The windows would be jammed and the balconies weighed down with women watching the procession and throwing hard candy and coarse grains of salt. The crowd would be like the Day of Resurrection, a monstrous body stretching out through the city, flexing its huge muscles and extending its trunk to shove it at last into the shrine of the Sultan.

Ahead of him, at the end of this human river, decorated on all sides with electric lights, was the resplendent, heavily made-up face of the bride—the bride of the tempestuous will that stretched through the streets of the city. The blood from the brown body of the countryside poured in an unending flow into this radiant heart. The eye of the believer could see it from thousands of leagues away, with all those lights. The countryside was covered in darkness and longed for a brightly lit night. What mechanical heart, what unbelievably powerful machine, could generate all this splendor and light on the face of the towering mosque?

He was drawn by an extraordinary force to the Sultan's shrine. All the way around the light-flooded structure the crowds of people were sitting so close together that there was no place left to step. He kept with the flow of the river. He was carried along by that single moving will created by the thousands of bodies walking toward the shrine. But he could not suppress the stubborn, persistent question in his mind. Where was he going? Why? Was it Hagg Karim's brown eyes soaring with longing? Was it those eyes that stirred in him this yearning to see the Sultan's shrine? Was it those eyes that made him unable to turn his back or to refuse, to stop and say "No!" and to get away from this crowd?

The people pressed through the door of the mosque. The attendants were busy moving them along with loud but painless blows to their backs and shoulders with whips made of flat strips of wood joined at the handle. They dodged them as best they could. Their faces were squeezed together. Faces and more faces. Their cheeks were almost contiguous, and their breath, their sighs, and their shouts almost blended into one. It was impossible to escape. The crowd was carrying him on to the tomb. That powerful and uncontrollable mass, almost bursting with the unused strength within it, was sweeping him along with it to the gate of the mausoleum and to the Sultan's tomb.

A huge grill of shining brass reflected in countless glints the light that fell from the great chandeliers hanging from the ceiling. The mass of people encircled the tomb—thousands of hearts, thousands of eyes, thousands of sighs, groans, and cries of anguish and love. Withered bouquets of flowers hung from the grill like lifeless bodies, choked by the breath of so many visitors. The people were pressed so close together as they surrounded the brass structure that enclosed the tomb that they seemed to be one mass of flesh with thousands of heads. They were a single body full of all the strange temptations that assailed mankind, temptations Abdel-Aziz's awakened senses picked up. The dazzling light could not penetrate the crowd of people or open pores in the compressed mass of flesh. Down beneath the surface, temptations and unspeakable desires that could not be controlled writhed like worms, moving, groping, and clinging, and then drowning in ambiguity.

"Help us, O Sultan!"

This was the burning center of the circle of passion and longing that extended for dozens of miles in every direction. From here the fervor spurted out into the arteries and smallest capillaries of the countryside—into the roads and the lanes, into the depths of houses and the reception rooms lit by lanterns. It was as though they were in an oven. Abdel-Aziz felt he was going to vomit. His eyelids were heavy. He could see Hagg Karim standing in the hall of the lodgings, beaming with happiness. He gestured with his hands and the big round trays were brought in. Then the flood of lust and gratified smacking of lips broke loose.

The throng carried Abdel-Aziz out of the tomb on strong, crowded shoulders. All his life he had been borne along on these shoulders, as millions of cracked feet in tattered shoes trod their path through time. He had been totally unable to resist.

Before the entrance to the tomb the *zikr* was held—two rows without end. The whole mosque was shaken to its foundations by the pounding of feet and the hoarse barking sounds rising from the men's throats. The roaring, crushing noise could not be resisted. No hesitation was possible before it. It overwhelmed every opposing echo and swept away every temptation. Those hoarse barks were bursting from hearts that had journeyed from every part of the earth and gathered here in one roaring cataract of human voices that could sweep away rocks and boulders and gouge the land with the strength of a huge hand of steel.

The two rows were jumping up and down and pounding the floor of the mosque with their feet. The heart of Tanta was a slaughtered animal beneath all those naked feet. The body of the city—thousands of old buildings, twisting alleys, and ornamented streets—was being crushed beneath this rumbling flesh. There was nowhere to flee from the thundering noise that stretched its arms in every direction and filled the space of the sanctuary.

The marble floor was carpeted with people sitting shoulder to shoulder. One would pull one's foot through two bodies only to place it between two others. The people were like grains of sand in a desert. Crowded groups sat in circles around hissing kerosene burners, big coffeepots, moulid biscuits, and *duqqa*. The men's turbans were of all shapes and colors—red, green, and white. Food was dispensed with generosity. Thousands of mouths ate, drank, and smoked without cease. The wide expanse of the mosque was a jumble of strange faces, immense turbans, iron chains, wooden swords, huge rosaries, and shouts, recitations, and prayers. But the hoarse barking of the two rows of men dancing the *zikr* overpowered everything else. Abdel-Aziz summoned all the resolve a human will possessed to separate himself from the crowd and say "No," but it was useless.

A light blow struck his shoulder, an insignificant tap. He turned to see before him a pug-nosed face with sparkling eyes. The man laughed a mock challenge, arrogant but affectionate, and held out his hand in a theatrical gesture.

"Give me a light."

He had no cigarette to light. Abdel-Aziz, as though mesmerized, handed him his cigarette. The man laughed at his easy victory. It was a laugh that caused Abdel-Aziz's heart to soar.

"May God light your heart with the love of the Sultan."

His piercing laughter trailed off as he made his way through the crowd. Abdel-Aziz watched his shoulders sway in time with his light, skillful feet until he disappeared.

He thought suddenly of Samira, as if she were there before him. Her clear laughter rang inside him, and he saw her bright, straight teeth and her eyes that always sparkled. But he quickly fell back into his despondent mood. He managed to reach one of the side doors and went out of the mosque into the street.

Even in the dark narrow alleys he could see the faces of country folk. They were wandering through the veins of the city, through all its tiny capillaries and to its nerve ends. The countryside had clasped thousands of arms around the city and embraced it. It had breathed its breath in a long kiss into its lungs. He walked, and walked.

In the darker corners had been set up burlap tents, oversized boxes with blinding white light bursting through the cracks and openings. They were packed with country folk, and the bright light of the mantle lanterns and the sound of the tambourines, drums, and flutes seemed to be imprisoned inside them. Glasses of black tea shimmered through the storms of water pipe smoke bursting from men's mouths. The eyes of hashish vendors glistened in the corners. A strong *zar* beat slaughtered the dozens of hearts that offered themselves to the rhythm, and the brass castanets flew about in the box of burlap like birds in a cage. The girl seemed pale under her heavy face paint. The glitter of her gold and silver spangles and the light splashing on her forehead dazzled the eye. The folds of her body were outlined beneath her yellow silk dress.

"Help us, O Sultan!"

He wandered out into the dark, quiet side streets, the unlit extremities of the city which the glittering electric blaze at the heart could not reach, the haunt of dogs and whores and police informers. His imagination was filled with the image of Hagg Karim making his way with longing eyes toward the train station. This was the city for which Hagg Karim's heart and his brown eyes yearned.

"You there!"

The voice split the darkness like the crack of a whip. It was stern and direct, an irrefutable accusation. Abdel-Aziz felt like a hunted animal. He wanted to run away and rejoin the huge body that was convulsing the city with its thousands of heavy steps. The cockroaches beneath the tiles raised their heads and their feelers from the decay and crept forward to attack him. He choked, dull-witted and glassy-eyed, like the sheep that had been slaughtered in front of the door of their lodgings. He ran as fast as he could to escape the sticks that had been raised in the air. He ran until he was out of breath and blinded by fatigue.

He started up the steps to the courtyard in front of the lodgings. It took all his remaining strength to keep from falling on the spot. Hagg Karim stood in front of the others, his great cloak falling loosely over his sturdy body. He was leaning on his cane. His eyes were full of serenity and contentment as he murmured a vague series of invocations. The men sitting on the mats were exhausted after dancing the many rounds of the *zikr* of the Big Night. The weary dancers—there were a great many of them tonight—were wiping the sweat from their faces with their handkerchiefs or the hems of their galabiyas. Mohammed Kamel's voice reverberated in the courtyard, calling for recitations of the Opening for brothers and friends. The windows were jammed with women watching what was going on. Their laughter echoed off the walls of the buildings. The trays were brought out, loaded with little glasses of cinnamon tea. They were passed around among the people, and an outburst of pleasure and boisterous conversation followed.

Hagg Karim stood proudly in his place, watching with contentment what was happening around him. Abdel-Aziz looked up at his father. He could not tell what it was in Hagg Karim that reminded him of Antara el-Absi in the Arab romance, whose dead body had been set up on his horse to face the enemy. For days the erect corpse had continued to strike fear into their hearts. But then the horse had bolted, and the mighty frame had fallen to the ground.

All the men were talking and laughing in one breath. Everyone seemed to be talking, listening, and laughing at the same time. The sheikh was sitting on his mattress and smiling with contentment, while the coffeemaker was busy listening to the hissing of the kerosene burner. The Dandy, as usual, was in stitches with laughter, and his grinning lips showed his teeth ruined by tobacco and tea. Iraqi turned around and laughed at nothing in particular. Ahmed Bedawi asked him what he was laughing at, and Iraqi cursed him. Mohammed Kamel smiled happily.

The women were sitting in the kitchen next to the extinguished burners and the empty pots. Rashida beamed, talking about the food and how those people had drunk a whole canal of *moloukhia*. Mohammed Kamel's wife, or rather his divorced wife, was sitting wide-eyed with an addled look on her face. She kept mumbling a stream of prayers and blessings upon the Prophet.

In the other room were the children and the girls. Samira was with them, laughing. She was teasing the girls from home, who had not lived in the city as she had. She enjoyed making fun of their ignorance.

Hagg Karim had sat down on a low wooden stool in the middle of the entrance hall. The others pressed close around him.

"Many happy returns, children."

A warm, gentle joy showed on his face as they sat around him in a circle of smiles and cheerful looks. But how would they sleep that night?

"The summer's mat is wide, children. Everyone sleep where he is."

Hagg Karim, too, would sleep wherever he could. He would fold his arms under his head and sleep. Abdel-Aziz watched him as he drew the last puffs of a cigarette.

With no preliminaries, someone greeted Abdel-Aziz from a distant corner.

"Many happy returns, Master Abdel-Aziz."

Abdel-Aziz could not understand the sudden, violent anger that exploded inside him. Perhaps it was the pungent stench of the toilet wafting toward him, or perhaps it was the hordes of insects that had begun to raise their feelers out of the cracks in the tiles, now that the bustle of the evening had subsided. He did not understand the secret of his sudden rage, but he managed to control himself. Meanwhile the man's voice kept croaking.

"Many happy returns, Master Abdel-Aziz. What a wonderful moulid it's been this year. It's never been like this before. Help us, O Sultan! And the people! Whole nations!"

Abdel-Aziz did not know why he blew up the way he did, but he was blind with rage.

"Nations with no mind! Nations that don't think. They move just like animals. They don't have any idea where they're going or where they're coming from."

His whole being was shouting, and the echo of his voice carried from one end of the lodgings to the other. The others responded with baffled faces and silent tongues and stared at him with mouths agape. In their eyes he could see the same dread the preacher stirred when he shouted at them. He blanched with fear and his limbs grew cold, but he kept on shouting.

"Is there anything you know? Where you're coming from? Where you're going? Idol worshippers!"

His voice trembled, but with an extraordinary effort he held back his tears. Hagg Karim's face went dark. He spoke firmly and with overwhelming power.

"Your people? Your family? Animals, Abdel-Aziz? God's people who have come here joyfully from the ends of the earth, whose steps cause the very throne of God himself to tremble. You are ignorant. Get out of our way. Get away from us with your unclean pants. Get away before the feet of God's people trample you and crush you into the ground. Unbeliever!"

Abdel-Aziz felt as though he were lying on the ground and millions of feet were treading over his body and his head, crushing his bowels and his brain and grinding them into the dust. He sat as though he were dead. Hagg Karim's voice was trembling, almost to the point of weeping.

"Idol worshippers? May God curse you! Our hearts are full of love for the saints of God."

Murmurs and sucking of lips spread through the gathering to the farthest corners of the hall.

"There is no power nor might but in God!"

"Be quiet, Hagg Karim. That's enough."

"God forgive you. Don't curse your son."

"There is no god but God! A father's curse is a terrible thing. The wrath of parents is God's wrath."

"It was just a moment of anger. O God, turn thy ear away!"

"He's a good boy, but Satan is clever."

Ali Khalil was sitting off in the far corner, pale as death. The Dandy was cowering like a dog, and Ahmed Bedawi looked on in disbelief. Mohammed Kamel, tears welling in his eyes, raised his hands in prayer.

"The Opening, men. The Opening so that the Lord may guide Abdel-Aziz, our son, and drive these evil spirits from him."

Eyes were closed, and the whispered recitation began. Hagg Karim raised his hands in supplication as he recited. Tears poured down Abdel-Aziz's face. He dragged himself away from the group.

They began to collapse one by one. Each one spread out his muffler and folded his arm beneath his head and slept—men, women, and children without distinction. The noise began to die down. A few eyes stayed open, and here and there in the corners one could hear the last remnants of the stories of the day. Hagg Karim walked about the room, arranging the positions of the sleepers, murmuring advice to those who asked him questions, and seeing to a variety of other matters. Finally he sat down totally exhausted and took the last few puffs on his cigarette.

Abdel-Aziz went into the children's room. He separated two bodies and lay down between them. He folded his arm and rested his head. The last bits of conversation scattered through the lodgings seemed sorrowful. He could not sleep. His face was covered with tears. The mantle lanterns went out one by one, and everything was dark. The only sounds were the monotonous breathing of the sleepers and the rustling of the insects in the night. He was unable to sleep. It was as if those insects were crawling inside his brain. There seemed to be no end to his agony. There was no way to sleep with that sharp pain inside him. His body was worn out, but his mind was wide awake.

Gradually the room began to be lit by a pale, faded light coming through the cracks of the window. He saw Samira's face next to his. She was smiling even in her sleep. She was pretty with her childish face. He loved her with all his heart. Warm tears flowed down his cheeks. He kissed her with trembling lips. He kissed her mouth. Her breathing remained calm and regular. He contemplated the serenity of her face. She had bared her body in the heat of the room. This was the first time he had seen her body naked like this. It had a dark, even color in the dim light. It was an exceptional body, full-fleshed, delicate, and harmonious. He pulled her to him, and her sleeping frame yielded.

He placed his arm under her head and drew her still closer. She was lying directly against him now. Trembling with desire he reached down and felt her naked belly. It was soft and tender. His heartbeats grew faster. With eyes closed he moved his face close to hers to kiss her again. Suddenly he opened his eyes. She was looking straight at him. There were tears in her eyes. It was all over. His hand fell, and he became a slab of ice. He got up sluggishly, dragged his legs through the sleeping bodies, and went out the door of the lodgings. A few frightened heads were raised and looked at him with questioning eyes. He ignored them, and they went back to sleep.

The street was slumbering too—a few streetlights at distant intervals and whores loitering in the recesses of buildings. Police informers moved about busily, like sudden gusts of wind. The regular policemen made their rounds with lethargic effort.

Suddenly he saw a drunk, a tall stooped man groping his way along as best he could and trying to run. He was shouting at the top of his voice:

"Help me, somebody! Help!"

Behind him came a group of unkempt children with disheveled hair and wearing a strange assortment of rags. Thieves and cigarette butt gatherers. They were chasing him and showering him with rocks, while he screamed at the top of his voice for help. Within seconds the informers and policemen fell on him with their sticks and the butts of their rifles and beat him until he dropped motionless in the middle of the street.

6

The Farewell

It had become part of Abdel-Aziz's nature. He would isolate himself from everything around him and immerse himself in his thoughts. But he found himself waking up every now and then to catch bits of what his father was saying to his cousin Habiba.

"The world is a marketplace. Some win and some lose. May the Lord take us away without loss."

"Not so soon, Hagg Karim."

"It's better to be with the Lord, Habiba."

"But it's so hard to leave the ones we love."

Death was the final outcome of the struggle between permanence and extinction, a small but certain truth. So why the pain? Inside Abdel-Aziz there was still the heart of that frightened little boy sitting huddled together with the other children around their big sister on top of the mud heating oven. The flame of the lamp had been like an unmoving eye drawn on the wall, and all the dogs in the village were howling mournfully in the night. Their big sister had whispered:

"The dogs won't let up. Someone is surely going to die tonight."

When Azrael, the angel of death, called on the village, no human being could see him. Only the eyes of the animals saw him. The old memory brought a smile to Abdel-Aziz's face.

Hagg Karim scrutinized everything around him—the couches with the worn-out covers, the faded carpet, and the ornate

Koranic verses hanging on the wall. He stared at everything in the old room as though he were seeing it for the last time.

Matter could be neither created nor destroyed. But when Hagg Karim died he would be destroyed. He was not made of ordinary matter. He was a unique substance. He was Hagg Karim. Abdel-Aziz loved him now as he had never loved him before.

The great tragedy was that scientific truth was devoid of poetry. It was simple and harsh. Abdel-Aziz had learned a great deal, and he had suffered a great deal in order to believe what he had learned. But he still did not know how to sit on the bench in the hall of the guest house and slap the bottom of his foot with his open hand, while the men, their faces lit by the yellow light of the great lantern, sat around him listening. He was unable, when he spoke, to keep the men around him enthralled.

Hagg Karim finished his cup of coffee. Now there was nothing left to do but say good-bye.

"Come again soon, Hagg Karim. Every time you visit the Sultan, come by and visit me."

"If I have time left to live, Habiba."

"If it were in my power, I would come to visit you every day."

"You've always been kind and thoughtful, Habiba."

Hagg Karim had told Abdel-Aziz how, when he was a little boy, he used to sit in fear on the mud bench in the Koranic school, reciting short chapters from the Koran with a chorus of other boys. They were terrified by the sheikh's stick, which would whirl about in the air and land with a whack on their little bodies, making them shout out the verses at the top of their voices. He had told him how in those days his eyes were always glued to the door of the school, waiting for his cousin Habiba to arrive. She came every day, wearing her long floral print dress and her blue shawl and carrying a little pouch with his lunch in it. After asking the sheikh's permission she would take Hagg Karim aside and give him his lunch. She always stayed long enough to talk with him for a while and quiet his fears.

She used to come every day until they married her off. He

was there the day she got married. She had hugged him to her breast in her wedding dress. He could still feel the silk on his face. She had wept and hugged him to her breast. He had slipped from her arms, choked with tears, and gone back to his village, to his father's big house, to that house teeming with children and women and animals, where he was friends with no one and where no one paid any attention to him. His mother had died the day he was born.

This visit was always the same. It was short but full of emotion. Holding on to the railing, they made their way slowly down the worn, dark steps. Habiba had this old house in Tanta, and she had fully grown children who called on her to pay their respects. Abdel-Aziz supported Hagg Karim by his arm. It was impossible to recall how many times he had run up these stairs when he was a child, or how many times he had walked them, respectfully following his father's dignified and sturdy steps.

In the light of the street Abdel-Aziz saw that his father's face was streaked with two lines of tears. The man was ashamed when he realized that his son was looking at him. He wiped away his tears with his hand. His lips trembled with what seemed to be a smile.

"Here I am crying just like a little child, Son."

As an infant Hagg Karim had been nursed by the breasts of many women. But the milk of strange women does not quench the painful thirst of a suckling child. Perhaps he was weeping for that thirst that had never been satisfied. Or perhaps he was weeping the tears he had suppressed the day of Habiba's wedding. Abdel-Aziz loved him more than he had ever loved him before.

They walked up a cool, damp side street, avoiding the pits that had been formed in front of the houses where the inhabitants threw out their dirty water. The foundations of the walls were so totally eaten away that it seemed the buildings were about to fall. But this was the way those buildings always were. They burdened every heart with the thought that they might collapse, but they never did.

Sidi Marzouq Street was empty, except for a few remaining peasants rushing to the railroad station with their baskets, their children, and their women. At the doors of the shops the merchants watched them with weariness and a certain fear. The children pursued them with insults.

"You've dirtied our town, you animals."

Omar Farhoud's huge camel was kneeling at the bottom of the stone steps.

His long, haughty nose, his big eyes, and his lips that hung loosely over his lower jaw were the embodiment of contempt and disdain. At the head of the street other camels had been loaded with other chests and were already dragging their heavy hooves toward home.

Omar Farhoud moved around the kneeling camel, arranging the gear on his back, pulling the ropes tight, and checking the straps. When he saw Hagg Karim his face beamed. Hagg Karim came up and greeted him.

"Many happy returns, Farhoud. May you come back to the next moulid in good health."

"Many happy returns to you, Uncle."

Hagg Karim climbed the stone steps slowly, leaning on his cane. In the windows of the three buildings were the women who had remained here year after year. Their pendulous breasts swayed beneath calico prints. Their laughter no longer rang as it used to, and it was no longer provocative.

"Good day, ladies."

"A good and blessed day, Brother. By the Prophet, light shines on you, Hagg Karim. Help us, O Sayyid."

The young girls had grown up. Many were married and had scattered here and there. The others were anxious and unhappy. They no longer had any place here. These apartments were no longer their homes. They wanted to escape and leave them to the wives of their brothers. The wind of departure was blowing everywhere, departure from the places one loved. The grief of separation showed on Hagg Karim's face. But it was mixed with the hope of coming back again next year.

"May God bring us back to you next year, children of God."

"A thousand returns, Hagg Karim."

A dark-skinned young girl came up the steps beating a tambourine and singing. Behind her, her aged father was blowing on a flute.

The yearly gift, O Prophet of God.
The yearly gift, like a year ago.

Hagg Karim stood for a while looking at the young girl and the old man who was her father. For years this same man had been coming on this same day to ask for the yearly gift. Hagg Karim smiled optimistically and called to the Dandy:

"Give them some of the Provisions, Dandy. Give them some. May the Lord never forsake us."

The Dandy filled the lap of his galabiya with pieces of bread and moulid biscuits and gave them to the old man. The neighborhood children began to jump up and down around the Dandy, begging him for bread and biscuits.

Hagg Karim smiled.

"Give them some, Dandy."

The Dandy distributed a few small morsels to the children's outstretched hands, but not without complaint.

"They've already had theirs. They've already had theirs several times over. Don't you think we should leave a little for the people we've been imposing on for the whole time of the moulid? 'Would you lend us your pot, please? Would you lend us your kettle? Would you lend us your kerosene burner?'"

The Dandy was wearing a cheap pair of dark glasses. He was losing his sight little by little, and none of those to whom he went for a remedy or cure could determine the cause. His eyes were growing dim. Some people said it was because of El-Gazyeh's death. From the day she died he had been as good as finished. Others said it was because of all the stolen food he had eaten. Abdel-Aziz observed the dying light in his eyes with grief.

"Load the camel, Omar. Load up, Son."

Omar Farhoud hurried into the lodgings. As Hagg Karim stood in the middle of the courtyard, leaning on his cane and holding his cloak over his shoulder, Oum Talaat came out the door with a chair and handed it to Abdel-Aziz. He gave it to his father, who looked toward Oum Talaat with an expression of thanks but did not say a word. Hagg Karim sat down on the chair and placed his cloak in his lap. Resting his hands on the crook of his cane, he sat looking straight ahead. Abdel-Aziz stood behind him. Oum Talaat was sitting on the steps in front of her house, and the women were at the windows around the courtyard. There were occasional shouts of people calling to each other and here and there the cries of children, but behind these sporadic sounds lay a powerful silence, like a solid black background with a few colored designs.

The men came out of the door of the lodgings carrying one of the two big chests. They moved with heavy feet across the courtyard and down the stone steps to the street, where they set the chest down beside the kneeling camel. Then they returned in silence to fetch the other chest. Iraqi the Deaf-Mute followed them in and out. He did not help them carry the chests, but his face was full of concern and his lips kept muttering inaudible words. His eyes were about to pop out of his head with worry.

The gear they had used in the lodgings was piled up around the camel and then loaded on and fastened with ropes. The men moved away and formed a wide circle around the great beast. Omar Farhoud released the hobbling cord and shouted at him. The men began to cry out in the name of God and the Sultan and to flatter him with words of praise. The camel did not frustrate their eager pleas. Raising his hindquarters and then his chest, he straightened up in front of them. He lifted his head haughtily and looked straight ahead. The men rubbed their hands and smiled. Omar Farhoud bid farewell to Hagg Karim and kissed him on the forehead. Tears came to Hagg Karim's eyes. Then Farhoud burst into uncontrolled weeping and raised his hands in prayer.

"O Lord, thou art the Lord and we are thy servants. Be gracious to us."

Abdel-Aziz refused to say good-bye to Farhoud in the courtyard. He went down the stone steps with him and walked beside him for a short distance.

Omar Farhoud was a good, kind-hearted man. His wife had been ill for a long time now. She would lie on a small mat on the mud bench in the central enclosure of their house, shooing the flies away from her face with a whisk made of palm leaves. Her only son had failed in his theological studies at Al-Azhar and now seemed to find nothing to do but to pester her with arguments and demands. Farhoud spent the whole day with his camel. If his camel had known how to talk, perhaps the old man would have done without human company altogether.

Abdel-Aziz climbed the steps again. The men were coming out of the lodgings. It seemed as though each man had a basket in one hand, a child in the other, and a wife following behind him. They stopped to bid farewell to Hagg Karim.

"Many happy returns, Uncle Hagg Karim. A thousand returns."

Hagg Karim looked at the faces around him and sighed:

"I'm finished, children."

A cloud of sorrow came over their faces.

"Don't talk like that. This world would be no place to live without you."

"Don't be foolish. As long as there are people in the world there will be good in it."

They paid their respects and went on down the steps. They were on their way back home. In their baskets they would be carrying some candy and perhaps a toy for a child. Their hearts were heavy as they contemplated the hostile faces on both sides of the street. In their minds was the same question as every other year. Had they been cheated in the things they had bought, or had they not? But the question would remain unanswered. There was no cure for their fears. This strange city left them dizzy.

Tomorrow at the break of day they would be back in their fields, with their feet sinking into the mud and the palms of their hands sore from gripping their short hoes. The sweat would be back on their foreheads, and the whirlwind of toil and misery would begin again. But for a few days to come they would still have the stories to tell, and the laughter. Sitting on the piles of topsoil or the mud benches in front of their houses they would relate the events of the days of the moulid. Out of these gatherings would come the seeds of longing for a new journey, seeds nourished by long days of hardship and suffering under the scorching heat of the sun, until, when the year had rolled around, the crier called them again to the moulid of the Sultan.

Rashida came and stood shattered in front of her father.

"Are you going home now, girl?"

"Many happy returns, Papa. A thousand returns. May I cook for your men a thousand years."

"You're your father's daughter, Rashida. God bless you."

He took a banknote from his pocket.

"Buy something for your children on the way. Your papa Mohammed the Dandy will go with you and your sisters to the station. Take them to the train, Dandy."

"Yes, sir."

The Dandy needed someone to take *him,* but this was their custom, and no one wanted to break it, even in the smallest detail. Rashida said good-bye to her father and kissed his hand over and over again. Abdel-Aziz knew that she would spend the entire trip home in tears.

Hagg Karim, with an altered expression on his face, followed those who were leaving for home with his eyes. Then he turned his head to the right and stared a long while before he finally realized that Mohammed Kamel was standing there with his basket and holding his little daughter by the hand. This was not the Mohammed Kamel who used to stand between the two rows of dancers with his arms and his flowing sleeves flying in the air as though he were a prophet. This was not the Mohammed Kamel who used to sit and listen to Hagg Karim's stories, his gaunt face bathed in the yellow light of the lantern. This was someone else, someone who was annoyed even at the formality of saying good-bye. He wanted to snatch the handshake and run. Hagg Karim looked at him with bafflement. This was the first time he was leaving before the brothers—before their farewell visit to the Sultan.

"Tonight we'll bid farewell to the Sultan, Mohammed Kamel."

"Pray for me there, please. It's not my lot to go."

"Why are you in such a hurry?"

"The water comes tonight, and I want to irrigate."

"Wait until tomorrow. There's something to say for every delay."

"It's the will of God."

There was nothing to be done. Hagg Karim held out his hand. Mohammed Kamel took the outstretched hand, but in the same moment his face became pale as that of a cadaver and his eyes blurred. He turned away and ran down the steps, not looking back. Without any doubt there were tears streaming down his face. Did not Hagg Karim have the right to see those tears? It was a small price for a lifetime, for the evening gatherings, the trips, and those good and pious words.

They were like two prisoners being pushed from behind as they came up to Hagg Karim. Their son, Shahhat, followed them. Sherkasi the Carpenter had grown extremely frail in his old age, and there was a gloomy, disheartened look on his olive face. He leaned on a cane. His wife was a huge, tall, frowning woman. Shahhat had the face of a madman. His left eyebrow sagged heavily over his eye and kept it shut, his lower jaw was enormous and protruded abnormally, his lips were thin and tightly closed, and his skin was covered with unpigmented splotches. Abdel-Aziz thought of the things that were said about the Sherkasis. This young man was the focal point in which all the residue of the family's madness had collected. He spoke to him:

"Why in such a hurry, Shahhat?"

"Just am."

"So you go. Let them stay."

"No!"

Only now did he turn and face Abdel-Aziz. He had his hands clasped behind his back so that the huge muscles between his shoulders were squeezed together, forming what looked like a hump.

Without saying a word, Hagg Karim extended his hand to them as they left. His face was dark. He got up to go into the lodgings. Abdel-Aziz supported him by his armpit. He sensed that his father was having difficulty breathing. A poisoned claw gripped Abdel-Aziz's heart. How long was it now that his father had been ill? But he would not consult a physician. He would only ask the brothers and traditional healers.

"Go and see a doctor, Papa."

"Don't worry yourself, Son. It's nothing."

The apartment was empty. Two big squares of filth outlined the spots where the chests had been. The chests had been the center of activity, with flat loaves of bread and handfuls of moulid biscuits being distributed from them almost without interruption.

The walls of the entrance hall were dirty and confining. Abdel-Aziz helped his father along in the silence. The only sound was the fall of their feet on the tiled floor. It was as though they were walking in an absolute void. They met Ahmed Bedawi going out, followed by his wife. He had been especially kind and gentle toward her recently, after their son had gone off to Cairo. He was going to take her himself to the railway station. His face was expressionless. He passed Hagg Karim without a word. Abdel-Aziz's father gave him a nod of his head, and the man was gone.

Next to the wall sat Ali Khalil. His eyes were the crystallization of sorrow, and his face had the pallor of death. All his life he had had to struggle against illness. Something seemed to be growing inside him in an unending effort to destroy him. Perhaps there was an intuitive perception behind the cry of the chorus of dervishes at the end of every gathering: "O God, spare us harm when and where it pleases thee, for thou hast power to execute thy will." Perhaps they had an intuitive perception of those tiny, microscopic beings that were part of their life and that devoured their bodies. They would work all kinds of spells to hold on to their lives, but there was no escape from the inevitable.

"Why are you sitting alone, Ali?"

Ali Khalil stood up, supporting himself against the wall. He and Hagg Karim walked together into the sheikh's room and sat down next to him on the mattress. Abdel-Aziz followed them and seated himself nearby.

Hagg Karim had spent his whole life amidst these men, amidst the rustling of their coarse galabiyas. Now they were sitting here sad and despondent. Mistikawi was coughing so loud he almost spit out his soul.

"Ah, the pain. Have mercy, O Lord. Take me to thy side."

Abbas gave no opinions on sacred law or matters of faith. Instead he pulled a variety of small bottles from his pockets and stared at them for a while. Then he took from them a few little tablets and capsules and swallowed them. The charm writer was as still and as pale as a statue. The coffeemaker pulled a big checkered handkerchief out of his pocket and wiped the tears from his eyes.

"Praise God, we have spent our days on the threshold of the saints."

The sheikh's hair had turned almost completely white. He sat on his mattress daydreaming. The sound of the prayer beads running through his hand deepened the silence.

They heard Saddiqa's deranged voice.

"It is not in our hands. What can we do? What can we do?"

The silence was total. They looked at each other without speaking. The charm writer took out his pen and a little piece of paper and wrote a charm. He handed it to the sheikh, who blessed it and gave it to Hagg Karim. Perhaps this was the first time in his life the man had ever written out a charm free of charge. Ali Khalil, who was hardly able to stand up, took the charm from Hagg Karim and went over to Saddiqa. He took her by the wrist and led her out. Most likely he would take her to circumambulate the tomb of the Sultan and then go with her to the train station to see her off. They sat quietly. Hassan Effendi could not restrain his tears.

When Ahmed Bedawi and Ali Khalil came back, the group was complete again. The old friends sat together for a while quietly. Finally Hagg Karim looked up with his longing brown eyes and spoke to the sheikh.

"The time has come, Uncle. You must bid farewell to the Sultan."

"Yes indeed, Hagg Karim. God willing."

The sheikh stood up and straightened out his galabiya. He took his green turban from the window and placed it firmly on his head. Then he walked slowly from the room, crossed the hall, and went out the door. Hagg Karim and the other brothers followed. In the courtyard in front of the building they all stopped for a moment and exchanged silent glances. Then the sheikh started down the stone steps, with the others close behind him.

Abdel-Aziz still did not know why this hour of the day burdened his heart with sorrow, this hour when the sun grew pale and covered everything with a thin film of gold. The broken shadows of the men on the rough pavement reminded him of the shadows of the palm trees before the porch of the guesthouse just before sunset. He remembered the day he had seen the men return, bringing her from Tanta. Everyone knew but her. Everyone knew that today Samira was going to be married to a young peasant. In the evening she had screamed like a caged lioness at the women who were with her in the room, refusing to authorize any representative to marry her to the man they had chosen. That day he had looked at her for a long time before he spoke.

"Name someone, Samira. Name someone. Don't make trouble for the men. Don't cause a scandal."

He had not known what he was saying. He had been feeble and indifferent. She had looked at him through her tears.

"All right. I name my mother's brother."

After that she had never cried again. But he had come to realize since that she would have been able to say no for the rest of her life—for him.

The shadows of the men on the pavement were long and broken, as though they were walking in a funeral procession. Ahmed Bedawi came over to him gingerly.

"Where's your gazelle wandering off to, Master Abduh?"

He did not answer.

"Tell me, Master Abduh, when we die will you remember to recite the Opening for us?"

"Every day."

"May God be pleased with you."

The earth had stored up the heat of the day and was releasing it now in foul-smelling breaths that bore the stench of filth, still wet from the water that had been sprinkled in front of the shops. The merchants were sitting around lazily or shouting back and forth to each other across the street. The waiter at the coffeehouse called out an occasional order. From a window a woman would yell down to a peddler, or hang out clothes to dry, or reach into a basket she had hanging there to pull out some onions for the evening meal. Occasionally a girl would appear in one of the windows and let her eyes wander without settling on anything in particular. The fronts of the old buildings seemed almost lifeless.

Was Mohammed Kamel happy now, or was he miserable? His legs were sinking into the mud and his palms were sore from gripping his short hoe. He was alone, separated from the brothers. The warm space on top of the mud heating oven was clamoring with children after so many years of silence. But his wife's eyes were empty of affection and love. She was concerned with her housekeeping. Did he remember Saddiqa? Did he long for the delights of the Path, for which he no longer had time? How could a mixture of blood, flesh and bones, and a variety of fluids, a man, bring on himself all this confusion and pain? Do we act out of complete knowledge or complete ignorance? Or do we have to struggle all our lives to learn even the most trivial lessons?

The group turned down Bathhouse Lane, a long, dark, covered passage occupied by tambourine makers. On both sides were piles of scraps of leather and wood, the materials from which they made the tambourines that created life in the evening gatherings. The workers were taking their time, talking and laughing a little.

From the lane a narrow alley turned off and led to the entrance of the bathhouse. The facade was covered with ornamentation in the medieval style, and the door was a great mass of wood decorated with the thick heads of huge nails. Abdel-Aziz was fascinated by this facade and by the great wooden door—by the stories of barren women who came to the bath in search of fertility, of impotent men with "ailing backs," and of the divine power of the steaming hot water.

Across from the western door of Sayyid Bedawi's mosque was a marvelous structure of marble. It was said to have contained the waterwheel that supplied the mosque with water. In it, oxen given as votive offerings had trodden in a circle, day and night, turning the wheel. The mosque, the waterwheel house, and the bath—what had been their surroundings in times past? What had the people been like? How had they talked? How had they bought and sold? Perhaps this group of men he was with had more in common with medieval times than they did with the present, when so many offensive buildings had crowded the square and destroyed its original beauty.

The narrow alley opened into the great square. Before them was the mosque with the lights hung around it. They had begun to shine in the evening twilight.

Hagg Karim's gaze seemed to soar with longing like a wild brown dove. The group broke into words of admiration, salutation, and prayer. Abdel-Aziz felt confused, uneasy, and alone. He was there with them, but nothing moved his heart. It was cold. The fire in it had been quenched. He looked about him with shame.

When the Dandy realized that they had come to the shrine, he wailed:

"O Sayyid, my whole life I have lit the lights at your evening gatherings. Give me back the light of my eyes, Abu Farrag!"

The square was quiet and almost empty. The huge mosque, with the electric lights strung around its sides, had something truly powerful and majestic about it, something in the solidity of the walls and the scintillating reflection of the lights on the huge brass windows.

As they moved slowly across the square, Iraqi could not take his eyes off the shrine. Overwhelmed by the sight, he muttered broken bits of words that bore no meaning. It was as though some unearthly spirit had inhabited him. His body was shaking with an extraordinary violence, with an uncontrollable desire to be united with that huge electrified building. Even before men had learned to speak, this kind of desire must have been present in them, and it must have been such desires that led them to spread cities across the face of the earth.

Abdel-Aziz had been a small child when, for the first time in his life, he saw a man step on the carpets of the mosque with his shoes on. He had been seized with dread and had asked his father about what the man was doing. His father had informed him that as long as one's shoes were clean there was nothing wrong with walking in them on the mosque carpets. At that time this answer had quieted him. But the question remained. There were people who walked on the carpets of the mosque with their shoes on. The clear crystal of which Abdel-Aziz's world was made had developed a slight crack. As he grew up and his eyes became sharper he began to see more pretexts and more excuses. They troubled his peace of mind, aroused doubts, and caused him pain. He came to loathe walking barefoot on the floor of the Sultan's mosque, which had been soiled by the feet of tens of thousands of peasants. But he clung to his love for these people. They were always there, looking at everything with simplicity and love.

He took off his shoes and carried them in his hands. He

walked behind the men in silence, lifting one foot and then the other from that filthy, sticky floor. Perhaps the secret of great halls, with their columns and soaring ceilings, was that they turned mutterings, quarrels, prayers, chants and recitations, calls, shouts, and cries, all these chaotic sounds, into something else, blending them and giving them echoes and reverberations in space, making of them one mighty, awe-inspiring voice. The vast halls of Sayyid Bedawi's mosque were the first thing that seized the heart after one came out of the little entrance passage lined with shoe wardens and their partitioned shelves. The group walked together. Abdel-Aziz knew the emotion that was shaking these men in the very depths of their hearts. How many times he had been overwhelmed by the mighty echoes he had heard inside great mosques. Something in the back of his mind smiled sadly, bidding farewell to the joys of childhood, to the profoundest joys he would ever know.

Those old men who stood on both sides with their wooden scourges, the attendants of the mosque, the guardians of the great halls, knew very well what they were guarding. They hit people, if only lightly, with those scourges. They were after their hearts. They wanted complete submission, and they allowed no false or wandering glances, no looks in which there was any trace of boldness.

"Be thinking of God, man. Don't be neglectful."

They distressed Abdel-Aziz. They were sticky and disgusting. Too much food and too little sun had given them a sickly, nauseating corpulence. They seemed anxious to him. In their eyes he saw avarice, and perhaps even a deep aversion for these people who were pouring into the shrine. The priests had their price—the piastres that were thrust into their palms and then quickly slipped into their pockets.

But the men were not disturbed by such matters. They were not concerned with the things that were troubling Abdel-Aziz. They were going into the immense halls of the mosque. These men who had lived for thousands of years in mud huts were filled with yearning for the splendor and beauty of these immense halls.

With this longing and devotion, with these rough hands, domes, columns, and great halls had been erected, and temples had been hewn out of solid rock. Coolness and shade had been created in the heat of the desert. The men stood still for a while, their hearts purring with prayer and praise. They exchanged glances and smiles of joy.

"Praise be to God! How beautiful!"

Ahmed Bedawi was carried away with childish joy.

"El-Khawarnaq Palace had one hundred and thirty floors, each one made of columns of marble."

They looked at him in silence. His face was beaming with happiness like a young boy's. Abbas did not want to miss the opportunity.

"Mosques are God's paradise on earth."

Mistikawi hastened to question him.

"Is that a saying of the Prophet or a verse from the Koran, Abbas?"

The sheikh and Hagg Karim moved on, drawing the other men behind them.

The two leaves of the door had been swung wide open. Inside loomed the great structure of thick brass latticework that surrounded the tomb. The polished metal scintillated in the light of the huge chandeliers with their hundreds of dazzling eyes. The men stood humbly in the opening of the door for a moment. Then they entered and moved counterclockwise around the tomb, holding on to the brass grill and rubbing their faces against it as they murmured prayers of abject supplication. Abdel-Aziz had been here on the Big Night. The crowds of peasants had almost pulled the brass structure from its foundation. Now there were only a few broken, shadowy figures moving around it, as it stood there lofty, powerful, and glittering in the light.

Ahmed Bedawi went over to the corner where there was a rock with the imprint of two enormous feet. The Prophet had stood on it barefoot and the rock had yielded and received the imprint of his feet to honor him. Images of the strange, rough feet of the Wanderers burst into Abdel-Aziz's mind, those feet that were a living challenge to distance and a mockery of hardship and suffering. Did the road yield to them? Were stones crushed under their steps? Ahmed Bedawi was searching for his own world in the things he saw around him, that world he had created for himself out of the books with the yellow pages. Every time he found something from it he was carried away with joy. He kissed the rock and looked toward Abdel-Aziz. He did not know what was in Abdel-Aziz's head. But something in him perplexed him and drew him toward him.

They sat down along the wall. Sunset was near and they wanted to pray in the mausoleum. The resplendence of the brass enclosure completely subdued all those present. They sat in a row against the wall, unable to take their eyes off it. Each one, in a whispering voice, was reciting words of prayer and praise. If Mohammed Kamel had been there, would he have been able to gather their intentions into a single will, one they could proclaim aloud before the tomb? Would he have proposed the Opening for the relentless disease that ravaged Ali Khalil and showed its effects in the glaze in his eyes, those eyes that clung so desperately to life? Would he have proposed the Opening for the Dandy's fading sight, or the illness of Hagg Karim? Or would he have sat against the wall murmuring his prayers to himself?

They formed in rows behind the imam to perform the evening prayer beneath the great dome. When the man next to Abdel-Aziz reached over to shake his hand at the end of the prayer, the youth's mind was wandering. He was embarrassed by his distraction, but he took the man's hand in silence. They left the tomb. But Hagg Karim's spirit remained there. His eyes were wet with tears.

There were only a few of them. They moved feebly across the floor of the mosque, carrying their shoes in their hands and looking about them. Hagg Karim's eyes were once again gazing intently at the things around him. It was a look that village healers recognized in the eyes of a man about to die. Abdel-Aziz felt a sudden anguish.

They entered a narrow, dark passageway and knocked on a door. The door was opened by a small, beardless youth whose eyes were full of graciousness and courtesy. The spacious room inside was spread with mats. At the head of the room was an enormous couch. On it sat a bareheaded old man. His hair and beard were so long that he seemed to be one of the Men of the Cave. The single galabiya he was wearing was tattered and dirty. As soon as he saw his guests, he stood up to welcome them.

"Welcome, noble visitors!"

He insisted on kissing the hand of the sheikh.

"The flesh of the Messenger of God! The flesh of the Sultan!"

Every time the name of the Sultan was mentioned, he would jerk and double over as if a stick had come out of the wall from the direction of the tomb and jabbed him in the ribs. He had been a master in the Institute of Secondary Religious Education in Tanta. Then love for the Sultan had possessed him, and had distracted him from his work and household. He had ended up here, living the rest of his life as a recluse. He was given a small pension from the endowments of the Sayyid, and he was served in his seclusion by this gracious, still beardless youth.

He had an unpolished roughness about him and a captivating lack of reserve. Abdel-Aziz listened with fascination to every word he said. He was a character out of legend who had burst forth from the yellow-paged books. He spoke with clarity and eloquence and the power of a prophet. He heaped upon their hearts mounds of his own singular knowledge, and he dazzled their minds with his profound thoughts, his embellished phrases, his feeling, and his serenity. Ahmed Bedawi could barely control his rapture. But Abdel-Aziz, little by little, lost interest in what the man was saying and began to watch his jerk. He would wait for it, laughing to himself when it came. Had it not been for the men he would have howled. But how could he, when they were sitting around the man, stunned and wide-eyed with awe?

They went out into the square again. It was wide and spacious, with only a few people passing by. The coffeehouses around the square were filled with light, but their customers were few. The men walked on quietly, looking. What had they done to New Street? They had torn it down and built in its place a wide avenue. They had ravished its former charm. The image of the two rows of old shops, with the roofing of awnings stretched between them, was still in his mind. The darkness and closeness of the street had given it intimacy. But they had torn all that down. Now it was exposed to the sun, and on the side that had been demolished there was a row of small, contemptible buildings.

They used to walk from the railway station to the shrine up a covered street filled with a fragrance that refined the soul. Now when they looked about, they saw a naked open space. They were strangers to this street. There were new merchants, and some of the old ones in new shops to which they were not yet accustomed. They seemed to be arranging their wares in bewilderment.

When would people grow used to this street and love it? And who would those people be? Not these men in any case, not this band of men who felt like newcomers to the street. Their eyes looked everywhere for something familiar, for some joy they had known in the past.

They were going to visit the Sayyid's staff. They followed the road down and passed through the tunnel under Seigar Bridge. At the height of the moulid this tunnel had reverberated with the falling of countless thousands of feet, the whistling of the boys, and the shouts of the policemen and the vendors. But now the tunnel was dark, and only a few people were going through. There were occasional beggars, mechanically reciting verses of the Koran over and over again. As the men walked, the sound of their footsteps echoed sadly off the walls.

The tunnel opened into the wide expanse where the fair that accompanied the moulid had been held. A frightening operation of demolition was taking place. Men were hopping about like monkeys on the remains of the structures that had towered over their heads the night before. They were gathering up the strands of electric light bulbs, the strings of banners and flags, and the signs with the catchy phrases and the strange pictures. All this was being taken down now and stacked on the ground. Sections of tents lay beside panels of dismantled kiosks. The games, rides, and shows were being disconnected at the joints and their severed members piled one on top of the other. The men, the dancing girls, and the clowns, who the night before had played on stage in bright costumes of all different colors, were wearing any old thing now and were working like ordinary laborers. They were dispirited, tense, and coarse. They would fly into fits of rage and curse in the foulest language. The few eyes that watched them with curiosity and amazement obviously annoyed them.

"The market has been held, and now it's over. What did you expect? It's just like life."

They called this street the Street of Sights. Hundreds of thousands of people had walked this way to look at all the things to see, while the loudspeakers blared at them from the tall structures set up on both sides. Where were they now to witness this total destruction? By now they were in their villages, sitting in the moonlight on the mud benches in front of their houses or on the piles of topsoil, and talking about the events of the moulid. Suddenly and all at once they had returned, leaving the moulid at its height. They had not waited to see this destruction. Perhaps they had wanted the image of the high point of the moulid, with all its excitement, to remain in their minds, so they could go on talking about it throughout the year. In the main street of the village they would meet those who had not gone. The eyes of the unlucky ones would be full of curiosity and eagerness to know what had happened. But in the eyes of those who had gone would be the joy of having seen for themselves. On the dusty earth of the lanes would be scattered colored candy wrappers and roasted chickpea skins. Some of the children would be carrying little flutes or rattles in their hands. The others would be watching them forlornly.

The street had become a wilderness of darkness. Here and

there they could see a dim lantern. The roof of stars twinkled brightly above. Abdel-Aziz breathed the light breezes of the wide moulid grounds. But he sensed that they had the force of a storm. They were going to the Staff.

Perhaps these staffs had their origin in the remote past, in the spear of a military leader fixed before his tent, or a pole bearing his banner in the midst of his camp. Today it was sheikhs who had staffs, and each sheikh had his own staff, a long wooden pole fixed in the center of the grounds where his moulid was held. These staffs varied in size and were larger or smaller according to the rank of the sheikh among God's saints.

What kind of staff did the Sultan have then? A giant column of wood fixed in a cement base and rising toward the sky. It was surrounded by a wide circle of people, some sitting and others walking around it in continuous, uninterrupted movement.

There were a few pale mantle lanterns on the carts of sleepy vendors. Then a band of Wanderers, men with no fixed abode, appeared around the Staff dancing a strange dance. Their long sticks flew in the air and their cries rent the night sky. There was a confusion of songs and shouts, joy, anger, and excitement, tears and pain. The Staff was the focal point of the moulid of the Sultan and the visible token of his being.

The group of men stood quietly, murmuring prayers and raising their hands and eyes toward the sky and the towering Staff. Here in the heart of the night, removed from the world, stood this great column, surrounded by a few scattered lanterns and these strange dances and songs. Suddenly the man with the chains around his body burst into the midst of them. He had a frightening, unearthly appearance, and his face was furrowed with age. But his eyes in the night and the scattered lights took on a compelling gleam. Sweat poured in streams down his face, and the chains rattled beneath his ragged clothing. The odor of his sweat penetrated the nostrils. He gazed intently in their faces and then broke into a wild dance on one foot, whirling his heavy iron staff in the air and crying out:

The mountains came to the Guide
and bowed to him.
A warning cried in the wilderness,
crossing the steppe and sea.
The lover slaughtered the heart of the beloved
with the tear in his eye.

At the end of every phrase a huge chorus of Wanderers shouted with a single voice:

"Hayy! God lives!"

Then the man wrapped in chains broke into uncontrolled weeping.

"Ah, Sultan, my beloved."

7

The Path

From the train station to the house, the way was engraved in his heart. How many times he had taken this way with his father's men, surrounded by the rustling of their freshly laundered clothes, their laughter, and their faces beaming with joy, and how many times he had taken it in solitude and silence.

When Abdel-Aziz stepped down from the train onto the station platform he was seized with anxiety. He turned around to watch the train pull slowly away. Squares of light were drawn across the gravel as the train moved off. The carriages closed in the light and the conversation or silence of the passengers. As the train rolled into the distance and the noise faded away, grief settled heavily over Abdel-Aziz's thoughts. He started off into the darkness.

The land around him was a maze of shadow, spotted in the distance with dots of yellow light. Here and there a flame danced on the wick of a lamp. The heavy darkness seemed to breathe as though it were alive. From time to time he heard the scraping of weary sandals, the sated snorts of animals returning from the fields, the croaking of an abandoned male frog, or the song of a sorrowful cricket.

The night did not intimidate him. He looked straight ahead with eyes that saw nothing, and walked. The road knew his footsteps. It smoothed his path and kept the stones from his way. Whenever the road led up a slight mound or headed down some shallow depression, he could see it in his mind's eye. He followed the road where it led, trusting his complete familiarity with it. But his heart was heavy.

The road stretched out before him, becoming smoother and wider. His feet moved rapidly, almost running. Along the side of the road the yellow dots following their slow path through the darkness increased in number, and the frames of the huts and the crowns of the palms and the other trees seemed even darker in the blackness of the night. The sister village, the twin of their own, lay silent in the gloom, giving off a warm, fetid odor that mixed with the cool night breeze.

There were not many of them, and even at this hour everyone knew or would somehow recognize everyone else. When a figure approached and his outline began to take shape against the night, you knew who he was, and he knew you.

"Peace be upon you."

"And upon you be peace and the mercy of God."

In the brief moment of silence between the two greetings the whole story would be told, and their hearts would be filled with sorrow. There was a lump in Abdel-Aziz's throat. He was hardly able to draw air into his lungs. Tears welled in his eyes. He went hurriedly on, as though he were fleeing from something. The pity and the sucking of lips followed behind him and struck his heart like a poisoned dart. He noticed the stars for the first time since leaving the train, shimmering white dots floating in a sea of soft, transparent light. How beautiful they were. The tears ran in hot streams over his cheeks. He did not wipe them away. He let them flow down over his heart to console it. Nothing was more compassionate than tears.

The Great Bear trailed its tail over the house, and the North Star was clear and bright. Hagg Karim was dead. He listened, but he heard only the monotonous breathing of the voiceless night. Had they not brought a loudspeaker and a Koran reciter? His seven uncles? And the men? The brothers and his friends—his companions of a lifetime? What had happened, then?

The man had rung his doorbell in the forenoon and come in quietly. He was wearing a wrinkled suit and a dirty shirt without a necktie. His vest was of the peasant type, and he had a peasant's woolen cap on his head. His face was veiled with mourning. Between his lower lip and his teeth was a gap filled with chewing tobacco.

"Go back to the village."

"Why?"

His eyebrows were thick and stuck out like an ape's, and his eyes were big and round. Abdel-Aziz knew him well. He was good-hearted to the point of stupidity. He would certainly tell him what had happened.

"Why?"

"It's nothing."

"Is my father dead?"

"No. He's not feeling well. That's all."

But Abdel-Aziz did not believe him. He lost no time. He almost ran. What could it be, Lord?

The road ahead of him passed between two rows of mud houses that seemed like the arms of a blind, aging mother. He threw himself into the blackness. The doors were open as they always were. Inside these low structures the flaming wicks of lanterns gave off a pale light. Through the entrances of the compounds the extinguished ovens seemed like collapsed, breathless lungs. Sleeping children were crowded on the mud benches. Near the roofs, just under the covering of cornstalks, gleamed the wary eyes of pigeons resting in their nests in the walls. Groups of women sat at the doors.

"Good evening."

"Good evening, Brother."

They recognized him in the darkness.

"Sweetheart, . . . Child, . . . My soul, . . . Be brave. . . . God make you a worthy son."

That unceasing sucking of lips! He ran like a pursued animal, plunging down the road. What had happened?

Suddenly there was a figure standing before him in the darkness. The man offered him a strong, rough hand. His face was solemn and his eyes were full of compassion.

"You're here. Thank God for your safe arrival. Who told you?"

"Selim."

"The Lord is gracious, Master Abduh."

"Praise be to God."

The words came to an end, and he ran on. From a distance he could make her out standing in front of the door of her house. Before he turned in her direction he head her voice coming through the darkness toward him.

"Abdel-Aziz! My brother!"

He hugged her. Her head came up to his chin. He wanted to absorb her frail body in his as he pressed himself to her compassionate bosom like a frightened child.

"Is your father dead? What's happened to him, Rashida?"

"It's nothing. It's nothing, child. There's nothing wrong with your father. He's fine, Brother, fine. Don't people get ill?"

But she could not control her tears and her body shook with sobbing. Abdel-Aziz wept with her, and they held each other again. In the darkness around them he heard sucking of lips, sighs of lamentation, and muffled words of condolence.

Abdel-Aziz broke away from his sister's arms and continued running.

"Take it easy, Abdel-Aziz. Don't hurt yourself. I'll come right away."

Inside the dimly lit houses he saw the women and the men. He heard the sucking of their lips and the expressions of their sympathy. He moved on through this maze of loving hearts, unable to hold back his tears. Omar Farhoud held out his hand.

"Praise God a thousand times for your safe arrival, Master Abduh. Praise God a thousand times."

Omar Farhoud's voice was broken, and his frame was stooped and twisted beneath his dark galabiya. He went back into his house, and Abdel-Aziz ran on. Ali Khalil's shop was closed. The big fifteen-candlepower lamp hanging from the ceiling was surely as cold as a corpse hanging from the gallows. Ali

Khalil was dead. Death lurked in the dark corners, peering with blind, lifeless eyes at Abdel-Aziz.

He could see the house now, the big outside door, the shadowy figures going in and coming out, and the square of light in the window—Hagg Karim's window. He pushed open the door and went in.

The eyes of his sisters, pale in the shadows and the dim light, watched him from the corners of the house. He went straight to the room. It was crowded with men, but they opened a path for him. Hagg Karim had been laid out on the big brass bed and his body had been carefully covered with a quilt. Nothing was revealed but his face. He lay still. His eyes were closed and he was silent but for the troubled sound of his breathing. Abdel-Aziz threw himself on his father's body and wept with his whole being, sobbing and wailing like a woman.

"Papa! Papa!"

A strong hand gripped his arm. The men pulled him away and he looked around, choking on his tears. In the shadows a dense circle of pale eyes and rigid faces surrounded him. Foreheads, cheekbones, and tips of noses glowed ominously in the lantern's faint light.

The brothers in the Path, his lifetime companions. Under their eyes the sun of Hagg Karim's days had risen and set. He had laughed with them and wept with them. Now they stood around him in his affliction. Abdel-Aziz wept with grief.

"There's no need to cry. The women have already done enough of that."

Someone had reproached him by mentioning the wailing of the women. Where had the voice come from? There was no way to tell. It seemed to be the spirit of their collective grief speaking for them.

"That's not why we sent for you. We sent for you to see to your affairs."

Here he was, seeing to his affairs. What affairs? Whenever he was able to isolate himself from his teeming worries he recalled that night, when the train had pulled away leaving him alone on the station platform, when he had made his way through the darkness to this house where everything had fallen apart. His heart was oppressed with the darkness of that night, with the faintly flaming lamp wicks moving slowly along their paths, the women sitting by the doors of their houses, and the men appearing out of the shadows to grip his hand firmly and offer him their sympathy.

He thought of Rashida. Her husband was now a stooped, feeble giant, nearly totally debilitated and constantly coughing. He sat all day long on the mud bench in front of their house, smoking and sucking on hard candies, never saying a word. All day long she would swear at him, cursing him for wasting money, and trying to get him to move and do something. But he just sat there, stiff and motionless, with an imbecilic smile on his face. All day long she worked in the compound in her tattered clothes, wearing on her head a dirty, worn-out kerchief that cramped her white, curly hair. She worked all day, carrying out the buffalo dung and spreading fresh topsoil under her feet, feeding their scrawny donkey, feeding all the hungry mouths, baking bread, cooking their humble meals, leading the animals out to water, and taking care of her eldest son Karim, a tall, thin boy whose bowels were infested with worms. Fear and compassion were always in her eyes when she looked at him. All day long, like a cow pulling a waterwheel round and round, she worked at the household chores. In the evening she would go to her father's big house and sit down with Abdel-Aziz.

"How are you today, my love? We're counting on you. Everything depends on you."

When she went back to her house she slept on the top of the heating oven with no mat, wrapping herself in a coarse woolen blanket. Perhaps she dreamed dreams of the past, shattered dreams of the days in Tanta, the moulid, the baking, and the evenings of joy.

Abdel-Aziz smiled bitterly. That night she had held him and said to him:

"Your father's fine, my brother."

Behind those words lay the tragedy that Abdel-Aziz was now living through in all its details. Rashida and he had laughed together so often in the past. Now it seemed the tears would never cease.

That night he had come running, and this is what he had found in the house. He was not going to run away. It was a yoke he had to wear, like their old black buffalo. He felt broken like Farhoud, but he would bear his burden quietly.

That night Farhoud had greeted him and then turned back into his house. But what kind of a house was it now? His wife was dead. Death was inevitable, and it robbed men's hearts of the things they loved most. It had taken from Farhoud the slight, fair-skinned woman with the clean hands and the narrow eyes, the woman who was always smiling and showing that row of small white teeth. When Abdel-Aziz had been little, he used to go and visit them in their house. She would smile at Omar Farhoud with affection.

"When the morning comes, load the moulid chests and trust in God, Omar. After your dawn prayer."

Omar Farhoud would nod his head in assent.

"God willing."

Abdel-Aziz had stood at the edge of their affection and watched. He was little, but he could sense the love between their two hearts.

Their son had grown up. He had failed in his studies and quit school. Fat now, with pallid white skin and a big gold tooth, he was rash and cruel. And he had married a girl who was fat with cruel eyes and enormous buttocks. Her footsteps shook the ground beneath her when she walked. This son terrorized the whole house, his father included, with his incessant yelling and screaming.

Poor Omar Farhoud would sit off in a corner of their compound, feeding his kneeling camel. He had nothing left but this camel. He would twist the animal's halter around his arm and walk behind him. The camel was a good-natured giant with a haughty, towering head. Farhoud, feeble and broken in body and spirit, would follow the fall of his hooves with hollow eyes.

A world was collapsing. Like an old building, its bricks were falling one by one. Dust had covered the spot that had always been so clean and tidy in front of Ali Khalil's shop. The wind had swept a pile of straw and filth into the place where the men used to sit together on the bench. Now there were other men who sat together in other places. The door of the shop was closed, like the eye of a dead man. Ali Khalil was gone.

They had said he was in his house vomiting blood, in that same room on the roof, that immaculate room with the small square down below and the narrow mud steps leading up to it. Trays covered with bowls of food for the dervishes used to be brought up from the hearth to that room. It would be so crowded with men and with joy that it would almost cave in. Up there he had sat twisting and bending over, spitting out blood all around him, while the men stayed with him, watching. They had told Hagg Karim he was in his house spitting blood. The cab had taken him to Tanta and brought him back, and it had brought the doctor from Tanta and taken him back. The men had wandered, pale with grief, into the guesthouse. Ali Khalil was vomiting blood. Hagg Karim had gazed intently at the great lantern hanging from the ceiling and said nothing.

Abdel-Aziz should have realized it then. Something had begun, and nothing could stand in its way. But he had failed to understand. He had gone off to study at the university in Alexandria, to argue and to laugh with the other students. From time to time he had published a sad poem in the handwritten student newspaper posted on the walls, or sent a letter to his father asking for money. Why had he failed to understand? Why had he not remained with them? Something had been needed—a cry, or a word, or a tear. But he had delayed, and a little man with long dangling arms had come and sat down quietly and said:

"Go back to the village."

Then everything had begun. He had refused to accept it, but it had happened. He had lunged into the darkness, where he saw only shadowy figures and spots of yellow light moving slowly along, making the blackness of the night seem even darker.

He was still living in the darkness of that night. The facts were dim and intangible. He had taken so many blows he could barely see.

The men were sitting around him in the central enclosure. They were all silent. From the mud shelf on the wall a lamp cast more shadow than light. In the background his mother and his sisters were moving around in obscure orbits. Vague utterances brushed against the fringes of his consciousness. The truth crept into his brain, framed with mourning and ambiguity.

Hagg Karim had been carried from the station in the men's arms. The little box of ambergris had been stolen from his pocket. All that way from the station to the house he had been carried along exposed to everyone's eyes. A shameless hand had made its way beneath his great cashmere galabiya and his striped satin vest to find out what he had with him.

Ahmed Bedawi sat cross-legged without a mat, scratching the earth in front of him with a little stick.

"I was with him."

They had gone to the district capital, to the agricultural credit bank, to borrow a sum of money against the harvest. There was no land left. His brothers had offered their own deeds and their entitlements to plant as security. The youthful employee had screamed at him, and Hagg Karim had stood humbly before him, listening to his curses and insults. Ahmed Bedawi had broken in.

"I said to him, 'Effendi, it's shameful and indecent, what you're doing. He's an old man, and he's well known and respected.'"

But the effendi had screamed at him again.

"Get out of here!"

And Hagg Karim had fallen to the floor.

Perhaps this is what had happened, or perhaps it was something else. His mind no longer sought to discover the details. He had ignored the facts when they began to take shape. What should he seek to discover now? He should have understood from the beginning that Hagg Karim's world had begun to crumble. He should have understood when he saw him sitting for long hours on the guesthouse porch, while people passed in the darkness of the late evening, murmuring their greetings and moving on. He should have understood when he saw him sitting alone for hours without speaking—the man whose special gift was conversation, fellowship, and love. Abdel-Aziz should have understood it at the time. But he had ignored what was happening. So what should he seek to discover now, when everything had lost its importance?

The men would gather next to the houses, on the piles of topsoil or on the mud benches, sometimes in the cool of the late afternoon, sometimes in the freshness of the forenoon, and sometimes in the soft light of the moon.

"Your father sold practically everything before he fell ill. The Lord help you."

They had brought him a doctor who had prescribed a great many drugs for him and said he should eat nothing but pullets and boiled vegetables. But there was nothing in the house now. They ate bread with cheese, while he ate bread dipped in sugar. It was all they had.

That night his mother had taken him to the storeroom.

"We have everything, Son."

She was as fat as she had always been, and her short, sturdy body was still active. Her constantly searching eyes never looked up. She went about her housework without ever tiring, carrying things, sweeping, washing, making dough, or baking. She never said no to any request. Her answer was always the same.

"Surely, right away."

He looked around in the storeroom. The containers were empty except for a few sparse remnants of what they had once held. She had hoped to deceive him. But he knew.

"We have everything, Son."

"Good."

The men would sit down with him on the mud benches or the topsoil piles next to the houses.

"Sell the few yards of land you have left. They're of no use to you. They're too narrow to be planted. The two feddans of the religious endowment will have to do now."

There were creditors of every breed—wandering peddlers, shopkeepers, and peasants whose word was past doubt. Abdel-Aziz knew they were not lying. No one would ever lie about Hagg Karim. Every day he paid off another debt, but the canal was drying up faster than he knew as he racked his brains trying to keep the big house running.

But why give himself over to his cares? This was a new day and a new confrontation with them. Abdel-Aziz moved slowly as he went down the stairs to the central enclosure. He was in no hurry to take on the hardships of the day. Why had he not been created in the image of his mother?

She never thought. She had been the same all her life, grim, dogged, and determined. The moment she got out of bed she would find something next to her to do. She would keep on working all day long until the activity around her subsided and allowed her to return to sleep. Did she really never think? Was she never assailed by worries and cares that caused her to lie awake most of the night?

Abdel-Aziz went down the stairs slowly. The house seemed like something new, although it was the same house he knew so well and awoke to every morning. His mother and his sisters were darting about like red hornets. In the girls' faces there was fatigue, despair, and anger. They were bitter and afraid. His father was sitting on the mud bench. One of his shoulders was somewhat leaner than the other and drooped more. His face seemed to be covered with dust. Perhaps it was the dust from the road. He walked every day to the railway station and back. But no amount of washing could take that dusty color from his face. His hands were clasped one over the other in his lap and his cane lay by his side. He was no longer able to do without his cane. The first stroke had left him half paralyzed, and it had left that dazed look in his eyes, those brown eyes that still shone with unquenched longing. He turned his head like a hunted bird. When he saw Abdel-Aziz he shouted:

"Open the door! Open the door! Let me go. I want to travel."

Abdel-Aziz's heart was rent for the thousandth time. He hurried over to his father. The girls could no longer bear him. They had begun to complain about the way he abused them. Only the two of them, Abdel-Aziz and his mother, still kept trying to please him. His mother would run over to Hagg Karim and stand in front of him as if she were helping him stretch out his turban cloth. To humor him she would ask him if he needed anything. Abdel-Aziz would sit down beside him and talk to him about the Path and the brothers and the shrines of the saints, and he would walk with him that long distance down the road and back. And so it went, day after day.

But this day his patience was exhausted. He turned to his father.

"It's not right to make me do this every day."

He shouted the words with a voice full of resentment and raised his hands in bitter protest. But his bewildered father thought he was about to strike him. He pulled back in fear, raising his sound arm to protect his face. Abdel-Aziz fell to pieces. The pain was more than he could bear. If he were to live a thousand years he would never be able to forgive himself for making Hagg Karim think what he had thought.

He went out and sat on the bench in front of the house. After a moment he asked one of his sisters to get the donkey ready for him. The donkey was old, but she still bore up under every task. He loaded the waterwheel gear on her back and then mounted her. They handed him the leading rope of the buffalo. It had been Hagg Karim's custom to buy the finest animals, and this buffalo was unique in the village. They still had the two feddans of land they rented from the religious endowment, and today was the day set for irrigation.

Abdel-Aziz rode off on the big black donkey toward their plot, leading the buffalo behind him. In front of him on the donkey's back he had situated the waterwheel gear. He was wearing a peasant's galabiya and had a cap of rust red wool on his head. The morning sun was still cool and heartening as he followed the way before him through the fields.

The doctors said that his arteries had become hardened and that the blood had difficulty flowing in such narrow paths. The capillaries at the end of the arteries were exuding water, which was collecting in a little pool on top of his brain and inhibiting its function. His veins had to be injected constantly with a solution of glucose, he had to follow a strict diet, and he had to take a great many drugs to help restore elasticity to his arteries. But where was it all going to come from? They did not have a thing.

Those were the bare facts. Hagg Karim had become a mass of congested arteries and veins and a brain with a little pool of water floating on it. His mind was muddled, and he would scream at them as though he were half crazed. And so the days went on until Abdel-Aziz frightened him by gesturing in the air with his hands. Abdel-Aziz would never forgive himself for that. Knowledge, pain, and impotence; a brain, arteries and veins, and tragedy. Where was the world of the past? Where were the miracles of the saints and the prayers of men and women? Their house would always be open for everyone, they had said. There would always be food and lodging for guests. But now there was nothing for Hagg Karim himself to eat. That world had crumbled and was gone. It had been smashed into pieces. What could he do? Nothing. No trace of hope remained to mitigate his depression.

The donkey was gentle and peaceable. She was a good animal, and she knew the spot. She stopped by the waterwheel. Abdel-Aziz got off, dropped the buffalo's halter, and set the waterwheel gear on the ground. The donkey sighed heavily. Abdel-Aziz stroked her neck and contemplated the sadness in her face. "Another Lonely Creature." He leaned his head on her neck and closed his eyes. Then he clasped his arms around her neck. She stood quietly, breathing slowly now. He tied her to a tree. Then he fixed the wooden arm to the waterwheel, harnessed the buffalo to it, and tied the blindfold over her eyes. He yelled at her and she began to walk around in a circle, turning the waterwheel. The grinding of the gears, which were badly in need of lubrication, and the splashing of the water in the irrigation ditch brought life to his heart. She was a magnificent shiny black buffalo with a sturdy, well-proportioned frame and a huge belly swollen with a calf. She would give birth soon. He felt happy. Perhaps things would get better and Hagg Karim would recover. The doctors said he could get well, that it was simply a matter of high blood pressure and that otherwise he was in good health. Abdel-Aziz began to sing, and the sound of his voice blended with the grinding and the splashing of the waterwheel.

When your loved one sleeps,
wake him gently,
When your flowers wither,
sprinkle them with juice of lime.

He laughed at his lightheartedness. Rolling up the hem and sleeves of his galabiya, he started to walk along the ditch to clear it for the water pouring from the wheel.

This was their land. It was part of the domain of Princess Fatima Hanim, but it was their land, yellow as gold with the stubble of the harvested wheat. The earth had been baked by the sun now, but the wide cracks in it were a rich, fertile brown. He lay down on his stomach and stretched out his arms and legs, trying to embrace their land. In its bosom were countless thousands of tiny veins and canals running between the particles of glistening brown silt. It was like a huge lung, breathing and renewing its richness and fertility. The Lord be praised! He was the son of this land and of these men.

He sat on the ground, clasping his knees to his chest. In the distance he saw Mohammed Kamel approaching. He was wearing his loose pants and his peasant's vest with a woolen sash wrapped around his waist. His face had a dark tan.

"Peace be upon you, Master Abduh."

"Welcome! How are you, Uncle Mohammed Kamel?"

His voice had its former sweetness, depth, and tenderness. It was the voice that had always fascinated Abdel-Aziz. His face, too, had the same unbounded goodness and gentleness. But something had changed, something Abdel-Aziz could not put his finger on. Something was different about this man who all his life had been their neighbor on the land and in the guesthouse, and their companion in the gatherings of the brothers.

He had divorced Saddiqa long ago and married another woman, a full-fleshed woman with enormous breasts. She had filled his house with children. She was a woman who never grew weary. From daybreak she was in the field, like the crows in the trees. She never tired of digging in the earth with her hands. She pulled Mohammed Kamel along behind her. You never saw him sitting any more. All day long, wearing his loose pants and his vest and with that woolen sash around his waist, he would be bent over in the field, turning the earth with his short hoe. He seldom spoke now. When he did, it was with the same old voice as before. But there were no longer any dreams in his eyes. He had a dejected look, and he kept his eyes on the ground. When he went off to the field carrying his hoe, he seemed at times a bit anxious or perhaps somewhat pressed, or at times he would appear shy and laugh falteringly. This was not the face that had been fashioned under the light of the lantern in the big hall in the guesthouse. It was a face that had been shaped in the scorching heat of the noonday sun. He did not ask about Hagg Karim. He wanted to talk to Abdel-Aziz.

"Are you going to irrigate today, Master Abduh?"

"God willing."

"May the Lord bless you and help you."

"I'll stand at the line between our field and yours. Don't worry. Not a drop of water will get on your land. You planted early, Uncle Mohammed. Our water won't get on your land."

The man spoke once more as he turned and went over to his field:

"Everything is in the hands of God. Don't put yourself out. I'm here with you. God will help us."

The water sparkled like hidden eyes suddenly appearing as it rose in the cracks in the dried earth. Abdel-Aziz walked back along the ditch to the waterwheel. The donkey was standing quietly next to the tree, and the big, sturdy buffalo was treading her familiar, monotonous circle, turning the noisy wheel. He yelled at her. She stopped blindly and listened, seeing nothing. Then she started to move again. But she leaped up suddenly and fell on all four legs. She stood up again silently, holding her left front hoof off the ground.

The grinding of the gears had stopped, and the stream of water dwindled until it seemed no more than a few tears. Abdel-Aziz stood for a moment dazed. Then he ran over to the buffalo and took off her blindfold. He undid the tie and removed the yoke from her neck. She stood where she was without moving. He tugged at her halter, but she was unable to move. He felt her front legs at the chest. She twitched with pain. A young peasant appeared out of nowhere. Abdel-Aziz did not even recognize him at the time. He was blind to everything.

"Get out of the way!"

The young man's experienced hand quickly discovered where she was suffering.

"Her leg is broken."

Abdel-Aziz was shattered. The peasant pulled the buffalo by her halter. She began to walk on three legs, but was hardly able to keep from falling. Two or three steps, and then she fell for good.

"We'll have to get a wagon to take her back to the village."

Abdel-Aziz did not even look in his direction. He untied the donkey, got up on her naked back, and rode off toward the village. Her back was long, and he sat exactly in the middle of it. With her own kind of wisdom, the donkey kept an easy pace. Perhaps she knew there was no use in hurrying.

There were no thoughts in Abdel-Aziz's head, nor any feelings in his heart. He was lightheaded and unmindful. Suddenly he started to sing.

We lived in ease, and fortune was our servant.
But now we cry, Who will shelter a stranger?
I am a stranger, my child.

Then he laughed at the top of his voice. He was alone. On the banks of the canals and along the little paths that led through the fields people were running toward the fallen buffalo. He did not know how they had learned the news, but they were going there by the hundreds, faster than the wind, gripping the hems of their galabiyas in their teeth. The donkey carried him along at the same easy pace, letting her head droop low. Her steady gait jarred him. His body shook as though it were made of jelly.

An eternity seemed to pass before he reached the edge of the village. One of his uncles was sitting with the men in front of the door of his house. The donkey passed them by, and Abdel-Aziz failed to notice. He got down and let her go on to the house. A tiny, sinewy woman with crossed eyes and disheveled hair darted out to meet him. Her arms and her fingers were stretched out as if she meant to throttle him. But she cried out:

"Don't worry, my son. Her rather than you. Never mind. Why are you so pale?"

In that instant Abdel-Aziz regained his awareness and understood what had happened. Tears streamed down his cheeks. He wiped them off with his muddy hand.

He looked in through the door of the house. They were rushing about like those poisonous red hornets. Something was wrong. Their faces were agitated and everyone seemed on the point of screaming. He turned back and threw himself on the bench. This was where Hagg Karim used to drink his afternoon coffee, where Ibrahim el-Gamal used to bring him the newspaper with the announcement of the date of the moulid. Ibrahim el-Gamal had left the village without saying good-bye. He had left his mark on people's hearts, but he had gone away without saying good-bye. Damn everything! Where was Hagg Karim?

One of his sisters came out to him.

"Your father has gone to the station."

So what can I do, he thought. Kill me if you like. There's nothing more I can do.

"And your father's wife has left the house and gone to your sister's."

One of his cousins came slowly up to him. He was winding his watch in his hand. Then he put it back in his pocket.

"What is it, Uncle Abduh? Have you had enough?"

He smiled at him.

"I only . . . no. . . . As the minstrel says,

If only once, O Fate,
you would spoil me and pamper me.
But misery comes in bushels,
to foil me and hamper me."

"Go and take care of your father. The days of the wandering minstrels are gone."

The days of the wandering minstrels were gone indeed. And so were many other things gone, gone without saying good-bye, just like Ibrahim el-Gamal. He set out for the station. The people he passed on the road were preoccupied with their own affairs. They cast sympathetic glances his way, sucked their lips, and went on.

In Ali Khalil's shop his young son was absorbed in his work. He was a green, fledgling copy of his father, weighing out staples slowly and meticulously and counting his money with care. Behind him was his mother, watching him with apprehension and love, just as she used to watch Ali Khalil. Abdel-Aziz smiled.

Here was Omar Farhoud's house. Farhoud was sitting in front of his camel and feeding it as he did constantly. The camel, with its big eyes and long nose, just kept chewing, like a feeble-minded child unable to feed itself.

Now he could see Rashida's husband. Where was she? Perhaps she was busy doing some chore inside the compound.

The row of houses came to an end. The open fields and the

road that led straight to the station lay before him. Ahead he saw Hagg Karim walking in the heat of the sun, supporting his frail body on his cane. His shoulder was drooping and his paralyzed arm hung lifeless at his side. He moved ahead falteringly on the long road stretching before him, but he did not turn aside, and he held his head high. Abdel-Aziz felt his heart throb. He quickened his pace until he caught up with his father. He put out his hand and grasped him under the armpit to support him. His body was feeble and unsteady, and his face was covered with dust. But his features were serene and gentle, and his eyes were full of longing that rent the heart.

"Where are you going, Papa?"

Hagg Karim answered with a soft, thin voice that sounded as though he were about to cry.

"I'm taking a trip, Son, to Sharqiya. I want to see my friends there. It's been a long time since I've seen them, Abdel-Aziz."

Abdel-Aziz tried with all the gentleness he had in him to change his father's path and lead him back along the road. The men in the fields looked up from their hoeing. A group of small children who had been playing forgot their game for a moment. Then they broke out laughing and ran off.

"Leave me alone, Abdel-Aziz. Let me go on my trip, Son. Please don't stop me. It's not right for you to stop me."

"It's too early for the train, Papa."

"I'll wait for it. I'll wait for it, Son."

"All right. But don't you want to change your clothes then? Are you going to go like this? In these clothes?"

"Yes indeed. Just the way I am. What's the difference?"

He took him back. The man was crushed. His whole being was crushed. But the longing was still in his eyes. Abdel-Aziz led him along as though he were a helpless child. They rested for a while on the mud bench in front of Rashida's house. When she saw her father, she was unable to hold back her tears. Her whole body shook with sobbing.

"What has happened to you, Papa? The grief in my heart, Papa, the water of the Nile can't wash it away."

Her father looked at her.

"Why are you crying, Rashida? Nothing has happened to me. I just want to take a trip. Let me take my trip. Please don't stop me."

Abdel-Aziz gripped him again under the armpit and helped him along as they returned to the house. They had passed Ali Khalil's shop when suddenly Rawayih appeared out of an adjoining lane, dragging the sightless Dandy behind her. She was moving too fast for him. He was stumbling and tripping, trying to feel the way before him with his cane.

"Here's your friend, Dandy. Here's Hagg Karim."

The Dandy flailed his arms pitifully in the air, trying to find Hagg Karim's hand. Abdel-Aziz caught his right hand and placed it in that of his father. But Hagg Karim's eyes were far away. They were looking beyond the Dandy into the distance. The Dandy was dressed in tattered clothes and had a dirty rag tied around his head so as to cover his eyes with the lower edge. He burst into sobs.

"I'm blind, Hagg Karim. I can't see, Hagg Karim."

Rawayih, choking on her tears, wailed at the same moment:

"You two have always been friends. You were the light of the village."

The Dandy kissed Hagg Karim's hand, and Hagg Karim said to him in a low voice:

"Don't cry, Dandy. We have to take a trip. We have to take a trip, Dandy. Get dressed and come with me."

Rawayih pulled the Dandy away and went off with him. Abdel-Aziz took Hagg Karim back to the house.

They had dreamed of Rawayih's death and of the feathers that would sprout on her face in retribution for all the fowl she had stolen. And now here she was, dragging the unseeing Dandy from place to place, wandering insanely through the streets and lanes and screaming her lungs out.

Abdel-Aziz let Hagg Karim go into the house on his own and collapsed on the bench at the door. There was not a particle of resistance left in him. He leaned his head against the wall and shut his eyes. But he opened them again when he heard a young voice calling him.

"Go and talk to your uncle."

He looked at the boy in silence. The child returned his look with fear in his eyes and then disappeared. He got up and walked reluctantly to the gathering of the men.

On the heap of topsoil in front of his uncle's house he saw the men sitting. They had not let the catastrophe fluster them. They were clever, alert men. He found them absorbed in thought, scratching the dirt in front of them and drawing figures. They made a place for him and he sat down. The buffalo was lying not far off and chewing her cud. She had been brought from the field on a wagon drawn by two mules. Both wheels had been removed from one side of the wagon and the buffalo had been rolled onto the ground. Now here she was, lying down and chewing her cud.

These were not his father's men. There was sternness in their faces, and their laughter was loud and strong. They sat together in the late afternoon, but not for the affectionate conversation of old friends. They came together to listen to the radio and the news broadcasts, and they commented with ardor and enthusiasm on what they heard. They were full of bitterness, and they were hasty and severe in their judgments.

Off to the side Abdel-Aziz could see Sherkasi the Carpenter. His face was pale as death and his eyes had no trace of their old luster. His body was almost totally emaciated, and the skin of his face seemed to be stretched over fleshless bone. He had been suffering for years from a liver ailment, and now each breath he drew threatened to be his last. Abdel-Aziz also saw Ahmed Bedawi there. His face was smiling. It was a smile that revealed his personal despair as well as his scorn for this new group of men, but it was none the less an affectionate smile, and it had the spirit of the old days. Abdel-Aziz scanned the men's faces, and they looked back at him with consoling glances.

The man came up to them riding his donkey. He got down and greeted them, and they returned his greeting.

"Welcome. How are you, Master Mohammed?"

He looked over at the buffalo calmly and asked the men to make her stand. They shoved long poles under her belly and gradually raised her until she stood. The man felt the spot where she was suffering. He thought for a moment. Then he rubbed his hands together and turned to the men.

"There's no hope. The tendon that comes from her shoulder blade is severed. We can't cauterize or stitch. She can live this way. She can stand or lie down with the help of the men. She can give milk and she can be bred. But she must not stand up on her own."

His uncle spoke with determination.

"She's no longer of any use to us."

The man replied:

"May God give you compensation."

Abdel-Aziz was watching a strange play on a strange stage. His uncle shoved his hand into his pocket and pulled it out closed.

"The price of a little tobacco."

"Forgive me. But when there is no hope, I can't take anything."

The man went over to his donkey.

"Wait a while so we can have a bite to eat together."

"Enjoy your meal."

Mounting the donkey he rode off and disappeared like a shadow in the distance. Ahmed Bedawi spoke.

"This buffalo should be slaughtered and divided up among us. If each one pays for the meat he gets, we'll put together the price of a sound buffalo. The price has to be set as if she were sound."

His uncle spoke again with the same determination in his voice.

"Hold on, Ahmed."

It was as though Ahmed Bedawi were ashamed of his idea.

"Hagg Karim used to do it that way. He would slaughter the animal with his own hand, distribute the meat, collect the money, and buy a buffalo better than the one that had fallen."

His uncle sighed.

"There's no need."

"Are we supposed to sit back and look on?"

"God is generous."

He turned to the butchers, who were sitting and waiting.

"Bless the Prophet. How much will you give for the buffalo, Seoudi?"

The man twitched and exchanged glances with his colleagues.

"We're all indebted to Hagg Karim."

"I didn't ask you to bid on Hagg Karim!"

The butcher grew bolder, and a cloud of disapproval came over the faces of some of the men sitting off to the side.

"The buffalo is pregnant. That spoils the meat."

"That's nonsense. Her meat is like white gold."

Abdel-Aziz closed his eyes and his mind wandered. When he returned to reality he saw his uncle putting the money in his hand.

"Take your money. The buffalo is yours, Saadawi."

Abdel-Aziz looked at the buffalo. She was lying down again, still chewing her cud. She no longer belonged to them. His mother used to whisper anxiously when she saw the sturdy animal coming sated back from the field, her udder swollen with milk:

"In the name of God. May God preserve her from harm."

And when she saw her going out to pasture, bellowing and eager to graze, she would say quietly:

"In the name of God the Merciful and Compassionate. In the name of the Prophet, may it protect you."

She used to squat beneath her with the milk bowl on her knees as the milk streamed from the buffalo's teats, filling the bowl and forming a thick layer of froth on the surface. Abdel-Aziz would sit on the mud trough in front of her and stroke her head and ears. She no longer belonged to them, nor to anyone else. Tomorrow her flesh would be dangling from the iron hooks.

His thoughts were wandering again. He smiled a pained

smile. Sometimes he thought about the face of Sherkasi the Carpenter. What a splendid face it had been, set off with such dignity and elegance by his tall, white cap. Now he was half dead. But he had made his way down the street, leaning on his cane, and joined the gathering on the heap of topsoil. No one noticed his presence. He sat at the edge of the gathering half asleep, unable to drive away the persistent flies that attacked his face. Perhaps the men were annoyed by his presence. Perhaps they were bothered by the presence of Abdel-Aziz himself.

The sun had grown pale and was about to set. It was time for another episode of the serial on the radio. Most likely the owner of the coffeehouse had already spread the mats out on his two benches and sprinkled the dirt floor with water. The teapot would be sitting on the kerosene burner, and the hot corncob coals would be ready for the water pipes. By now the men were no doubt longing to leave. They would crowd into that room where the radio was blaring and where playing cards were being slapped with excitement on the low wooden tables set out on the earth. The glowing coals would be heaped on the clay bowls of the pipes, and the men would become engrossed in a conversation that never ended because you never knew when it had begun. But it was not the conversation he had known. It was a marketplace jumble of words, cries, and noise.

Perhaps they had grown weary of him by now and were merely sitting with him out of civility because of his misfortune. His uncle settled the matter with few words. Now it was time to go to the coffeehouse. In the old days the men used to speak slowly and deliberately. They lived without all this bedlam. But these were boisterous, exasperated men. They talked about politics, cooperatives, feudalism, oppression, Kennedy and Khrushchev. Abdel-Aziz felt he had to leave.

But he took his time. He liked sitting with them. He only wished that that awkward reticence and hesitation they felt in his presence would go away and that they would burst forth with their usual bitterness and sarcasm. But they remained uncomfortable and inhibited. Abdel-Aziz started to get up. As he was half standing he looked around him and noticed Ahmed Bedawi getting up too.

Where the houses came to an end, the open land stretched before them, rising gradually across the brown fields and the golden lines of trees to meet the sky at the horizon. The sun cast long, soft shadows that tripped over the pebbles in the road. Ahmed Bedawi sighed.

"Why is everything changing, Master Abduh?"

That short frame, the childish face with the narrow eyes, the white hair beneath his cap that had replaced all but the last traces of black. Everything was falling down around this man, and he was still smiling. His elder son, who had married early, had taken his wife and left the village for Cairo. No letters ever came from him. Ahmed Bedawi was dismayed by what he saw happening around him, but he kept on smiling with his childish smile of amazement.

"What is it that's happened? I don't understand it."

He still went to the gatherings of the men, although he sat at the edge of the group. When they talked he would listen amazed, and smile. When he was totally bewildered by what he heard, however, he would speak. He would speak as though he were sitting in the hall of the guesthouse under the light of the big lantern. They always brushed aside what he had to say. Humbled, he would say no more. But he kept on smiling.

Abdel-Aziz answered him with another question.

"What of Sherkasi the Carpenter? He seems to be doing very poorly these days."

Ahmed Bedawi's face grew a bit sullen.

"Since the day his wife died, he's been a broken man."

It had been a strange day. In the morning the whole village had been convulsed with laughter. Everyone coming back from the market had told how Shahhat Sherkasi had been driving his doddering old maid sister in front of him, kicking her and jabbing her with his fists. Everyone had told how funny it had been to hear the poor old girl whining and wailing like that, while Shahhat beat her like an animal and showered her with the crudest insults. The story had been told dozens of times over. In the end they had learned that Shahhat's mother, having discovered there was not a single scrap of bread in the house, had decided to sell a turkey hen in order to buy some grain to grind. But the turkey belonged to Shahhat's wife. It had been given to her by her family on one of the feasts. They had told with a great deal of exaggeration how Shahhat's wife had wailed when she noticed that her turkey was gone, how Shahhat had become insane with rage and rushed off to the market to find the turkey and his sister, and how he had brought her back along the road, beating and cursing her, while she carried the frightened, screeching turkey on her head.

In the morning the whole village had laughed over this story. But in the afternoon the wailing had begun, announcing the death of Sherkasi the Carpenter's wife. She had tried to push Shahhat away from her daughter and he had kicked her in the stomach. She had spit up blood, and in her last breath she had begged the men not to harm her son Shahhat who had killed her.

In the evening they had held the funeral reception, and Shahhat had sat sullenly among the people who came to pay their condolences. His left eyebrow sagged down over his eye, keeping it shut, his huge lower jaw jutted forward, and his lips were thin and tightly closed. The skin of his face was covered with unpigmented splotches, and swollen muscles gathered between his shoulder blades in the shape of a hump.

"Master Abduh, I don't understand a thing. I used to think I was a wise man."

Sherkasi the Carpenter had come to the Path out of longing for a male child, and he had made his wife wear an iron collar around her neck so that Shahhat would live. And that child had sat at her funeral reception just looking on.

Abdel-Aziz had not eaten anything all day long. His stomach was empty, but he had no appetite for food. Someone called him. He took leave of Ahmed Bedawi and went off.

In his sister's house he found his father's other wife sitting cross-legged on the bench and dressed for a journey. She was wearing her black silk dress, and her headcloth was wrapped tightly around her face. She sat resting her chin in her hand, while her daughter stood beside her, silent and despondent. Abdel-Aziz seated himself next to her on the bench without saying a word.

"Your mother insulted me and made fun of me."

She began to cry. Abdel-Aziz knew she was weeping for his father. All those years she had sat in a corner of the house watching him without saying a thing, hoping that he would speak to her or find his way to her room, the room she tidied so carefully day after day, and where she slept at night alone without a man.

"I'm going away, Abdel-Aziz. I have family, and there is no place for me anymore in your father's house."

Her face was wet with tears. It was a withered, wrinkled face. There was no longer anything there that called for bathing with blusher soap. Abdel-Aziz smiled bitterly to himself. His sister's whispering voice interrupted his thoughts.

"She'll go away for a couple of days, till she quiets down a bit. Then she'll come back."

Abdel-Aziz was sure she would never come back. Her eyes had already flown away, like two migratory birds. His sister and he went together to see her off. When the old woman hugged him to her breast, he knew it was for the last time. He never saw her again. She died among her own people.

It had been a strange day. Abdel-Aziz thought about it as he sat on the roof, contemplating his surroundings in the clear night air. The stars were shining brightly in the sky, and a gentle northerly breeze brushed against his face. He looked at the familiar things around him—the bundles of corn and cotton stalks piled on the housetops, the crests of the willows and the old sycamore figs, the single room on their own roof, the food and milk containers, the little mud towers for grain that crowded the roofs of the houses in the village, the homely, squat minaret of the main mosque, and the distant dome over the tomb of his grandfather's wife in the village cemetery.

It had been a strange day. The buffalo was dead. Now their animal pen was empty except for the big black donkey. She might be hanging her head now in the darkness and mourning.

He stretched out his legs and leaned back in his chair. They had put down a mattress for Hagg Karim. He was lying on it, covered by a quilt. His regular breathing was the only sound to be heard as they sat around him in silence.

Abdel-Aziz's mother was sitting with them, collapsed in a heap. She was fast asleep. When she could not find something to busy her hands with, she always fell asleep. He never saw her distracted and absorbed in thought, or sitting down to enjoy a conversation with the others. If she had not been so inhibited, she would have left them by now and gone down to her room to sleep.

Rashida and the girls were sitting quietly, but they were as alert as owls perched on the branches of trees in the darkness. What was Abdel-Aziz going to do? Something had to be done. Should he give up his studies and look for a job so he could take them all to the city? Would he be able to manage a household on new ground? Should he go to the city alone and send them money and his suggestions and advice by mail?

The gatherings that included both Rashida and Hagga Showk had always been the most delightful of all. A bitter smile came over Abdel-Aziz's face when he saw Hagga Showk coming up to them.

"Good evening, children."

They returned her greeting in whispered voices. Abdel-Aziz's mother woke up in an instant. She seemed to be asking for a fight. Hagga Showk sat down quietly on the mat. She looked over to Hagg Karim lying under the quilt. Good-bye to the good old days, to the affectionate words, to the glances filled with longing, to the radiant cheeks. Those days were gone.

"Such is life."

Things had been different then. Now Hagga Showk was infatuated with all kinds of essences and plants, strange herbs, and little magical objects. But she could find no cure for her constant headache nor for her bad temper and low spirits. She hung a golden fish on her kerchief and fastened an amulet to the strips of cloth woven into the end of one of her braids. Against her temples she had tied the leaves of a special plant. She had things to boil, the liquid from which had to be drunk before taking anything in the morning, things to rub her body with, and a whole stock of complicated remedies and charms. She used henna on the white locks that hung over her temples. Hagga Showk could not bear to have white hair.

She handed something to Abdel-Aziz's mother.

"Here, Oum Abdel-Aziz. Boil it, and then rub the arm that's ailing him with it."

"Fine."

Without bothering to conceal her hostility his mother took the packet from Hagga Showk and placed it nonchalantly at her side. Showk got up to leave. Abdel-Aziz did not try to make her stay. Perhaps she would be a little less despondent among her grandchildren and her things.

"I hope I leave you in good health."

The packet was abandoned on the mat. Possibly such things had had their use in the old days. Abdel-Aziz smiled to himself.

One night long ago Iraqi had come to visit Hagg Karim when he was suffering from a slight illness.

"What's wrong with you, Papa?"

When Hagg Karim pointed to his aching head, Iraqi shrieked:

"Your head is 'open,' Papa."

Then he asked for a wooden key, a big handkerchief, incense, candles, and some cooking oil. Leaping up and down, he performed a series of strange rituals and recited a few shattered incantations with his twisted tongue. The others nearly died with laughter. Finally he burned the incense and rubbed Hagg Karim with the oil, which he had heated over one of the candles. Tying a knot in the handkerchief, he placed it over Hagg Karim's head. Then he inserted the key under the handkerchief and began to twist it. As the handkerchief grew tighter around his head, the poor man screamed with pain. Iraqi shouted with joy at his success in "closing" Hagg Karim's head again. Everyone there was convulsed with laughter.

Now none of these things were of any use. What was needed was expensive drugs, a special diet, and constant visits by the doctor. And they had nothing in the house. Neither Showk's remedies nor Iraqi's medicine could help. Iraqi's whole life had become a comedy routine that no longer interested anyone. He would tear off to work on his bicycle and speed home at the end of the day without even glancing at the guesthouse. The benches were covered with dust. No one sat there anymore.

It had been a strange day. He looked at the sky. As the Great Bear turned slowly around the bright North Star, the stars seemed to betray the same bewilderment and longing he saw in his father's eyes. After the calm and stillness of the night would come the dawn and a harsh new day, with a new set of problems.

He heard the shuffling of slippers on the stairs. Samira came onto the roof, tall and plump. On her shoulder she was carrying her son, who was holding on to her scarf. Abdel-Aziz's eyes clung to her. His mind was distracted and he could think of nothing to say or do.

"Good evening."

The others replied with reluctant whispers:

"Good evening, Sister. Welcome."

When she saw Abdel-Aziz, she was unable to suppress a cry.

"Abdel-Aziz!"

She hurried over to him and knelt down, placing her hands on his knees.

"Abdel-Aziz! I've missed you so much, Abdel-Aziz. I've wanted so much to see you."

She laughed as she spoke. Her voice had a clear ring amid the silence that surrounded them. It was as dazzling as the North Star in the darkness of the night sky. Something came over Abdel-Aziz, a feeling that spread through his entire being and made him tremble, a simple, innocent tear he had not known for a long time. He placed his hands over hers.

"Welcome, Samira! Welcome!"

She went on talking, isolated in her exuberance among the silent faces around them. Suddenly she looked about and saw them. It was though she had been screaming among voiceless grave markers. She fell into an embarrassed silence. Then she turned around to find her slippers. Putting them on, she started down the stairs. Abdel-Aziz watched her leaving and realized that the happiness he had felt was being taken away from him. He called after her, trying to hold on to the moment:

"What's the hurry, Samira?"

"Never mind."

He stood up, heedless of the gloomy, silent faces around him. He was thinking only of her.

"Wait a second. I'll come along and see you home."

The shadows of the houses on the street were black, and the bright moonlight cast a greenish tint on the walls. The tips of the bundles of cornstalks, wet with the evening dew, hung in twisted fringes from the rooftops. It was a delightful evening, and Abdel-Aziz longed to express his feelings.

"How have you been, Samira?"

"Just fine. And how have you been?"

She was tall. Her shoulder almost came up to his. They used to walk along this street in the early morning to catch the train for school. She had grown up now, but her heart was still the same. She still had her old smile, her bright, even teeth, her cheerful nature, and her serene spirit. He had to shed the burdens that were oppressing his soul.

"Just as you see me, Samira."

Laughter filled his breast.

"The day before yesterday I was passing by, and I saw you out in the street. You were running. I wondered what could have happened."

She laughed with surprise.

"Did you really see me? How embarrassing! I was barefooted and I didn't have anything on my head."

He laughed back.

"I saw you all right. What were you doing?"

"I was running after the goat, damn her. She'll be the death of me. There must be sixty devils in her legs."

She could hardly go on, she was giggling so.

"She eats other people's things, and there's always a scandal afterward."

Samira calmed down a bit, and a childish seriousness came over her face.

"By the Prophet, Abdel-Aziz, I really do have my troubles. Goats, sheep, cattle, and calves. I work myself to death taking care of them all day long."

Suddenly she went into stitches, and Abdel-Aziz, without knowing why, broke out laughing with her.

"Let me tell you what a funny thing happened the day before yesterday. I went into the animal pen and found the cow lying on her side with her eyes closed and her legs sticking straight out. I said, 'O my God, the cow is dead,' and I started to scream. But as soon as I started screaming like that the cow jumped up. Good Lord! The cow had only been sleeping. Everybody came and stood around me. What was I going to tell them? I was laughing so hard I almost choked. Everybody else just stood there, slapping one palm after the other. 'Has the girl gone mad, or what?' they were saying."

Abdel-Aziz nearly died with laughter. He had not laughed like that for a long time. What if he were to put his arms around her, to hold her laughter against his breast and press it into his heart?

"Tell me, Samira. Do you still remember anything of the subjects we used to study in school?"

"Forget that, Brother. My head is upside down. I tell my son, 'Let me see your books, and if there's anything you don't understand I'll explain it.' He says, 'Never mind, Mama, the things you used to learn don't have anything to do with what we're doing.'"

"He's big now, Samira. Let him fend for himself."

"I do!"

"You're wearing the iron collar so he'll live. Do you believe in those superstitions, Samira?"

"It's what people say. I'm afraid for my children, Abdel-Aziz. They're wonderful, especially when you sit and talk with them."

Abdel-Aziz walked all the way with her, and then turned back down the street. The shadows were darker and the light of the moon had grown brighter. The sound of his own footsteps was all that he could hear in the silence. He moved on at an easy pace. For some moments he gazed at the face of the moon. He felt he wanted to raise his voice and sing. He had no desire to return to the house and bury his joy in that room of suffering on the roof.

He turned off into a dark lane. It was impossible to make out the way, but he kept on walking until he sensed that the lane had come to an end. He was there. The threshold of the door was a good deal lower than the level of the lane. He stepped down, holding on to the lintel of the door to support himself. The courtyard was totally dark. He felt out the path with each step. Before him, through the cracks of an old wooden door, gleamed narrow slices of a brilliant white light. He made his way into the coffeehouse. The small room seemed to be ablaze with the light of the mantle lantern, the shouts, the cries, and the excitement. It was a little parcel of boisterous life buried beneath the silence of the village, but its power was overwhelming. Without any interruption in the noise and the activity, a place was made for him between two of the men. The radio was turned all the way up, and the shrill voice of a woman singing provided an earsplitting accompaniment to the clamor of the men. There was hardly any room left in the place, either on the benches lining the walls or on the reed mats and gunny sacks that covered the floor.

Each of the low tables was surrounded by a little circle of enthusiasm—the excited gestures of the card players, the graceless sound of their lips slurping tea, and the hollow gurgle of their water pipes. The air was thick with smoke, and the heat from the mantle lantern and the hissing kerosene burner was stifling. The owner stood in front of a high table next to the wall. He was constantly pouring tea or piling live coals on the tapered clay bowls of the water pipes. Whenever he handed a glass to one of the men, it was accompanied by a scornful volley of outrageous insults.

He was a thin, wasted man with dirty clothes and lusterless eyes. But his pallid face was full of life. His teeth were black, and he had a strong, insolent smile. He handed Abdel-Aziz a glass of tea without a remark. It was hot and very sweet, and it was so strong it turned his mouth inside out. But the flavor was exceptional. The bitterness of the boiled leaf dissolved in the syrupy sweetness of the sugar and spread through his body like a feeling of joy and exhilaration. His loneliness melted into the overpowering din. He heard his uncle slapping his cards on the table and showering his opponent with curses and threats of inevitable defeat. The men seemed to be speaking of almost everything, and almost in a single breath. Their words were strong and bitter, full of frustration and anger.

"Change the station. Let's hear the news. Gag that woman who's singing!"

The owner reached up to turn the knob. But he did not forget to answer the man who had spoken.

"The news? You don't know any more about politics than your good-for-nothing father did."

"I want to find out, idiot. Are we going to go on being donkeys for the rest of our lives?"

The solemn tones of the newscaster clashed with the unabated din. No one seemed to be listening. But an occasional comment here and there revealed that the men were following what was being said.

"Sir . . . arrived today at Cairo Airport."

"What does he want, that son of a bitch?"

"If I had been there I would have spat in his face and sent him home."

Abdel-Aziz found himself speaking, quietly at first, but then excitedly at the top of his voice. As the broadcast continued its struggle with the boisterous voices of the men, his excitement increased. Everyone was talking. Someone would remark on what he had said, and he would come back with an answer or a new opinion. The room was a confused uproar of arguments, laughter, and insults.

He lost himself among them. He felt the same bitterness, anger, and pain that they did. The harsh phrases kept coming. His forehead was covered with sweat. Someone handed him a water pipe. He filled his lungs with the thick, rich smoke. It went to his head immediately. He became dizzy and coughed. But he went on talking, and he kept going back to the pipe. The taste was extraordinary, like a hundred cigarettes in a single breath. Only that heavy blue smoke could interrupt the incessant storm of his words.